Return of the Father

Book Six
of
The Abyss Walker Series

by

Shane Moore

Editorial services for this edition provided by Edward Gehlert.

Beta reading by Calla Patton.

Design by Kendall R. Hart and © 2014 New Babel Books

Return of the Father

© Shane Moore

A New Babel Books Release
381 High Point Drive

Holiday Shores, IL 62025

www.newbabelbooks.com

Genre: Fantasy / Series

ISBN: 978-1-63196-023-9

Revised Edition; First printing.

Printed in the United States of America.

Other Abyss Walker Works

White Wraith—Origins

White Wraith—The Lock of Requ *Coming soon!*

White Wraith—Maelstrom Serpents *Coming soon!*

The Wererat's Tale—Book One: Of Rat's and Men

The Wererat's Tale—Book Two: Ring of the Nonul

The Wererat's Tale—Book Three: Collar of Perdition

The Abyss Walker series

The Plea of Apollisian

The Trial of Innocence

Darrion-Quieness

Death of Kings

Tides of Winter

Return of the Father

Swords and Plowshares—Patrick Tomlison *Coming soon!*

Other Abyss Walker Works
Dwarven Cookbook

Other Works by Shane Moore
"I am Villain" I, Hero magazine #2
Apocalypse of Enoch I: Rapture
Apocalypse of Enoch II: Scourge

Table of Contents

To the Abyss Walker fans. Despite the bankruptcy of a publisher, the collapse of a major chain, and the evolving industry--you made this happen!

"There will come a day when the heavens turn their back on us as the shadows rise up to claim our lands. Only the humbled one can be our salvation when he discovers who walks for death. Yet, even then, if his love is lost, the darkness will be lasting."

~ Hiramem's Prophecy

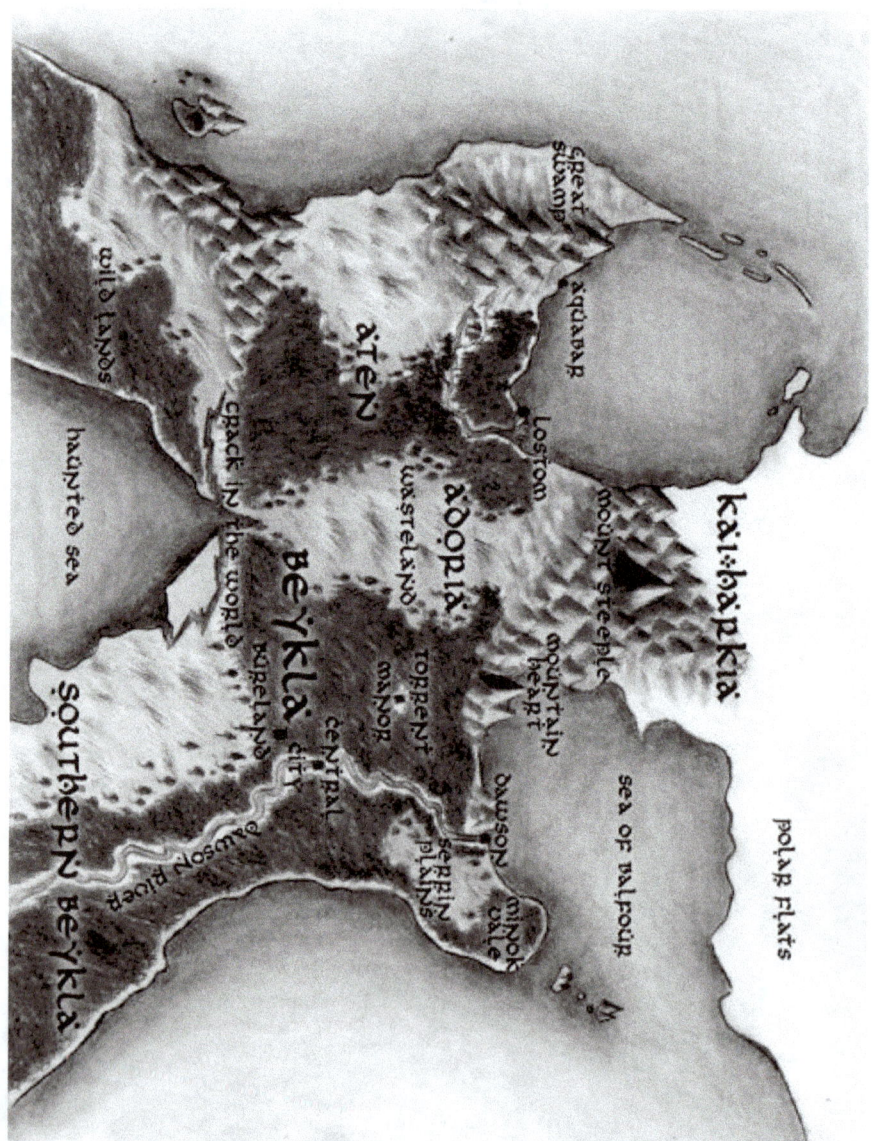

Songsinger

The cold air whipped across the road blowing Amerix's long silver streaked greasy hair about his face. The starlight sky had given way to cloud cover and by the drop in temperature, the old general expected snow. He had grown to detest the white stuff. It covered the land in a cold sheen of misery. It crunched under his boots, slowed his travel, and made hunting more difficult. Though, it did make tracking easier, the grizzled dwarf had yet to figure out how to make that useful.

Amerix continued along the road for some time. It had not changed direction that much, but he had little choice. If the clouds continued to cover the stars, he had no way in determining what direction he was going. It was strange to the old dwarf. Somehow, in the under mountain, he always knew what direction he was going. He could tell if he was traveling up, or of he was traveling down, but here on the surface world, he was lost. He might as well been in the realm of Limbo. The only constant that he noticed was the stars. And they even seemed to change as the night and season progressed. The only benefit to the dwarf was that he could estimate the time of year and direction from their placement in the sky. It was not an easy skill to learn but after a decade or so with the stone hearts he had figured it out.

As the night progressed the temperature dropped. Amerix could see his hot breath as he marched in his brilliant gold colored armor. The thick steel skin was lighter than chain, though based off its size, it should weigh four times as much. His plates did not creak when rubbed together like normal plate armor. They were smooth. It reminded Amerix of leather armor.

The old general marched down the road for several more hours. He was happy he did not see any merchants or other wanderers. They would surely attack him and he was eager to test his axes and armor, but he was not quite ready for the hassle. He must be getting old. The grizzled general chuckled to himself and made his way to a small clearing next to the side of the road. It was covered in short green grass that was trying to grow for the approaching spring weather. There was a small crumbling stone structure. It was nearly twenty foot tall and was covered in dried vines and moss. The vines had an unusual leaf that resembled a hand and snaked around the building, like a python around its prey.

Amerix stepped over old wooden debris and around the side of the tower. It was missing its northeast wall revealing a small flat area that would be perfect for a camp. There was an old fire pit that was overgrown with vegetation showing the site had not been used to camp in since last summer.

Amerix walked in and dropped his pack. The empty leather bundle landed lightly and collapsed in on itself. He started undoing the straps to his armor as the wind blew the vines. Amerix froze. There was no wind, just a soft cool breeze. He turned quickly and drew his axes. The old general's hawk-like eyes scanned the darkness, but he saw nothing.

"I know yer there, ye ragged cur! Come to yer death!" he shouted as he moved around the corner of the collapsed wall.

The grizzled dwarf stared out towards the road. He did not see any horses, or any sign of life other than the chirp of springtime birds. Just as he started to run back to his camp, something hooked his foot and jerked him to the ground. He landed on his belly as he was pulled back towards the interior of the collapsed structure. But before he could roll over and chop what had a hold of him, he was released.

Amerix jumped to his feet and sliced the air with his razor sharp axes.

"Show yerself, you gullysmite!" he shouted into the darkness. Yet nothing answered. The birds quieted and the forest was deathly silent. Amerix glanced around the camp when something snatched him around the neck and jerked him up into the air with tremendous power. His heavy frame was flung against the stone wall. The dwarf's metal armor clanged against the old bricks as his feet kicked furiously. He tried to cry out a threat and promise of death, but his throat was lashed so tight he could not speak. He could make out leaves around his face and he realized someone had used a vine to ensnare him. Amerix smacked the stone wall with his arms and flipped around facing the wall. He could see a single thick vine that was wrapped around his neck and was anchored to the top of the old wall. The renegade general dropped his left axe and tugged at the vine that was around his neck while he reared back to slice the hangman's cord.

To Amerix's horror, another vine shot out and snatched his wrist before he could sever the thick cable-like vine. He tried to get his fingers around the vine that had his neck, but it was so strong and tight, he could not. The grizzled general chuckled to himself. He knew he had only seconds left before he lost consciousness. He had survived battles that normal dwarves would have died of fright, yet here he was. Stuck to a wall by some carnivorous vine, like a fly in a spider web. Amerix wished he could go back to the bridge at Central City and die at the hands of the human champion. He was a good man, worthy of falling to.

The thought roused something inside of the old dwarf. He kicked his legs up against the wall. With his free hand, he snatched the vine that had his neck, just as another encircled his waist and another around his left arm. Amerix growled and with all of his strength he pulled down. His powerful legs flexed and within moments, the top of the crumbling wall gave way. Amerix landed hard on his back as a shower of bricks rained down on him. Several hit his armor and a large one bounced off of his helm. He rolled to his feet and snatched up his other axe. It did not take the vine long to recover and it stated tugging again.

Amerix slashed furiously. His razor keen axe's severed a new cord with each swing. He cut the one around his neck first and then began systematically cutting the rest. In a few short seconds, the killing vine was no more.

Sweat dripped from the old general's brow and he was

covered in a sticky white substance that drained from the severed vines. Amerix walked around the structure to ensure there were no more vines before clearing a spot of broken rock and debris. On the back side, he discovered several skeletal remains. Two of them human and one appeared to be that of an elf. Their equipment had long since been ruined by the elements, but after rummaging through the remains he did find a small fortune in gold coins and some jewels. One of them humans must have been wearing chain armor when the vine attacked. The armor looked as if it had been pulled apart in some areas and smashed into thin lines of wire in others.

The old general ignored the imaginations of their death and poured some water from his waterskin and wiped himself down. Despite the drop in temperature, the wet rag felt good on his hot skin. When he was finished, Amerix laid the rag out on one of crumbled rocks he had used to build a fire pit and then began to gather up some deadwood that was laying about. After piling the wood in the small ring he tossed in some dry grass and sat down on a fair sized log he had carried into camp. He rummaged into his near empty leather pack and pulled out an old flint rock. It was small from the years of scraping, but Amerix liked it and it had served him many a cold night.

A quick flick from his axe and several small sparks fell into the dried grass. Amerix placed his old calloused hands around them and blew lightly. Then a flame quickly burst from the sparks and Amerix lowered it to the small sticks he had prepared in the pit.

As the fire grew, Amerix flipped open his bedroll and then circled he camp, dropping small pointed four pronged spikes. Anyone, or anything, that tried to sneak up on him at night was in for a nasty surprise.

Amerix laid down and snuggled into his bedroll. The crack of the fire seemed to comfort the lonely old general and he drifted off to sleep.

Trinidy surveyed the damaged area. His glowing blue eyes revealed the myriad of black stinging insects that skittered and scurried across his rotted face. Three score of his ghouls had been obliterated by a powerful magical blast. It had severed trees and splintered their trunks. The caster was more skilled than all of his liches. If he could find and convert this wizard, his army would grow remarkably stronger. Based off of the tracks in the snow the spell weaver traveled by carriage. This would make him difficult to catch.

The death knight glanced up at the storm that seemed to follow them. His first attempt at controlling the weather wandered away on the winds, but the most recent moved when he did. The creation of it was simple, really. It was anchoring it to his body that was difficult. Trinidy found that the snow storm kept his zombies from rotting so rapidly and the thick grey clouds blocked the sun, allowing his shadows and other creations to move freely with the army at all hours.

Trinidy watched with pleasure as his army shambled across the snow covered earth like an army of ants on the move. He found it peculiar that his soldiers enjoyed bashing the skulls of those they recently killed and found it more fascinating to watch as they ate their brains. He animated the corpses by fusing their tortured souls into their rotting carcasses, but now it seems they were enjoying a bit of their new life. It brought a cracked deathly smile to the undead king's face. He had brought his soldiers some sort of pleasure. He knew he was a good leader.

The wind whipped around Trinidy, blowing his dark dirty yellow cape. It was the same cloth he had procured from the yellow tower in one of the first cities he had sacked. Though it bore the symbol of some god he had never heard of, he found the symbol comforting. It was a setting sun on the palm of an open hand. It seemed as if the symbol should have been important to him in his past, but he could not recall exactly how.

He shook his helm covered head and pushed the thoughts aside. He had decided that he deserved a steed. All kings had a magnificent steed. He had thought of a horse, but an equine was not befitting someone of his power. Almost as if by thought, the dark black energies started swirling around Trinidy. Their snake like wispy strands began to glow with an orange hue. The gray clouds above him turned black and the snow beneath his feet churned like a bubbling cauldron. The wind increased as the strands rocketed around his body like a tornado of power. The snow at his feet spread and formed giant runes that extended out from the death knight, forming a large circle, and in a massive orange flash it all stopped.

Bits of snow and debris fluttered down around Trinidy. Dust eddied into small whirlwinds that quickly died out. The death knight glanced around. His army was gone, the snow was gone and the forest was gone. All around him was a dark gray blasted landscape. Above him was a deep red sky with black and yellow sulfurous clouds that churned overhead like an angry storm. Small insect like creatures burrowed from the rocks under his feet and then writhed in agony.

The Abyss. He was back in the Abyss. Trinidy felt rage inside of him. There was no fear, only unbridled hate and rage. He would find Bykalicus and destroy him once and for all. The death knight started forward but struck a barrier that held him fast. He glanced around and noticed that the runes that had encircled him in the snow were also engraved here in the rocks.

Trinidy smiled. He must have opened a portal to the Abyss. He existed in both places, an overlap in the planes of existence. He had heard of evil necromancers and summoners that were able to call forth demons in this manner.

Trinidy quickly encircled his fingers and drew forth bright yellow energy. He deftly weaved it and channeled the force into the cold slate of the Abyss's rocky floor. The rock shuddered and twisted. With his other hand, Trinidy began to create dark brown weaves and encircled the yellow that gripped the mass of Abyssal rock. They squeezed until small drops of red colored metal dripped out and floated in the air. The death knight repeated this process until he had a sizeable amount of the raw Abyssal steel floating before him.

"What are you doing?" a feminine voice called out.

Trinidy turned to see a powerful horse standing just outside of his portal. It was jet black with bright pupil-less red eyes. The animal's mane and tail were burning flames that flickered in the cold Abyssal wind. Dazzling jets of flame shrouded the back of the animal's feet, near the hooves, like long wisps of fiery hair.

"I am crafting me a sword fit for kings," Trinidy answered in a deep and guttural voice.

The animal snorted a blast of flames and replied, "You should not be here."

"Oh, says who?" Trinidy countered as he shaped the steel into a long broad sword.

The animal stepped closer. "I was coming to you. Soon, you will need me again."

Trinidy stopped and turned to face the powerful steed. "Need you against who?"

The horse pawed the ground sending out bits of gray slate. "Against the Abyss Walker."

Trinidy's rotted face frowned and his eyes flashed brighter. "I hate him. That is the wrong I am to right, isn't it?"

The animal stepped forward. Its glaring red eyes seemed to penetrate the soul of the undead knight as she spoke, "No, Trinidy. The Abyss Walker is your son, Lancalion."

Trinidy gritted his teeth together in rage. "No!" he screamed as he slapped his hands together sending out a blast of magical energy that split the Abyssal earth hundreds of feet in all directions. The dark yellow clouds began to swirl above him as wind whipped around him like he was in the eye of a tornado. "My son is dead!"

The beast lowered his head and walked through the wind, even as the energy around it burned her hide and peeled the hair from her flesh. "I served you once. Years ago," she said.

"Eckwin?" Trinidy asked quietly. The torrent of air began to weaken and the blast of energy started to die away. "I think I remember you."

The beast bowed her head. "Yes, he has turned to the dark arts and is in love with a succubus named Delania. Bykalicus has sent her to warp and manipulate his mind. As hard as it may seem, we must kill him before his soul is completely lost."

Trinidy nodded as a cold icy tear dripped down his rotted face. The hundreds of stinging insects that scurried about from his nose to his ears avoided the tear. As it ran down the death knight's cheek, it briefly added color to his rotting form, but was quickly overcome by dark gray flesh.

"I will join you soon. Dicermadon has ordained it. We are to be rescued from this hell and we will be able to serve him in his glory," she said.

Trinidy nodded solemnly and kneeled before the bright crimson blade that had formed in front of him. The blade was as long as it was broad. It bore great runes of the archaic language of the gods down both sides of the blade. The hilt was made of gold and shaped like a horseshoe of thorns. Each side of the crimson blade was serrated like a cutting knife. The blade could be wielded by one hand or two and the pommel had two open hands that held a setting sun. Trinidy smiled at the symbol. It was like the one that was on the back of his cloak. The death knight removed his old sword and threw it down. It clanged harmlessly off of the cold Abyssal floor. He sheathed the new blade into his scabbard and turned to Eckwin. "I shall see you soon, my friend. The world is not like we left it. There is evil everywhere. Mankind has stumbled and we must return to smite down the wickedness that has spawned forth."

Ekcwin nodded as Trinidy faded from view. The runes around his portal began to slowly fade. Eckwin stepped into the portal and watched as bright red magical weaves began to unravel revealing the massive form of Bykalicus. The arch-demon smiled wickedly. "One of your greatest performances ever, Nefertora. Make sure he kills the boy."

The steed nodded. "It may have been foolish to tell the fool that the boy is his son. He may resist."

Bykalicus shook his horned head. "No, had he found out on his own, he might have. But a true deceiver tells parts of the truth and hides the lies among them. They will convince him the only way to save his son is to kill him. Only through death, will Lance be able to be controlled. And then I will use him against Dicermadon, or Azkarnicus as he calls himself now."

Nerfertora's equine form began to fade from view. "What if I am forced to reveal myself on the field of battle? Trinidy had not traversed the Abyss much, but I am sure he will know of me. I had my fun with him while he was in the Iron Fortress."

Bykalicus chuckled and waved his hand in dismal at the fading image of Nefertora's equine form. "So what? Kill the boy yourself. Just make sure he is dead. If you are killed there, you will reform back here. Just make sure the boy dies!"

In seconds, the portal was gone and damage to the Abyssal slate was the only evidence that it was ever there.

Vlargcar awoke in his cell. The dark room was not lit and the smell of feces and blood hung in the air. He sat up and ran his head through his thick black mohawk. The top of his head had been scarred by his mother and he could only grow hair right down the middle. Vlargcar never thought of it much. He just accepted it as another one of the things in life that just were. Like the sun shined. He often pondered how far away it really was and if the gods lived on it, but the thoughts were too much for his head, so he simply decided that the sun just was. There was no need to explain it. He could not affect, or change it, even if he did figure out how and why.

This massive orc got up from his bunk and stretched as he yawned. The men of the arena had given him quite a large cell for his victories. He had a bunk, with a blanket and pillow. He had a wash basin and fresh straw every few days. The soldiers were ordered not to get too close to his door, which was not even visible from his bunk.

Vlargcar belched and scratched his belly. He could hear the shouts of men outside of his cell. Normally soldiers did not come near his cell, let alone hoot and holler. The orc made his way into the short hall from his room. The exterior hall was empty save for two soldiers dragging the strangest animal Vlargcar had ever seen. It was small, maybe as tall as the men's knees. It walked on all fours and was covered in fur. It kind of looked like a wolf, except its hair was real short. It had strange markings, like a tiger, except more blended, that were mixed with large patches of white. The animals head was almost as large as its chest. It was covered in blood and did not appear as if it could walk. The men were dragging it down the hall kicking it and shouting curses. The animal had its tail tucked between its legs and it was in obvious pain.

"Stupid filthy cur!" one of the soldiers snarled, "I paid nearly five gold for you and you get all messed up fighting a lioness."

The other soldier chuckled and kicked the animal. It did not whimper, but tried its best to walk as the other man jerked on a leash that was connected to its collar. "And it took him long enough to the kill the bitch!"

Vlargcar's blue eyes shined in the darkness. That small animal fought and killed a lioness? The orc found that statement hard to believe. The animal was formidable looking, and was severely injured, but if it won, why were they treating it so poorly?

The men stopped in front of Vlargcar's cell. The complete darkness prohibited the men from seeing the seven foot monster that lurked inched away from them through an iron bar door. The stench of ale, smoke, and body odor wafted from the two men. Their words were slurred and it did not take Vlargcar long to figure out they were intoxicated. Their words were hard to understand, he only spoke a bit of the human tongue. The other champion, Jude, had been trying to teach him when they were in the training room together, but he only got to go there once a week.

"Let's not waste our time. Just kill the fool dog here," one soldier called out.

The other drew a dagger from his belt and kneeled down and placed the weapon under the dog's neck. It offered no resistance, accepting the fate that was about to befall it.

Rage erupted in Vlargcar. How dare they kill this animal? He had defeated a foe that these two soldiers could not
and he had no armor, no sword to do it with.

Vlargcar did not think as he shot out his tree trunk like
arms from his bar. Both of his vice like hands seized the
necks of the two men. With tremendous force he jerked the
two men back into the bars. The veins in his arms bulged as
he pulled and squeezed with all of his might. The soldiers
tried to cry out, but the iron grasp that held their necks prevented them from uttering a sound. Seconds later the pop of
the soldier's necks preceded their bodies going limp. Vlargcar tossed the men to the floor of the hallway. Warm blood
ran down his hands and dripped onto the floor. It was the
first time in his life he had not offered an enemy a chance to
surrender before he killed them. Vlargcar pondered the truth
briefly and quickly dismissed it. They should not have been
trying to betray the warrior animal.

The dog looked up at the hulking figure and turned
his head to the side. He sniffed the dead soldiers and then
sniffed at the orc.

Vlargcar kneeled down and stuck out his hand. "Hi."

The dog struggled to his feet and staggered on shaky
legs to the great orc. Vlargcar patted the animal on top of his
head. The dog wagged his tail and the orc scooped him up.
The dog did not protest as Vlargcar took him back into his
cell. He made a small bed of straw and fed the dog some of
his gruel and bread. Vlargcar laid down and covered up. He
rolled over and found himself face to face with the dog. It
was sitting and wagging its tail as it looked him in the face.

"What do you want?" he asked.

The dog did not say anything, but wagged his tail a bit
ore furiously.

Vlargcar reached down and grabbed the animal by his
collar and helped him into his bunk. The dog quickly circled
and laid down, placing his head on Vlargcar's leg. The orc
marveled at how the touch of the animal made him feel. He
reached down and examined a small metal tag that hung
from the dog's neck.

"E-D-G-E," he said to himself. He did not know what

that meant, but he knew his friend Jude would be able to read it for him. Within moments, the two were asleep.

"Do the gods really exist? My mother often spoke to me about the Goddess of Mercy. She had been a loving goddess that forgave all and understood why some men were driven to great evil by being victims of it themselves. She had explained to me that evil only begot more evil, that it was a long chain that sometimes never ended. She explained to me that when someone wronged us, it was better to find why they wronged us. What had they suffered to cause them to act so?

My father loved my mother so, but he argued it mattered little. Their wickedness was a chosen action and by their own decision they brought the hammer of justice down on their own heads. I used to listen to them argue for hours about it. My mother always seemed to win, much to my father's dismay, but he loved her for it. He used to brag he had never met a man with her wisdom, let alone another woman. I miss my mother. I will do as she says and pity the men that took her from me, but as my father taught; I will pity them to the dark recesses of the Abyss!"

-Lancalion Levendis Lampara-

2
Friends and Foes

Jude sat in his cell and crunched on a juicy red apple. He had access to food whenever he needed it. He guessed it was a bonus for being one of the premier fighters. His cell had not changed and he stared at a king's board through the bars of his door. Copel was not as foolish as he looked and he had Jude under check and into a tight spot. If he moved his queen, he would be in check. If he moved his king, he would lose the queen.

"Never liked the bitch anyway," Jude growled as he moved his king.

Copel smiled and eagerly moved his castle and captured Jude's queen. "I think I have finally beaten you, Iratus."

Jude nonchalantly took another bite of the juicy apple. He hated being called that. He knew some of his ancestors were Iratus, but he located the fact he had their talents. Jude favored intelligence over brawn. The large swordsman chewed the oversized bite and moved his cleric diagonally, defeating Copel's castle.

"Checkmate."

Copel jerked his head in shock. "How did you…? I had you beat, gladiator."

Jude smirked and leaned back in his cell. "I am not defeated until my king falls, jail keeper."

The hint of his current situation was not lost on the portly keeper. "So what is Jude's king?"

Jude chewed the reminder of the oversized bite and placed his massive arms behind his head and he leaned back against the cool stone wall. "I don't know. I have never followed a king."

Copel shook his head as he began to pick up the finely crafted kings set. "Surely you would die for someone."

Jude swished his tongue around his mouth for a minute. "Probably my friend, Lance. Assuming he still lives."

Copel placed the last king piece into the case and gently closed the wooden lid. "You have mentioned him many times. He does not seem significant. Why do you follow him?"

Jude shrugged. "Eh, I don't know. He was always a nice kid. Several years younger than I. He had a rough go of it growing up. I guess I always felt sorry for him and wanted to keep an eye out for him. Like an older brother, maybe."

Copel stood and scooted the old wooden chair back against the wall. "I am saddened that you will most likely die in here."

Jude took a deep breath and spit. The globule escaped he bars and landed on the stone floor near Copel. "You are not my friend, jail keeper. You are my master, I am your slave. If killing you would allow me to escape, you would already be dead."

Copel lost a little color in his face and his hurt expression said it all. "That saddens me, Jude. I am not your enemy."

Jude leapt from his cell and thrust himself against his bars. Bits of stone broke loose near the ceiling and crumbled down into his dark black hair. His powerful arms flexed and the veins in his neck bulged.

"Listen to me, fool!" Jude growled, "The day you let me escape is the day that you can work on calling me friend. Until then, sleep with one eye open!"

Copel nodded solemnly as a knock on the door echoed in the chamber.

"Sir, is everything okay?"

Copel opened the door and was met by two roving

guards. They had a look of concern on their weary faces.

"Yes, everything is fine. What do you need?"

"Sir, we found John and Gordan dead in the hall outside of the giant orc's cell."

Copel but at his lip. They were off the last two days, "Why were they in the coliseum?"

"They, uh. Well sir, they, uh."

Copel glared. "Dogfighting again?"

"Yes, sir," the men answered.

"And is the hallway to the orc's cell off limits?" Copel asked.

"Yes, sir, it is."

"Then send them to the undertaker. Send the rest of their month's pay to their spouses and tell them that they were killed in a slave uprising and that the slave was tortured and killed."

"But, the orc is in his cell," the men answered.

"Do you have a problem with following orders?" Copel asked through the crack in the door.

"Uh, no, sir."

Copel did not say anything else. He slammed the door closed and shook his head.

"The orc killed two guards?" Jude asked.

Copel nodded and started to pick up the apple cores Jude had tossed into the room.

"He is a good being. There is no wickedness in him. The guards must have been tormenting him," said Jude.

Copel nodded. "Regardless, the men will demand justice."

Jude nodded slowly. "Perhaps you can give him a fighting chance? He deserves that, at least."

Copel pondered the thought. "I would have to pit him against an enemy so powerful that no one would suspect he would survive."

Jude nodded. "Yes, but he would have a chance. His fate would be his own."

Copel picked up the case and scooted the small wooden table next to the wall near the chair, "I can see about that. That is a good idea, Jude. You are a fair man."

Jude spit on the ground again. "Save your compliments, jail keeper."

"I am sorry, Jude," Copel said as he opened he heavy wooden door and started out into the hall.

"To hell with your sorrow, jail keeper!" Jude answered as the wooden door closed shut.

Copel wiped a lock of his greasy hair from his face as he started down the long corridor. "I tried to be your friend, Jude," he said to himself, "Perhaps it is best both you and the orc pass on to the afterlife."

The portly jailor made his way to the end of the corridor and muttered to himself. "Both of you deserve a fighting chance. I shall give you both what you deserve."

Amerix awoke from his sleep and sat up. A great pile of snow fell from his head and around his sleeping roll. It had snowed in the night and large flaks were still falling. The trees had been covered in bright white lines of icy powder. He grumbled to himself and rolled over to check the fire.

"Damn," he muttered to himself as he looked at the cold fire pit and half burned logs.

With a sigh, he got up and dusted the flakes from his small clothes. It did not feel cold enough for the snow, though it clearly had gotten colder. It was certainly an odd storm. The old general gathered up his gear and began the arduous task of placing his armor back on. It may have been as light as leather, but it still went on like plate.

After several minutes, Amerix had donned his fine set of plate. It seemed to have repaired itself from the scratches it had gotten from the sharp stones and the vice-like grip of the carnivorous vine. The renegade was not sure he liked that about his armor. Repairing itself as good and all, but how was he going to tell the great tale if he had no scars. As Amerix began to imagine telling the story, the sad truth fell over him like a crushing wave. He had no one to tell his stories too. The general gritted his teeth and hefted his pack over his shoulders and started back out to the trail.

It did not take long for the snow to stop and the sun to

come out. It made the ground a bit muddy, but Amerix did
not mind. He didn't really like the snow much anyway. As
he continued marching throughout the day, Amerix stopped
little. He occasionally snagged some berries from a bush, but
for the most part he marched on through the day and well
into the night.

He camped several times, and groaned as he made his
way around many small settlements. He was sure he was on
the road that would take him to central city. It was a wide
road and he frequently had to duck into the woods to avoid
being seen by merchants. He initially wanted to fight some
humans and test his new axes and armor, but he realized
that would bring trouble and attention that would slow him
from finding the Beyklan boy.

Amerix marched up the dirt road in the starlit night. The
cool wind blew by and the branches shook, creaking and
popping in the moonlit night. He was beginning to doubt his
god. How foolish was it to march into the very Beyklan city
he had tried to destroy. They surely would not accept him
with open arms. And if he did find this Beyklan, what was
he going to say? This plan seemed more and more ludicrous
as the days went on. Yet, the old dwarf plodded on, one foot
in front of the other.

Amerix heard a rustle up in the trail to his right. He narrowed his eyes and crouched low. He silently cursed himself for not camping hours ago. He was tired and not in the
mood to fight anything. To the old dwarf's bewilderment, a
stunning white horse stepped from the forest and into the
trail. It was a thick chested animal with a long wild mane
and tail. Its forelock was long and blew lightly in the breeze,
revealing a stout ivory horn that twisted around itself into a
perfectly straight point.

"Great," he said to himself, "That stupid horned horse
again."

Amerix stood up and waved his hands in the air. "Arrrgh!
Get outta' here, ye stupid horse! I got no treats fer ye!"

The unicorn did not seem upset or even remotely startled. She merely lowered her head as a small elf stepped
from the forest. He was wearing a breast plate that appeared

to be made from wood. He carried a long gnarled staff and had a long green bundle under his arm. It was clearly heavy and the elf struggled to carry it.

Blasted elves, Amerix thought to himself.

"Amerix Stormhammer?" the elf called out in dwarven, "Amerix Alistair Stormhammer?"

Amerix smiled and drew his axes. The brilliant bladed weapons shined in the pale moonlight. "Yea, that's me. So, what. Ye want to meet yer maker?"

The elf tossed the green bundle on the road. It did not bounce and seemed like it was heavy by the way it hit the cold dirt.

Amerix noticed that his comment seemed to infuriate the unicorn. He chuckled to himself, "Stupid horse."

The elf frowned in clear disgust. "As much as Ehleesha and I would enjoy sending you to the deep bowls of the Abyss, we are here to bring you this… on Leska's instructions."

"Send me to the Abyss?" Amerix said with a chortle, "Ye and what army?"

The elf did not respond, but the unicorn pawed at the ground furiously.

Amerix spit. "Bah! Even if ye were able to send me to the Abyss, I would become king there."

The elf shook his head and started back towards the forest. He paused at the edge of the road. "Leska demands that you return this to its owner. You will find him in the human village called Central City."

Amerix sighed and shook his head. "Piss on ye, elf. It just so happens that I am on me way to Central City, but I ain't yers, or the bitch Earth Mother's, stinking courier. Take the bundle yerself."

The elf shook his head again and vanished into the thick forest.

"What about ye, horsy? Ye want some?" Amerix said with a middle finger gesture.

Ehleeshuh reared up and kicked her front feet before landing in thundering heavy hoofed charge. Her mane shook in the cool night breeze.

Amerix spread his feet wide and gripped his axes tight.

"I owe ye a cutting, ye stupid horse. Steal from me when the boy and I were trapped."

Great clods of dirt erupted from behind the unicorn as she charged. Amerix gritted his teeth and charged back. His stubby legs propelled him forward. Ehleeshuh lowered her head and prepared to spear her dwarven enemy.

Just as the two met, Amerix swung his axe in a wicked strike. He missed and hit only air, as the unicorn vanished into a puff of small white powdery mist. The force of Amerix's strike propelled him forward and he fell to the cold dirt road. The deadly dwarf rolled with the momentum and popped up with his axes in a defensive posture. His old blue eyes scanned the forest of any sign of the elf or the unicorn, but he saw neither.

After a brief scan, the old dwarf sheathed his axes and starred back up the trail. When he reached the bundle he starred down at it for a few seconds.

Pick me up, stupid, a feminine voice called out in his mind.

Amerix jerked his head and looked down at the bundle. It sounded like the voice he heard at the sandbar at the bottom of the Dawson River.

"Ye just talk to me, bundle?"

There was no response. Amerix shook his head and kicked the bundle with his foot. The wrapping fell away, revealing the glimmering blade of a sword Amerix recognized immediately.

"Songsinger," he said to himself.

Amerix reached down and gently removed the wrappings to gaze at the beauty of the sword. It was like gazing at an old friend. He picked up the sword and held it. It did not hum and it was warm to his touch.

I missed ye too, he thought to himself and then wondered why he would think that? But, he did miss the sword.

"Are you talking to me, sword? Me father mentioned rare weapons that could speak to their owners."

You do not own me, the voice answered in Amerix's mind.

Amerix started down the trail holding Songsinger out in front of himself. "Well, I have ye now and the only way someone is getting ye from me is to kill me, so that kind of makes ye mine, sword."

Nonsense, Songsinger countered.

"Nonsense?" Amerix asked, "How do ye figure?"

I needed to get to the druid grove and speak to my followers. It took me many years, but I succeeded. And now, you are doing my will to return me to the man you took me from so I can serve the purpose I created myself for, the sword echoed in his mind.

Amerix chuckled as he walked up the trail in the darkness, "Okay, sword. I must be delusional. First, ye said followers. Who worships a sword, for one. Two, ye said created yerself. How in the bloody hell did ye make yerself?"

It doesn't matter, Athodrin. Get me to Apollisian as soon as possible.

"My name is Amerix, ye stupid sword," the renegade general countered.

The grizzled old general camped that night and started off early in the morning. Songsinger did not speak since their conversation on the trail. The radiant weapon never seemed to dirty or become tarnished. It was simply perfect. As Amerix started to place his armor on, he noticed that the metal from the sword was the exact color of that from his armor. He picked up the blade and held it next to himself. It was a perfect match. The old general never really studied the sword before. Its blade was long, almost as long as he was tall and it tapered to a perfect deadly point. The hilt was made of the gold colored metal that was exactly like his armor. The ends of the hilt flared up a bit on each side and under them was a carving of a woman that appeared to be tied up. Her hands were positioned over her head in such a way to suggest they were bound. Her legs were together and slightly bent in the middle. Her right foot was position on top of her left.

The handle of the sword was made out of some kind of marble, but it felt like leather and was easy to hold. The pommel of the sword was shaped like a crown, but unlike any crown he had ever seen. On top of the crown was the symbol of two open palms laced together and a rising sun between them. Amerix thought he should recognize the symbol, be he could not recall what it was from. He had seen it many times in his youth, but he just couldn't recall it.

The grizzled old general shrugged and slid the sword over his back in a make shift scabbard he made the previous night. As he marched, the cool spring winds blew from the west and shook the trees that now had budding leaves. Amerix took a deep breath and closed his eyes. The air was refreshing. The one thing that he liked on the surface world was the wind. It always brought fresh air and fresh smells. Amerix opened his eyes and sighed. Another human city. This one was going to be hard to avoid. It was quite spread out and appeared longer than it was wide. Maybe he would slip through the middle and no one would give him a second glance. He took a deep breath and stuck his thumbs in his pack as he started forward.

The town was fairly small as human villages went. The structures were almost all one story, save for a huge building in the middle of the town near a stone well. The first few villagers did not pay Amerix more than a passing glance. A few had some lingering stares, but nothing more.

"Hmph," Amerix mumbled under his breath, "Maybe this town is a bit more tolerant. I might be able to get some supplies here."

The old general made his way toward the two story building. It had a brick foundation, but everything else was made of wood. Several people made their way in and out. Amerix stepped onto the rickety wooden porch and clunked his way inside. A few of the humans spoke to him, but he did not understand what they were saying, so he nodded and smiled. The inside of the building was a large expansive room. There was a set of stairs on the north wall and dozens of tables and chairs that were scattered about. A few humans sat around. Some playing cards, some were eating and drinking. Amerix smiled, and realized that this establishment served food. He clanked up to the bar. He was tall enough to see over the counter, but not by very much.

A middle aged human came up to him as he was wiping his hands on a cloth. He was balding and a bit over weight. He wore an apron and loomed over Amerix in a threatening way. The old dwarf ignored the man's tone and made the motion of soup and patted his belly.

The barkeeper shook his head from side to side and pointed toward the door. Amerix bit his lip. A swift axe slice and he could cut the man down and take what he wanted. In fact, based off of what he saw, he could probably cut down every man in this stupid one horse little town.

Amerix smiled and tossed a gold coin on the counter. The barkeep stared at it for a bit and then back to Amerix. Amerix watched patently as the barkeeper frowned and snatched up the coin. He began shouting back into the room behind the bar. Amerix stood where he was until the barkeep looked at the old general and pointed to a table. Amerix nodded and made his way over to one in the back. He dropped his pack on the floor and removed Songsinger from his back and leaned the enchanted sword against the wall. He hopped up on the chair and removed his armored gauntlets and his shining new horned helm.

A young woman came forward and timidly set a wooden mug in front of Amerix. She smiled and scurried off. The renegade smelled the mug. It was some form of ale. He shrugged his shoulders and took a drink. It was human ale. The stuff was normally so weak that you could put it in a baby bottle, but this was pretty strong. At least by human standards. He glanced over the rim of the mug at the barkeep. He was watching Amerix intently.

The grizzled dwarf took a sip and nodded to the barkeep, who then seem satisfied and started back to his task of washing mugs.

Amerix sipped the ale a bit longer when a large human walked in. He was well over six foot tall. His skin was bronze and he had long black hair with black bear claws that were woven into it. Amerix made him out to be Kai-Harkian almost immediately. Of all the humans, he liked them the best. They were a hardy folk. They could eat anything, drink forever, and most of them spoke dwarven.

The man made his way to the counter and ordered a drink. He dropped a few copper coins on the table and was given a mug. He turned and examined the room until his eyes fell on Amerix. He smiled and made his way over.

The man loomed over Amerix's table briefly. Amerix glanced up and made eye contact. The man had piecing brown eyes that seemed to look deep into Amerix. When the man met Amerix's gaze, he smiled.

"Can I sit?" he asked in dwarven.

Amerix did not answer; he just kicked a chair out next to him. The large man sat down and placed his drink in front of him.

"I didn't expect to see yer kind so close to Central City," the man said.

Amerix eyed him suspiciously with his steel blue eyes. "How far from Central City am I?"

"'Bout three to four days," the man said as he took a sip, "Prolly make it by the end of the week if you travel hard."

"What makes ye think I am going that way?" Amerix asked.

The man took a long draw from his drink before answering, "I seen you come in from the south. You got to have a death wish to be heading north. So I figured if I was a dwarf with a death wish, where would I go? Central City of course."

The serving wench came over and placed a large plate of roast meat in front of Amerix. There were small white bulbous things next to it and three long orange looking vegetable spikes. The plants were obviously boiled and there was a rapidly melting pad of yellow lard like substance that as dripped down between them.

"You like beef, huh?" the Kai-Harkian asked.

Amerix glanced up with a disgusted look on his face. "I like food. This is food, so I like it."

The Kai-Harkian was silent for a moment and watched with earnest as Amerix tried his food. "I see you like beef."

Amerix chewed slowly and eyed the man. He was growing quite annoyed by his presence. "Don't ye have some ibexes to hunt?"

The man chuckled, "I have seen many dwarves in my day, but never one your size. You are older than Old Man Mountain so you must be the rogue general, Amerix."

Amerix stopped eating and suddenly became aware of his surroundings. He began to count the number of patrons their weapons and in what order he would cut them down as he made his way out of the building.

"What if I am?"

The man smiled as his soup was delivered by the serving wench. He thanked her and slid two copper into her palm. She smiled and glanced back. He said some words that Amerix did not understand. Was he telling her to rouse the guards?

"Answer quickly, boy, or die. Yer choice," Amerix warned.

The Kai-Harkian did not seem distressed. "Settle down, General. I don't think the folks here have seen enough dwarves to know that you are grossly oversized."

"I saw ye alert the serving girl and palm her some coins. Just know that if the guards come in here, I will kill ye first," Amerix growled.

The man shook his head from side to side and chuckled. He brought his spoon to his mouth and carefully sipped the soup. "I gave her a tip, General. It is called a gratuity. Humans don't pay their workers well, so it is customary to give them a little extra."

Amerix frowned and glanced back at the bar. No one was paying much attention to him. "I have a lot of enemies, dog. I have not lived this long by being reckless or offering them any advantage."

The man nodded and blew on another spoonful of soup before putting it into his mouth. He savored the watery concoction before swallowing. "This is true. Your entire clan is killed-twice, and you manage to survive every time. So tell me why you are doing the exact opposite of what has kept you alive, and going to Central City?"

"Are ye saying Clan Stoneheart is no more?" Amerix asked with interest.

The man nodded and took a bite of bread. "Yep. The King of Beykla marched the entire Western Army to their door. Killed them to the last. The wily dwarf king had a surprise for them. It was a giant white dragon. It decimated half of their numbers before the battle even began. The idiot Beyklan king charged on in anyway. I think of the thirty-thousand strong army, only a few hundred survived. The dwarves were nearly completely defeated when the roof caved in on them. General Bodrell spent months digging out the bodies. They found the king and several of his best warriors in a circle. They fought to the death. Quite heroic, if you ask me."

Amerix felt sick to his stomach. He should have been with them. He could have died a hero with his brothers. No, they would not have accepted him. He lied to the king and took his army.

"Bah. They were girly dwarves. The lot of 'em. Had I been there, I would have cut that army down single handedly."

"I suppose that is what you are planning to do at Central City? It has grown a bit since your army was defeated. Seems after the Torrent, it fueled their love for Duke Blackhawk. When he defeated your army, people flocked there by the hundreds. I bet it is nearly twice as big as it was before."

Amerix took another bite of meat and then stuffed a bite of the white bulbous vegetable in his mouth. He decided he liked this dish very much. He chewed and swallowed and washed it down with a big gulp of ale.

"No, I am going there to return something that I should not have taken."

"Don't waste your time, General. They won't let you get into the city before they try to kill you."

Amerix frowned. "I have no choice, it is the right thing to do. If the filthy murderous dogs kill me, so be it."

"My people have a saying that might make some sense to you, General," the man said, "Everyman is perfect in his own sight."

Kellacun stepped from the blazing bright orange portal that took her from Kalen's study to the cool night atop of the Central City civic building. She expected the air to be warmer and the signs of a recent snow fall confounded her.

The assassin made her way around the side of the dome and ducked under the stone archway that led to a group of stairs that extended down into darkness. Her trip brought crushing memories of her childhood love, Joshua. She had traversed this way when she confronted her fiancé after she discovered her parents had been murdered. It was the last time that she embraced him as a lover. He was always an estranged enemy after that.

She deftly moved down the stairs to the heavy wooden door at the bottom. She examined the exterior of the door with her delicate fingers. Sliding them up and down the smooth wood finish and smiled when they ran across a small ridge. She pulled her thin silver dagger from her hair and pried on it. The wooden panel popped loose quietly revealing a small poison needle trap that was set to spring launch when the door was opened from the outside.

She stepped to the side and prodded the trigger pate with her dagger. The dart shot out and landed harmlessly on the stairs. Kellacun picked up the dart and placed the end in her mouth as she set about the task of picking the lock. In seconds, the door was unlocked. She diligently placed her lock picks in her belt pouch and pulled out a small brown jar. She unscrewed the lid and placed it against the door, with her ear on the other end. Satisfied when she did not hear anyone on the other side, she silently opened the door just enough for her to slip through. She hastily reset the needle trap and used a bit of tree sap glue to place the panel back over the trap. When she finished, she slipped into the stone hallway and used her picks to relock the door.

The assassin used her finger to place a lock of her dark black hair behind her ear as she moved down the middle of the bright red carpet that extended to the end of the hall. It had not been opened in many months. There was a fine layer of dust on the stone floor, but the rug was free of debris. She removed the cone from her pouch and listened to the door. She could make out guard's voices from the other side.

"Midnight already?"

"Yep, the taverns are still open. You gonna go chase Susie?"

"Nah, got me a new squeeze."

"Really? New as in Susie doesn't know, or new as in Susie dumped you."

"She didn't dump me. It was a mutual break up."

"Right," the voice chuckled, "So tell me of the new number."

"Well, while Dolin is away, I have been spending time with Seirra."

"His granddaughter?"

"Shhh. Yea, so?"

"How old is she?"

"Old enough to be treated like a lady."

"The duke will have you hung if he finds out."

"How can he? He won't be back until tonight and yesterday's snow storm is likely going to keep him another day."

Kellacun moved away from the door. Dolin had a granddaughter? That would mean that Joshua must have married. Kellacun felt a burn in her nose as her eyes watered and a warm tear trickled down each of her cheeks.

She moved away from the door and placed the cone back into her pouch. She knew that Joshua would likely move on after he was reassigned. She had not seen him since she was sixteen, but he was her only love. She would love him forever.

As she slipped back through the door to the rooftop, she did not miss the irony that she was about to kill the father of the only man she had ever loved.

Kellacun climbed down from the rooftop and made her way into the alleys behind the civic building. She moved silently and deftly. Her sleek black leather outfit seemed to meld into the shadows as she searched for a sewer grate.

In minutes she located a grate and tried to lift it. The heavy grate resisted her. Kellacun frowned and noticed that it had been locked. That struck her as odd. The assassin quickly picked the lock and slid under the heavy wooden grate. Once inside, she carefully relocked the small metal fastener and climbed down the rusty metal sewer rungs.

When she stepped down into the sewers, it brought back a wave of emotion. She used to live down here, in the Severed Hearts Guild. She detested Pav-co, but he paid nicely.

She suspected that he was the one that hired Grascon to kill her. When she survived the attack, she figured that she could not trust Pav-co any longer.

She would pay a visit to ole Pavie and let him know she was working on a mark from the king of Nalir. The last thing she wanted was the guild rogues trying to trip her up.

Kellacun deftly moved through the sewers. She avoided a few of the fetid corridors natural inhabitants and was shocked when she came across the guild door. The secret door in the wall was left wide open. When she stepped through to the other side, the long corridor was littered with debris and pieces of wood. At the far end of the hall, the great wooden door that held the beholder had been smashed. Bits of wood and other debris was scattered over the floor.

Kellacun kneeled down and a lock of her sleek black hair fell in front of her face as she examined the broken door. She used to marvel at how beautiful it had been. One of the few things of beauty in the guild.

She quietly placed the piece of wood back down and stepped into the guild chambers. She found dismembered skeletal remains of the guild in a large pile in front of the main chamber area. Kellacun covered her mouth as the stench of rotting flesh washed over her. She slowly moved into the room. By all appearances, the guild hall had been sacked a year or so ago. Why was there the smell of rotting flesh? She moved towards Pav-co's chamber. Her vision was keen and allowed her to see in the dark, a fact that was shared by all lycanthropes. *Who did this to the guild? How did they get in? Couldn't the guild have seen their torches, or could the attackers see in the dark?*

Kellacun started to turn when a flash of movement to her right caught her attention. She ducked low and drew her silver dagger.

Rushing from the shadows was a large ten foot long green grub worm. It had dozens of tentacles that extended out in front of it, like a squid. It had a single wide mouth, like that of a human, and was filled with hundreds of needle-like teeth. Outside of the mouth were two large pinchers, like that of a stag beetle.

Kellacun transformed into her wererat form and leapt over the creature. Its tentacles flailed up at her and caught her boot. She landed safely on the other side. The creature seemed to have a slow time trying to turn, so she rushed out of the chamber and back into the hallway. Her foot began to tingle as she ran and she soon found that her foot was going numb and the tingling was beginning to spread up her leg. A loud splash behind her told the assassin that the giant grub had made it into the sewer corridor.

By the time Kellacun had reached the ladder, she was nearly numb from the waist down. She struggled to climb the grate to the surface. Her chest began to tingle and itch and her arms were getting weak. She fumbled with her lock picks and managed to open the lock. She weakly pushed the grate up and slid under it as her useless legs drug behind her. She rolled over and fumbled with the lock. She slid it through the iron hasp and slid it in with a resounding click. She weakly rolled over away from the grate as thin green tentacles began to reach out from between the bars. They patted the alley floor searching for her. Kellacun could feel the paralyzing poison flowing through her veins. She rolled over a few more times until the poison over took her. She laid there in the alley staring up at the starlit sky. It did not take the grub long to realize it had lost its meal and it abandoned the hunt. Kellacun had heard of those monsters, but they stayed much farther down in the sewers. There must be next to no activity in them for one of those creatures to venture so far to the surface. She sighed and hoped that no one would find her before morning. The poison usually took a few hours to wear off and getting picked up in an alley could have disastrous consequences.

"Do the ends justify the means? Often this wisdom comes to light in life. If it has not, it will. There will come a time when you must ask yourself if the results of the methods you use to achieve a task are worth the end result. I wanted justice for my parents and was willing to break the law to find that justice. I do not know if the thief killed anyone to get those parchments. I do not know who he stole from, or if he stole at all. Is that wrong? I could easily say I paid him to retrieve the parchments. The methods he used are beyond my control, but were they?

I was wrong for hiring Grascon to steal those parchments. Had he not, I might have never been set upon the path I would un-intentionally walk. But had I not, would I have walked down any path, or would I have become a victim like the Ecnal's before me, a great person in time, lost to senseless murder. Of these things I will never know.

Do the ends justify the means? I guess it is a question best answered by those who suffer the means."

-Lancalion Levendis Lampara-

3
Apollisian's Second Flea

The carriage bounced and jostled down the trail. Fehzban was becoming more comfortable with his return to nor-
malcy. He had a full three day growth on his chin and he
spent most of his days sitting up with the driver and visit-
ing with Apollisian. Ian and Alexis rode to the front looking
for potential dangers while Stieny huffed and pouted about
anything he could come up with.

Lance read in the Necromidus and wove partial spells,
marveling at how it was all beginning to make sense to him.
He would summon forth several snake-like tendrils and let
them dance in front of him. He could begin to see the pattern
of how they fit together and how certain patterns created
certain effects. Today he had summoned a small weave of
Abjuration. The bright orange threads seemed to bend light
around them.

"Delania, why do abjuration threads bend the light
around themselves? Almost like they are here and some-
place else at the same time."

Delania was roused from her daydream. She turned to
see Lance fooling with some Abjuration weaves. "I am sorry,
my love. What did you say."

Lance frowned and dismissed the weaves. "You have
been acting weird the last couple of days. What's wrong? I
do want to marry you, but I told you it is my people's custom

that the man propose with a ring."

Delania shook her head in dismissal. "No Lance, that is not it," she said as her nose burned and her voice cracked.

Lance scooted closer with a worried look on his face. "You can tell me. We have no secrets between one another."

Delania turned. Her bright blue eyes met his emerald orbs. Could she tell him? Would he trust her, would he *love* her? "Lance, do you love me?"

"Of course," he said with a chuckle.

"No, I mean love me forever. Do you love me no matter what happens?" she said, trying to think of way to prepare him for the truth. Could she tell him she was with child? Could she tell him that she was a demon from the Abyss?

Lance took her hand in his and turned her cheek toward him with his other hand. "I love you like the sun shines, like the moon turns, and like the rain falls. Nothing can stop it."

She smiled and kissed him tenderly. "Lance, I think I am with child."

"What?" he said, "Are you sure? We only did it a few times."

Delania nodded. "I think so. Fehzban is skilled in knowing these things. He told me he believes it so. He offered to marry us. If you would ask me, that is."

Lance nodded. He felt so close to her. He got down on one knee and began to summon several threads of bright yellow conjuration. They swirled and twisted in the carriage, tumbling and falling over one another, until they formed a two small rings of magical energy that were joined together to form the number eight.

"Delania, my love," he started with a trembling lip, "Will you marry me? Will you join your soul to mine?"

Delania felt tears welling up in her eyes. "Does it bind our souls? Will it bind them forever?"

Lance smiled, "Of course, my love."

"But what if we lose our souls?" she asked worriedly as tears streamed down her face, "What if our soul is taken from us?"

Lance nodded and summoned a power from deep inside of himself. Thin clear divine weaves shot out from him. They extended out through the carriage and into the forest. They were heavy and clumsy, but he strained and brought them into one another. Once they touched, they bent and twisted to his will easily. Lance narrowed his eyes and encircled the two conjuration rings with a divine one and looped them onto his and Delania's soul. He tied the weaves off and made them permanent. "There, my love, our souls are bound together. No one can take your soul without taking mine."

Delania grabbed him by both cheeks and giggled as she kissed him. Lance wiped her tears away with his thumb. "So will you marry me?"

She frowned. "Yes! But, you do not have a ring like your people say you need."

"Nah, I just made two rings that encircled our souls. Those are better than any ring a man could make."

Delania giggled as she wiped a tear from her cheek. "So you can see my soul?"

"I don't really see it, but I could feel it with the magic, so I circled it and linked it with mine," he said.

Delania took him in her arms. She could feel his strong embrace. Lance was not a warrior, but he still had a masculine hug that made her feel safe.

Ian signed as he rode down the trail. His butt was getting sore at the hard pace they were making. He had not rode this much since his adventuring days. Life at the keep had made him a little pampered when it came to trail life. He was used to a hot and a cot every night.

Alexis glanced over and looked Ian up and down. He did not seem to fit into the group of Lance and Delania. "So how did you end up with those two?"

Ian glanced back at the carriage, then back at Alexis. She was beautiful, even for an elf. "My home town was sacked by the death knight and his army. I left the keep and warned the townsfolk. They did not take my warnings for heart. They believed, and foolishly so, that Lord Brightson would be able to defend them," he said as his voice trailed off.

"So what happened?" Alexis asked.

"The monsters were like nothing I had ever seen. They ran as fast as a man in sprint, but they did not tire. They could paralyze a man with a claw or a bite. Not sure which.

Then, as the men lay there screaming, they were eaten alive."

Alexis shuddered and leaned back to make sure there were not any following them. "So how did you survive? Were you able to outrun them?"

Ian nodded. "Me and Knotts ran down the pier. I had a single mast boat there. The fool horse jumped in it. I don't know how long I was at sea, but I put to ashore and started southeast when I met up with them."

Alexis nodded and glanced back at the dwarf that Lance had healed. He was happy and jovial and stroked his short beard every few seconds. "So where did you find the dwarf?"

"I found him on the trail. I didn't think he would live past the night, but he stayed alive."

Alexis frowned. "So Lance did heal him and it was not some trick?"

"It seems that way. I don't know much about the ways of the godly, but he does not seem to follow the guideline that I would expect a man of the cloth to adhere to."

Alexis nodded. "Yes, he surely is something else. I think the undead monster follows him."

"Why do you think that?" Ian asked.

"Alexis, we should be nearing the junction this afternoon," Apollisian called forward to her.

She nodded to Apollisian and then turned back to Ian. "It doesn't matter, he is coming with us. Let's just hope he is as innocent as my foolish husband believes him to be."

"I don't think he believes he is innocent. Your husband just strikes me as the guy that puts principle above practical."

Alexis chuckled. "You have no idea."

Fehzban climbed down from his conversation with the driver and entered the carriage cabin. Delania and Lance glanced up at him as he entered.

"Am I interrupting something?" Fehzban asked.

"No," Lance said, "Do you think you could marry us?"

"Sure," Fehzban said with a smile as he hopped in, "Do you have rings?"

"Uh," Delania stammered, "We have already exchanged them."

"Oh. No big deal," the dwarf said as he mumbled to himself.

"Everything okay?" Lance asked

"Yep. I just need to remember what to say. I have not done a wedding since I was with my clan," he said, rubbing his rapidly growing beard.

"How long ago was that?" Delania asked.

Fehzban chuckled, "Too long."

"So you have seen many couples married? Do you think we will be a good one?" Lance asked with earnest.

"Lance, there is no way you can tell if a couple is good for one another. Only they can determine that themselves. If you have doubts or worries, then perhaps you should not marry."

"Oh no! We don't have any doubts," Delania interjected as she smiled and patted her belly.

Fehzban smiled, "Okay then. Take each other's hands."

Lance took Delania's hands and held them. They felt so warm. He gazed into her eyes as Fehzban spoke.

"Lance and Delania, do you take each other's soul to meld with your own? To have and to hold, from this day forward, for better or for worse, for times in wealth, and times in poverty, in sickness or in health, to love and to cherish until death do you part?" Fehzban said with a smile.

"No," Lance said.

"No?" Fehzban frowned, "How can you say 'no'?"

Lance did not take his eyes from Delania's. "It's easy. Because not even death will take my love from me. I am linked with her soul. We are one, together. Our souls are linked. So change that last part to forever."

"Okay," the befuddled dwarf said, "Forever."

"I do," Lance said with a smile.

"And do you, Delania?" Fehzban asked.

"I do," she said as a tear ran down her cheek. She had waited for a moment like this since the very day she could last remember. All of those thousand years in the abyss and now she had found love. She had found a true friend.

"Then I pronounce you husband and wife. You may kiss the bride," Fehzban said.

Delania pounced on Lance and smothered his mouth with hers. She forced him down on the bench and started fumbling with his belt.

Fehzban blushed. "Oh my! I guess you want some privacy!"

The dwarf quickly closed the curtains and hurriedly climbed out of the carriage and made his way back up to the driver. "They, uh... They don't want to be disturbed for a while."

The driver nodded. "Not the first time on this trip."

"Obviously," Fehzban said as he popped the cork on a small keg of spirits.

They rode on for several hours. As the sun fell into the western sky, they arrived at the Junction. It was an odd settlement at the meeting of three roads. One was not used any longer that lead to the old Torrent Manor. The road to the northeast lead to Dawson and the road southeast led to Central City. There was a three story building sitting directly in the middle of the odd settlement. There was a stable to the south of it and several long hitching posts set up in a grass lot outside where wagons and horses were tied, marking this building as an inn of some sort.

"Alexis, take the others down the trail. I will warn the men and women here that the death knight is coming. I cannot spend too much time. If they will not listen, I cannot stay to convince them," Apollisian said.

Alexis nodded and leaned over from the top of her horse and kissed Apollisian on the lips. He closed his eyes and exhaled. She breathed in and placed her hand on his cheek. She could become lost in his embrace.

Apollisian pulled away and smiled warmly at her. "Go, my love. I won't be long. That fool, Dolin Blackhawk did not listen to me when the dwarves were attacking. Surely he won't make the same mistake twice."

"Do not dally, husband. I have a horrible feeling about this army. I want to spend as much time with you as possible," she said.

Apollisian nodded and turned his Vendaigehn steed and hurried down the hill toward the junction. He made his way to the north building and knocked on the door. The sun had set and the feint glow in the western sky was being washed away by the dark blue cover of night. He could hear someone rustling around inside.

"Go away, you drunkard! The inn is behind you!" a tired voice called out from inside.

"Sir, I am no drunkard. My name is Apollisian Bargoe of Westvon Keep. I am here to warn you. There is a mass of undead marching this way. Get your things and flee to Dawson. You will be safe."

"Beat it, you drunken gutterspuck!" the voice called back.

Apollisian sighed. "Mind the snow, sir. If it snows, you have only a few hours."

"Piss off, before I alert the militia," the man called back.

Apollisian did not say anything else. He did what he felt he should do. He hit every structure in the Junction and got the same response. No one wanted to hear what he had to say. No one wanted to be inconvenienced from their lives to open the door, or pay attention to his warning. He started to untie his steed when he glanced at the inn. Why should he bother? They would not listen. Why should he even bother? But before he could rationalize any further, he found himself walking toward the front door.

As he walked in, the entire place reeked of ale and sweat. He had been here once before on his way to the Torrent a few days before the dwarves sacked it. The common room was a bit rough, but he did not recall it being this rowdy.

He made his way to the bar and snatched up a chair. The bartender looked at him and frowned, but did not say anything.

Apollisian took it into the center of the room and climbed on top of it. "Good people of the Junction. I am Apollisian Bargoe of Westvon Keep. I have just traveled at haste from the western Andorian wasteland. There I met a force of undead lead by a death knight that dwarfs the power of the necromancer from Calito."

The bar was silent for a few seconds before it erupted in laughter. Patrons tossed drinks and pieces of bread at him.

Apollisian climbed down and wiped the ale from his face. He returned the chair to the bar and started to leave when a firm hand grasped his arm. He turned to see the bartender had snatched his wrist.

"Unhand me, sir. I have returned your chair. My job here is done," Apollisian said.

The bartender leaned close. "Are you the paladin that warned us about the dwarves in Central City?"

Apollisian frowned. "Yes, how do you know that?"

"I was the militia guard that took you to the waiting office," he said solemnly, "You are one of the rare honest men in this world. If you tell me again that this army is indeed coming, I am going to take my family and flee to Dawson immediately."

Apollisian looked the man in the eye. There was true worry and concern on his face. "I understand this will be financially trying," he said as he handed the man two gold coins, "I wish it was more, but this ought to be enough for you to recover some losses and hold you over until it is safe to return."

The man looked down at the two coins and nodded his head solemnly. "You are a great man, Apollisian. My family and I will leave tonight. What will you do?"

"I am on my way to Central City to speak with the duke again. I hope he is more receptive this time."

The barkeeper handed Apollisian a skin of water and a fresh towel. "Do you need provisions? I have food I can give you."

Apollisian took the towel and wiped the ale from his face. "No, keep your food. You will need it more than I. We have provisions and we are only three days from Central City."

The man nodded and started packing things up from the bar. Apollisian glanced at the crowd one more time and shook his head. In a few days they would know a hell like no other.

The cool night air greeted Apollisian as he left the inn and untied his horse. He untied the steed and mounted up, drying himself off the best he could. He packed the towel in his saddle bags and spurred his horse south to catch up with the group. He missed Alexis already.

Doogan Raymer gently closed the door to his city stateroom. The duke had put him and Edgar up in the civic building. He was hoping for lavish inn accommodations, but it seems these quarters would be sufficient. He tossed his bags on the bed and surveyed the room. It was nicely done. It had a large rug, bathing tub, dresser, coat rack, chamber pot, and mirror. He checked himself in the mirror and sucked in his belly. He frowned when it did not move and quickly dismissed his fatness.

"Women want money more than muscle," he said to himself.

After a quick once over, he closed the door to his stateroom and walked down the smooth polished floor. He passed the guards with no greeting and made his way into the bustling streets. Central City was turning into a haven since the defeat of Amerix. Crowds of people stirred through the streets. Tent merchants set up shops throughout the city, making every day seem like a fair. The economy boomed, and the coffers grew. The thieves' guild vanished, likely killed by the dwarves and life was good for Beyklans here.

Raymer glanced about as he made his way down the street. Merchants and street hucksters beckoned to him, but the fat noble ignored their calls. He examined the street until his eyes spied a large crowd of patrons standing under a balcony of a small two story villa flat. Sitting with his back to the crowd was a man dressed in black. He wore black leather pants and a black cotton tunic. He had long black hair that hung down from under his dark black fedora. He held a paint brush in one hand and a palette in the other. A large canvas sat on an easel in front of him. Doogan made his way through the crowd and pushed his way to towards the front to get a better view.

He made his way towards the front of the crowd and marveled as the Duco-Letum applied paint to canvas. The painting appeared to be some fantastic zombie but the piece was devoid of all color. Doogan poked the man to his left. "He is better than I had ever imagined."

The man nodded and quickly averted his eyes to the street painter. "He is quickly becoming a legend."

"Does he always paint with just black and white paint?" Raymer asked.

The man gave Raymer a disgusted look. "He does not use black. Any good painter never uses black. He just uses deep blues."

Raymer shrugged and shook his head as he glanced back up to the painting. *Sure looks black to me,* he thought.

In a short while the Duco stood and turned to the crowd. An attractive woman stepped out onto the balcony. She had brownish red hair and she was dressed in a nice silk robe. She held her hands up to hush the crowd.

"What is she doing?" Raymer asked.

"Shhhhhh!" several people in the crowd answered angrily.

Raymer started get angry. Did they have any idea who they were shushing? Before the he could fire back an egotistical reply, the woman started speaking.

"William has completed his latest portrait." she said.

Duco stood and held his painting up for the crowd to see. There were many silent whistles and some gasps of awe from the crowd.

Raymer stared in wonder at the piece. It was the side of a mountain that had carved faces in it. Five in all, but the faces were grossly exaggerated and made to look like zombies. Raymer was initially turned off by the work, but the more he looked at the piece, the more brilliant it appeared.

"We will open the bidding at five silver pieces," the woman announced to the crowd.

In seconds the crowd was alive with bids.

"Ten gold!" Raymer shouted out.

The crowd hushed quickly and some kicked the ground angrily. The woman waited for a bit and the crowd watched expectantly, but no one else offered another bid.

"You win, sir," she called out, "Approach the door and you will be let up."

Raymer made his way to the door of the building. It was an average door and did not seem to be made of fantastic quality. In a short moment the door opened and the woman let him in.

Raymer went inside and was offered a seat. The interior

of the home was quite lavish. There were many plush seats and velvet cushions set about. Various works of macabre art were hung on the walls, as well as some more traditional work depicting the great Laricin West. The piece that caught Raymer's eye was a huge orc that was standing in the arena with two swords drawn. The beast had a large wild mowhawk and tattoos on his face. He looked much like a cross between an ogre and an orc, except for his bright blue eyes. He wielded two huge swords that dripped blood that he held out in front of him. He had a few minor wounds and his dead enemies lay around him amid a dark torrential sky in a packed coliseum setting.

"I am Heather, William's assistant. Do you have the payment?" the woman asked.

Raymer opened his coin purse and counted out ten gold coins. Heather accepted them and handed the painting to him. "It is still a bit wet. You will want to set it in the sun to sure the paints."

Raymer nodded and took the painting. "What of these other paintings?"

"They are not for sale," Heather said.

"Who is the orc?" Raymer asked pointing to the painting on the wall.

"That is Vlargcar. He is one of the current gladiator champions. They say he was trained by the Darayal Legion," she answered.

Raymer scoffed. "It is fitting that the elves would train an orc. I can't stand the damn self-righteous, pompous, long eared freaks."

Heather opened the door. "William will be putting on another show this weekend. Be sure to stop in. He is going to start at nightfall. Said he had a dream that he would be inspired that night."

"I'll be town for a week or so, I might stop by," he said as he stepped out into the street. He figured his son would like the painting.

"The Duco Letum. Surely an interesting character. His fascination with the macabre has been a discussion by many a magistrate. With warrants for his arrest in several countries-the painter of death ended up in Central City of all places.

While the artists seems harmless-some say those he paints always meet an untimely death sometime later on. I can say for certain I know of several portraits he has painted that the ...victims later died. Some of their deaths were quite horrific.

I once visited the halls of the Ducom Letum for my own portrait. What I found fascinating was that he once painted himself. The sad irony of this oft makes me ponder the fate of the painter of death."

-Lancalion Levendis Lampara-

❧ 4 ❧
Promises of Blood

Sir Oswald Thorrin made his way through the city. There seemed to be a strange tension among the people. He surmised it was the big gladiator fight that was coming this weekend. He had to admit that he was excited to see the event. The orc that was trained by the Darayal Legion was supposed to fight a ogre. He doubted the green skinned monster could defeat such a foe. But, he would have never believed that an orc could have blue eyes either.

As he casually strolled he spied a large robust man wearing nothing but silk standing under the balcony of that horrid street painter, William Tackett. The corpulent man was loaded with jewelry and seemed to have a ring on every finger. He appeared to be traveling alone and was a fool to advertise his pockets to the commoners. Sure, the thieves' guild had been inactive for well over a year, but dressed as he was, even a common cut purse would flock to him like flies to a dung heap.

He street painter held his painting aloft for the crowd to see, and as he surmised, the fat noble outbid everyone. The artist handed the painting to his wife and went inside his balcony door. Oswald despised the creepy man. Had he not been a soldier of principle, he would have invented some charges to get the man tossed into the city dungeons where he belonged. Though the captain figured such news would only add value to the detestable artist's work.

Oswald stared back towards the Blue Dragon inn, when he was met by one of his guards.

"Sir, the Central Army has building inspectors looking at the bridge," the man said with tired breaths, "But it looks like they are making some kind of modification."

Oswald sighed. "Your report is noted."

The guard nodded and headed back to his post hesitantly. Oswald glanced at the inn and back to the bridge. *A quick bite or should I speak to the bridge engineer?* he thought to himself.

Oswald debated the idea for a few more seconds before heading into the inn for lunch. The inspectors no doubt had some sort of work order, and if it was not in order, the bridge sergeant would have sent word.

General Bordrell walked through his camps talking with his men. They had set up the staging site just a mile from the Dawson River. Two units consisting of thirty scouts and ten soldiers each were staging on the north and south road from central City. Though it pained him to hold his own citizens as prisoners in a city, he knew it to be for the best. The person, or thing, the undead king was looking for must not be allowed to leave the city. Bodrell smiled, as far as he was concerned not a single walking corpse would leave it. As he made his way through his ranks he saw men, excited for battle. Some told stories and wild tales about how many undead they would cut down. Others seemed excited that their enemy would not scream as they died, or that they would feel no remorse dispatching the crippled foes. A few men were a bit concerned about the stench, a truth, he had not considered.

Bodrell made a sharp turned and walked past the camps of the legionnaires. They did not resemble a close-knit fighting force. They lacked uniformity and he could not distinguish rank or file. He knew who the leaders were, but could not make out a specific tent, or main operations stage point.

He did not see a meeting house, or the other normal military locations that he was accustomed two. Bodrell surmised that since they were such a small fighting force, that they were able to avoid such complication. But nearly two thousand legionnaires were worth an army of twenty thousand men. His father had told him stories of how the legion ripped a bloody whole in the side of the horde during the orc wars. He recalled the story of the legionnaires that went into battle with General Laricin West, knowing that they would all die. The Darayal Legion possessed an unnatural courage that he fond both disturbing and invigorating.

Bodrell nodded and waved a few more times to some of the troops and ended his stroll at the mage camp. This area resembled nothing like a war camp, and looked more like a carnival of moppets. Every tent was multicolored with bright reds and blues. Some were covered in stars and others with weird round balls floating in the night sky. Some of the balls were encircled in strange bright rings that were tiled on their sides. He ignored the lavishness of it all as he made his way to the arch mage's tent. He ducked under the flap and walked in to find Jon sitting by a hearth reading a book. He had a table next to him that held a bottle of Osimar wine and a crystal goblet. It was half filled with the bright red fluid.

"Jon, my men prepare for death and you sit in here and sip from a crystal goblet filled with wine that costs more than their homes," Bodrell said frustrated.

Jon smiled and picked up the goblet, swirling its contents before sipping again. "General, some men prepare for death in different ways. This is how I do it."

Bodrell scoffed. "Not likely."

Jon smiled and reached down beside his chair. He opened a small chest and pulled out a second goblet with one hand while closing his book with the other. "Pull up a chair, General."

Bodrell glanced behind him and dragged the easy chair over next to the wizard as he poured he second goblet full. Jon handed it to him as he sat down.

"So what brings you by, General? Surely not a casual visit. You are not a man of such things."

The general nodded. "I need to be sure that when we cross, your magic will be able to drop the bridge."

Jon smiled and sipped more wine. "Of course. I am assuming your engineers are drilling the holes and packing them with the fire powder?"

Bodrell nodded. "And another thing. Some of the men seem to be worried about the stench from the undead. I want your mages to whip up some kind of salve that we can place under their noses that will counter act their stench."

Jon nodded. "Shouldn't be too hard. Have your men gather about three hundred pounds of bitterroot and milkweed. I should be able to make a paste out of that which they can use."

Bodrell nodded, and then in a single gulp downed the wine, before setting the empty goblet on the small end table.

"You know, you are supposed to savor that," Jon said with a chuckle.

Bodrell stood and started towards the tent's door. "I will savor it when the undead king is dead for good."

Jon opened his book as the general left his tent. "I will hold you to that, General."

Apollisian and the others rode well into the night. The southern stars shined brightly amid a dark sky of black and blue. The group was weary from their steady pace. They took turns sleeping in the carriage when possible. Delania seemed as unaccustomed to riding as Lance did, while Ian seemed to enjoy it.

Ian rubbed his chin as he an Apollisian rode ahead, while Alexis and Delania slept in the carriage. Steiny rotated driving with the carriage master, who seemed afraid to say anything to anyone other than his repeated notifications that he was skipping the group once they made it to Central City.

"So, the elf is your wife?" Ian asked.

Apollisian glanced over at Ian. He was not an old man, but he was surely in his middle years. "Alexis is my wife. Her race is not important to me."

Ian nodded. "I thought I heard her call you husband. It is an unusual marriage. You must be a great man to earn a wife of such magnitude."

Apollisian nodded, unsure if Ian was complimenting him or insulting him. "I met her many years ago. In the service of my church long before the breaking."

"So it is true, the churches are broken." Ian said. "What churches were affected? Do they know why?"

Apollisian shook his head sadly. "We do not. At first, I thought it had something to do with taking Alexis as my bride. But, as time went on, I noticed it was everywhere. All churches, good and bad. Even the dark cults are powerless."

"So tell me of this Abyss Walker that Alexis is talking about," Ian said.

Apollisian hardened his face and narrowed his eyes. "It is my wife's custom that only those of her kind call her familiar. You must refer to her as, Overmoon."

Ian nodded. "My apologies, I had forgotten that custom. I had heard of it before in my travels. I was saying, tell me of this Abyss Walker that Overmoon speaks of."

Apollisian glanced back at the road briefly before turning back to Ian. "Her people, and many others from many different races, believe that the titans of old created evil to tempt men away from their gods so they would worship them instead. It is said that evil was new and was not feared then and took hold of the realms like a plague of wickedness. The gods were desperate to stop the titans who would enslave mankind, so one of them took in the world's evil and created a place for the wicked. They called it the Abyss. The god who created it, then formed masters of this world to imprison the evil souls there. But the god did not realize how corrupting the evil was. It turned the Celestial Keepers into twisted monsters of great power. They later became arch-demons. He called on his angels to battle the arch-demons, but the god himself had been corrupted. He fell into the Abyss and took his angels with him. Fearing that the evil might escape, Rha-Cordan sealed himself and all of his angels into the Abyss, dooming them to an eternity of suffering and damnation."

"So who is the Abyss Walker?" Ian asked.

"The titans were defeated and evil had been contained. But prophecies said that a small bit of the evil had managed to escape the Abyss and taint the heavens. It is said this evil would grow and manifest itself as a man. It is written that this man will call forth the power of the Abyss and lay waste to the world, just as the titans had tried hundreds of thousands of years ago."

"So this undead general is the Abyss Walker?" Ian asked.

Apollisian nodded. "I believe it to be so, but Alexis seems to think that the boy is, or has some connection to him. Before the breaking, which I believe to be the breach of the divine crown, I searched his heart and there was no evil in it. He is tied to the Abyss Walker somehow, but I do not know at this point. I hope I am able to figure it out before it is too late for him, and for all of us."

Ian bit his lip. "I saw what those undead monsters did to my friends, Apollisian. If that general is not the Abyss Walker, then have mercy on us when the real one arrives."

"I can imagine the horrors you must have faced. I have fought the twisted vileness of undeath many times in my life. Though I know you will not wish to speak of what happened, it is important for us to know what kind of monsters he has," Apollisian said.

"Aside from the normal walking corpses that my countrymen faced at the Battle of Calito, he has many more gruesome ones. My friends and I were attacked by the things that were chasing us in the snow. They had the power to steal a man's ability to move with the smallest scratch. They tore our horses out from under us and ate some of my friends while they were still alive. We did manage to cut a few of the beasts down, but there were so many," Ian said as he trailed off.

Apollisian caught a glimpse of a silvery moon and narrowed his tired eyes. "Were there any others?"

Ian jerked his back as he was roused from his nightmare. "There were walking shadows. They could pass through solid walls and their touch seemed to pull your very soul from your body. I am not sure how they did it, but they killed men the quickest. I am guessing the foul magic that creates them is poisonous to the touch."

Apollisian nervously glanced around as he imagined the very shadows of the night coming to life to attack them. "How do you fight shadows? Were you able to kill any of them?"

Ian shook his head. "No, but I am sure the sorceress of the West Tower were able. They stood much longer than those of the keep. I am guessing that their magical energy damaged the power that animated them. I know no normal axe or sword could affect them."

"We must hurry. I do not know the width of the undead army that bears down on us, but if we are not careful, the edges of their army will overtake us," Apollisian said.

Ian nodded. "To be honest, what is the difference between now and then? Once that storm cloud comes, it is only a matter of time."

Apollisian did not respond. He rode south with Ian and they both mulled over the grim task that they were soon to be standing against a wave of death that would most certainly consume them. Apollisian glanced back at the carriage and felt worry fill him as he thought of Alexis. He had dragged her into danger so many times. Perhaps he should send her back to her father. This would be a battle he would most likely not survive. The warrior felt the pang of worry in his heart and then glanced to the sky. The worry was soon overcome with dread as dark gray clouds began to hide the moon. The storm was soon to be upon them.

Vlargcar stood in the waning light of the evening sun. The bright orange and yellows that peeked through the thick purple clouds that hung just above the horizon gleamed off of the battle-marred armor of the green skinned warrior. He had been a prisoner of the arena for almost a year. Since that time he had defeated countless foes, vanquished monsters far worse than those appearing in the nightmares of babes, and battled the demons that dwelled within himself. The orc had made but two friends in his life. One was taken away from him, and the other was a fellow prisoner that stood beside him now.

Vlargcar glanced over at his only friend, Jude. The swordsman fought with such ferocity that even sometimes amazed a brute like himself. Though Vlargcar towered over Jude at over seven feet tall, the human was much larger than any of his own folk, being just a hand or two shorter than him. Tonight Jude was adorned in his breast plate armor, ignoring greaves or any other type of armor that others were accustomed to. His thick muscled arms bugled with rage and seemed to swell with the beatings of his heart. Yes, Jude seemed more of a monster to Vlargcar, than he was. The swordsman said nothing or looked Vlargcar's way. He kept his iron gaze forward toward the gate that would soon raise and unveil their enemy. They had fought together once before about a week ago, and the two had easily vanquished a horde of dwarves that the magistrate had captured north of the city. It seems the bearded folk were not liked by the humans because they were frequently set against him. Vlargcar had tried to speak with them in the past to try and get them to throw down their arms and not fight, but when they realized that he spoke their language it always infuriated them. Vlargcar never understood why they were angry. Amerix had taught him to speak dwarven fluently before their capture, and he was sure his words had been chosen right.

Vlargcar's thoughts were interrupted by the clang of the thick iron gate across from them as it slowly raised. Jude growled something unintelligible and drew his two-handed great sword, holding the great blade aloft. Vlargcar slowly drew his long sword and short sword as sweat began to drip down the side of his face, only to become mired in his coarse black sideburns. His chain armor chinked as he shifted his weight and prepared to kill the enemy that was presented to him. Vlargcar often tried to speak to his enemies to offer quarter, but they were either monsters that did not understand his speech, or were too vile, or filled with hatred to care. Either way, he still felt obligated to offer his enemies a chance to save their lives before the fight, if they wished.

As the iron gate reached the top, it boomed into its locked position. The crowd in the arena roared in anticipation of the battle. To Vlargcar's surprise, the largest thing he had ever seen stepped out. It was almost ten foot tall and had dark green skin, mottled with large brown spots. Its head was somewhat oblong with an oversized nose and dark greasy hair that hung loosely about its head. The monster wore no armor, but had a collection of furs that was loosely strung about its body covering its waist and groin area. The monster was as muscled as he and Jude in a comparable body type, telling Vlargcar the beast was probably much stronger than the two of them combined. The monster had a single club that was the size of a small tree that it hefted around easily.

"Ogre," Jude said flatly under his breath.

Vlargcar nodded. He didn't speak the same language as Jude, but some monsters had the same name regardless of what language they were spoken in. "Must want us tough fight to have," Vlargcar answered back in broken common.

Jude frowned and nodded slowly. He had been teaching Vlargcar the common tongue for some time, but the giant orc wasn't the smartest pupil. Jude was used to teaching Lance things. Jude almost smiled as he recalled the boy's mind and how when it came to learning things it was more akin to a steel bear trap.

Vlargcar frowned. He guessed Jude understood what he was trying to say, but his language was so confusing. It had words that had no meaning, except to change the meanings of words it used before, that then had different spellings. The whole language made little sense to him, but he felt better about learning it, than Jude learning dwarven. Vlargcar knew his captures spoke common, so if he was ever to have an upper hand on them, he would need to speak their tongue. "Knowledge is power," Amerix always used to say.

"Tough fight, my ass. They are trying to finish us off," Jude said as he motioned to the gate.

Vlargcar squinted his eyes to see. He did not have very

good eyesight and seeing far distances was difficult. But what he saw was more than unnerving to the green skinned warrior. To his dismay, not two, but three more ogres stepped from the gate. Each was ten foot tall with clubs as large as the first.

The crowd erupted in awe and eager anticipation of the approaching battle. Jude and Vlargcar were well known as undefeatable warriors, but four ogres could wipe out a hundred men easily before they were felled.

"We need to get them in close, orc. Make their long reach a disadvantage to them. Their only attack on a close opponent will either be a kick, or an overhand swing. Overhand swings are much easier to dodge and manipulate," Jude said quickly as the four ogres marched purposely toward them.

"If kick at us, stab foot. Then they only use clubs," Vlargcar answered back, hoping Jude understood.

Jude eyed the blue eyed orc for a brief moment with his hawk-like visage. "Sometimes when I think you are the dumbest creature to walk the earth, you say something with a bit of wisdom that surprises me," Jude said, "Now hurry up and ask them to surrender so we can get to killing them."

Vlargcar smiled and placed his great helm over his head that hung loosely behind him. The bright green plume dangled down from his helm, and hung loosely down his back. He stepped forward and called out in his native tongue, "Throw down your weapons great warriors, and we will spare your lives. If you do not, the crows will feast on your eyes and the worms will eat your brains."

Jude smiled nervously. The orc language was so guttural and threatening sounding, he wondered if any orcs ever offered such a bargain to a human, but it was misunderstood as a threat.

The largest ogre stopped and raised his club out to stop the others. They gave him an angry glare, but offered no protests. "You must be the half-breed that killed Chief Slargcar's top war party," the ogre offered back.

Jude nearly fell over in disbelief. The ogres actually stopped. Never had he seen any foe stop at Vlargcar's quarter.

"I am no half-breed, nor did I slay the war party, though

that is of no importance. My name is Vlargcar, son of Slarg-car of Glargcar. But you can call me the bringer of death if you dare approach me or my companion," Vlargcar stated angrily.

The ogres nearly fell over with laughter, but the largest one found no humor in the orc's threat. "You dare threaten me half-breed!" The ogre shouted angrily as he waved his tree trunk like club through the air.

"I threaten no one, ogre. I only speak truths. Come at me then, so I might teach you the power of truth," Vlargcar said with an angry growl.

Jude gripped his weapon tighter and prepared to release the monster within him. Guttural language or not, he was sure the last exchange was not a friendly one.

"I will make you eat those words, half-breed!" The ogre said as he charged forward.

"Here I am then, fool!" Vlargcar taunted.

Jude understood the last exchange even though he didn't know what was said. As the huge hulking beasts charged forward, Jude loosed the rage that was inside of him. He felt it erupt into every muscle from his jaw all the way to his feet. He felt his strength double and his body swell. He felt his mind beginning to numb, though it was nothing like the first time when he blacked out, though his senses were dulled.

"Get ready," Vlargcar said to Jude in dwarven as he pre-pared to rocket forward through the ogres initial swing. If he and Jude could survive the first swing, they might have a chance.

The ogres thundered forward as the pounding of their heavy footfalls on the coliseum floor was drowned out by the blood-lusting roar of the crowd. The first ogre reached Jude and Vlargcar swinging his club from side to side. His flat yellow teeth were clenched tight as spittle erupted from his mouth as he swung.

Vlargcar rushed in, deflecting the crushing blow with a powerful strike of his long sword. The force of the heavy club knocked the orc to the side, but before he could recover Jude buried his great sword into the hip of the great beast. Jude felt his blade sink deep into the ogre's flesh and lodge itself into bone. The ogre howled in pain and kicked Jude in the chest. Jude stumbled back and lost the grip on his sword. The weapon remained impaled in the ogre's hip as Vlargcar slashed in with his long sword. The blade made a deep slice down across the ogre's ribs and hot red blood splattered the orc's face. The beast howled in pain and swung his club overhand, bringing it crashing down toward Vlargcar.

Jude jumped to his feet and wrenched his sword free as the ogre swung at the orc. The heavy club struck the ground sending up a shower of rocks and dirt. Jude wanted to slice the beast again, but the other three were closing fast. Jude side stepped a strike from a second ogre, stepping in front of the first ogre, he and Vlargcar fought. The beast would have an easy strike to kill him, but the swordsman trusted the orc to deal out his wicked death.

Vlargcar easily dodged the overhand strike, bringing his short sword across the fingers of the ogre. The razor sharp blade, coupled by his strength, severed four fingers. Before the ogre could call out in pain, Vlargcar leaped in the air and drove his long sword into the throat of the beast. The blade sunk to its pommel, only to be wrenched free a split second later. Vlargcar had no time to relish the death of the first ogre, as another brought its club crashing down.

Jude felt the shift in the dying ogre's weight and side stepped next to the falling body. The ogre's swing was deflected by the first one's falling corpse. Jude took advantage of the beast's exposed ribs with a two-handed strike and a mighty roar. His great sword tore into the inside of monster's thigh, severing its blood way. Great gouts of bright red blood erupted from the wound as the wounded ogre dropped its club and grabbed its leg as it tried to staunch the flow of blood. *Not just a mindless brute's if he is trying to stop his own bleeding,* Jude thought to himself.

The crowd roared at the first ogre's death.

One of the ogres launched a kick at Vlargcar instead of swinging his heavy club. Vlargcar met the kick with his long sword. He jabbed the sharp blade into the soft part of the ogre's foot and buried the blade all the way to the hilt. The ogre dropped to the ground clutching his foot, howling in pain.

Jude turned to the next foe when the ogre struck him in the side with his club. The weight of the weapon hit Jude hard in the side, lifting him from his feet and sending him head over heels through the air. Jude felt all of his air leaving his body and heard several of his ribs pop. He felt little pain though. He never felt much when he was raging. His hurts only became aware to him after the battle was over. Jude hit the ground hard and rolled for what seemed to be an eternity to him. He realized he no longer had a hold of his sword and his right arm seemed useless. Jude sat up and struggled to see as one of his eyes was clouded with blood. He noticed he was over thirty feet away from the battle, and the orc was alone against three of the beasts.

Vlargcar watched in horror as Jude was blind-sided by one of the ogres. The blow sent the swordsman through the air, knocking his blade from his grasp. The ogre turned toward Jude to finish him off. Vlargcar could not reach the ogre in time so he hurled his short sword at the beast. The lighter blade whistled as it cut through the air, end over end, striking the ogre in the small of the back. The thin blade made a popping sound as it buried itself into the ogre's spine. The beast roared and struggled to reach the small weapon and pull it free with its huge bulky arms. Vlargcar quickly turned to the other two ogres. The one with the wounded foot almost had the long sword free and the one with the slashed blood way had staunched the bleeding and was on its hands and knees preparing to stand. With a groan, Vlargcar hefted the ogre's club. Though the ogres wielded the great clubs that easily weighed two hundred pounds, Vlargcar wasn't much smaller than they. Though his swing was awkward and easily predicable, the wounded ogre never saw it coming. The great club came crashing down with tremendous force, crushing the ogre's skull and splattering his dark pulpy cranial tissue across the dirt floor of the coliseum.

The crowd roared even louder at the death of the second ogre.

Jude struggled to his feet and staggered over to his sword. Though he felt little pain, his muscles and body was not reacting well with his commands for it to move. He was sure he had many broken ribs, a broken shoulder, and he even thought his hip may be shattered. A broken hip would surely mean death as a gladiator fighter. The injury would not heal right and he would develop a definitive limp, limiting his range of movement and speed. Jude pushed the thoughts from his mind and rushed toward the downed ogre with a small sword sticking out of its spine. Jude hurried his steps and brought his heavy two-handed sword down on the neck of the ogre. His left handed blow was weak and the sword needed to be wielded two-handed to be effective, but the sword still sunk into the ogre's shoulder. The monster howled in pain and shot out its giant hand and caught Jude around the neck. Jude instantly felt the air to his brain stop and he felt his collar bones snap from the strength of the ogre's grasp. He tried to pull his sword free from the monster's shoulder, but he could not move either of his arms. Jude knew he was about to die.

Vlargcar roared at the ogre and it roared back. The two were akin to brothers, save Vlargcar was slightly smaller. The ogre's muscles tensed as it brought it's club crashing down. But to its surprise, the club did not kill the orc. The green-skinned half-breed had caught his club and he was now in a tug of war with him.

"Let go 'uh my club!" The ogre growled as it pulled with all of its might backward.

Vlargcar amazed himself with his strength, though he knew without a doubt the ogre was much stronger. When he felt he was about to lose the tugging match, he let go of the club, sending the ogre tumbling backward. The beasts tried to catch itself, but the wound in its foot was too great and the beast fell to its back. The ogre rolled to its hands and knees with the club in hand.

Vlargcar quickly picked up his long sword that the ogre had plucked from its foot. The blade was covered in warm blood and slippery, but he kept his grip and brought it down on the ogre's neck. The sword made a shrill ring as it cleaved the ogre's head from its shoulders. The head tumbled over and came to rest on the dirt coliseum floor with a look of disbelief that it had been slain by an orc.

The crowd roared in disbelief as the third ogre was slain. They started chanting Jude, Jude, Jude...

Just as Jude started to lose consciousness, he felt the blood starting to flow back to his head. The eyes of the ogre became glossy and it released its grasp, falling over dead from the weak left handed blow Jude had dealt it earlier. Jude gasped and struggled to his feet. Vlargcar walked over and offered Jude a hand. The swordsman took it and fought to his feet. Neither of the two warriors missed the contrast of Jude's bronze skin, and Vlargcar's dark green as they were grasped in friendship. Even the crowd was silent for a fleeting moment, before roaring in great pleasure at the power and fighting prowess of the two gladiators that had done what no man, save for those in legends, had done. Only the great General Laricin West had been known to slay ogres in battle.

Vlargcar ignored the approving shouts from the crowd and searched for his swords, while Jude walked very slowly toward the portcullis that led them back to his cell. He knew his rage was about to expire, and once it did he knew he would most likely not be able to walk.

"You think you will ever grow to like their admiration at how we kill?" Jude asked through a grimace as he forced one foot in front of the other in his slow, but deliberate march out of the coliseum.

Vlargcar glanced up at the tens of thousands that had arrived to watch his possible death, then looked back at Jude. "Nah," Vlargcar said flatly, "Besides, I don't understand their words so well anyway."

Jude marveled at the raw unbridled goodness that dwelled inside of the orc's bright cobalt blue eyes. It was at that moment the swordsman realized why the gods created a being with such a low intelligence. Hate was never inherent, it had to be taught. And fortunately for the world, Vlargcar seemed to be a poor learner.

As they walked down the long cold damp corridor of the coliseum Jude thought about Lance and his ability with magic. Jude shuddered uncontrollably. Lance was a much better learner than the orc. Jude wondered what would happen if he learned to hate.

"Family. Did Amerix turn his back on his family by ousting the wicked Therrig? My mother would have said that the old general owed it to Therrig to find out why he committed the evil acts. But, I argue some people just do not want to be helped. They are content in their dark hearts. My mother was the goddess of mercy. Her empathy often blinded her to the real motivations behind me. Actions do not make men, their hearts do. Tragedies could be seen as sunlight. If you have a heart of butter, the sunlight will melt your heart until it goes away, allowing you to form a different shape. But if your heart is clay, the sun will harden it in the shape it is in and mold it that way forever. It matters little if you understand why they are evil. The fact that they are is unchanging. I loved my mother, but it frustrates me that despite her unfathomable wisdom, she lacked the serenity to grasp this truth."

-Lancalion Levendis Lampara-

5
Snows of the Fallen

"It's snow!" Jacob said as he stumbled out of the common room of the Junction Inn.

Another standing next to him glanced to the orange glow from the eastern sky. He frowned drunkenly and belched, "Look. The clouds end there. We can still see the sun."

"That's not the end," Tracy said as she untied her apron from her night shift, "That would be the beginning. The storms come from the west."

"Damn weather," the two mumbled to themselves and wandered into the remaining night.

Tracy stared ominously at the storm clouds as they slowly crept farther east, threatening to cover the sunrise. Her long red hair fluttered in the cold western breeze. "Father is going to be pissed."

Tracy turned and smiled as her blue eyes fell on her brother. "Hey, Travis. Heading to the field?"

"Yea. Father is on a warpath again."

"Is he still pissed about plow strap?" Tracy asked nervously.

Travis nodded as he clasped his hand on her shoulder. "Yea, but it is okay, Peanut. I took the blame. He will get over it. You know how he gets. It was a good idea, you just had bad luck."

Tracy nodded as she distantly recalled pushing wide to

create another plant row, "Thanks, Travy. Do you think Father should plant today? With the snow and all?"

Travis scrunched his nose and shrugged his shoulders. "I don't think it will hurt. This late snow will come and go. I'm sure of it. Besides, if we get the planting done this week I can play ball with the Bells."

"You and your ball games," she said with a wry smile, "How is Matt doing? I have not heard from him in a while."

"He is good. Still a bit sore at you over that whole mess you made with his friend."

Tracy punched Travis in the arm. "I didn't do anything wrong."

Travis rubbed his arm and smiled. "I know. I was bit mad at you too, but whatever makes you happy, Peanut."

Tracy smiled and hugged Travis. "Thanks, brubby. That means a lot."

Travis hugged her warmly. "You going to the leeches this afternoon?"

"I am on my way now. Jenny and I are both working today."

Travis frowned. "What? You just worked all night at the inn. You need sleep."

Tracy shook her head. "I will get a nap this afternoon. Plus, Harvard is bringing in his daughter. And since the clerics can't heal anymore, the duty has fallen on us to figure out is wrong with folks and heal them."

Travis shook his head. "I don' know, Sis. What if she has the plague or something?"

Tracy frowned and punched him in the arm. "She doesn't have the plague, brubby. She has some kind of foot infection. Besides, remember when I went to Central City to enter in the hurdle race?"

Travis nodded. "Yea, yea. You beat the whole city. You tell me that story every month."

"Well, this is like that. You might understand why I want to help people, and just like the hurdles, you didn't know I was good at it. If I am half at good at helping hurt and sick folks as I am at hurdling, then I will be great. Besides, you didn't think you were the only one in the family that was fast."

Travis smiled and glanced up at the tree behind them before trailing off. "I know…"

Tracy turned to see what Travis was looking at. She saw a large black vulture sitting in the tree behind them. It was unusually close and just sat there. Its black feathers were in stark contrast to the increasingly heavy white snow fall.

"That's weird."

Travis nodded. "I think I am going to tell Father about this. Very weird."

Tracy nodded and hugged her brother, keeping a wary eye on the buzzard. She couldn't seem to take her eye off of it. The animal seemed so foreboding and ominous. "Tell mom I will be home this afternoon."

Travis smiled and punched Tracy in the arm. "Be careful, Peanut. See ya tonight."

"Hey," the guard called out as he kicked Kellacun's unconscious form.

The other guard glanced around the alley. Their red silk capes fluttered in the breeze.

"She drunk?"

"I don't think so," the first guard answered as he gently kicked her again, "Hey, woman."

"She ain't no peasant. Not with that get up."

"Look there. On her leg." the guard said as he pointed at the red bloody wound just above Kellacun's foot. A thick green syrupy fluid drained from the deep gash.

"Bet she has been in the sewers. Think she is one of those rat people? Ain't seen or heard from one in a while, but she fits the description."

The first guard rubbed his chin. "She may very well be. She has the sewer stink on her, that's for sure."

"Let's take her in. The duke's new inquisitor ought to be able to make her sing," the guard chuckled.

The guards removed their silk cloaks and wrapped Kellacun's unconscious form in them. They each grabbed an end and started towards the magistrate building.

"Yep, I heard that inquisitor is some monster. A reject from Clan Stoneheart, right before the war. What was name, again?"

"Fraitizu, I think."

Kellacun opened her bright blue eyes. She was still groggy from the poison but found she could move her arms and legs. She sat up and looked around. She was no longer in the alley and was covered with a single white sheet. Her armor and weapons had been removed leaving her nude. Kellacun scanned the small room. It had white painted walls and several wooden cabinets that were also painted white. There were several counters that lined the room with a small wooden door at the far corner.

Dried blood stained the floors and areas of the counter. The blood was old, Kellacun's nose could determine that, but there was an odd smell in the room. Like an alchemists laboratory. She climbed down from the hard marble slab she had been laying on. It was cold to the touch so she wrapped herself in the sheet. The thief had difficulty moving her legs so she stumbled to the counter. After resting her head on the cool countertop she opened one of the cabinets. Instead of finding her gear, she discovered several blood stained leather pouches. They were extremely dirty and were in stark contrast to the cleanliness of the room. There were several odd iron attachments. One seemed to fit over a person's head, yet the inside of the iron contraption had rusted barbed hooks. There was a strange long bar that would fit under the person's chin.

Kellacun closed the cabinet door and moved to the next. Each time she discovered another contraption that seemed geared for causing great pain or torture to the wearer. After several minutes of searching, Kellacun advanced to the door. She dropped the white sheet and her ferocity replaced her modesty. She stepped to the side of the door to avoid any shadow to be cast on the floor. The master thief placed her ear to the door, tilting her head just slightly and listened. She could hear footfalls coming down the hallway. She could tell it was made of stone by the sound of the footfalls. The dank smell told her she was underground, and the lack of other ambient sounds told her this was a room of seclusion. Clearly she was to be tortured and killed. Anger erupted in her as she narrowed her eyes. If the fool magistrate thought they could kill her so easily, they were sorely mistaken.

The brass handle on the smooth wooden door turned slowly and opened. Kellacun tensed her muscles and let the rage flow. It poured through her heating her limbs and heightening her senses. Her sallow skin became overgrown with hair. Her fingernails elongated into smooth black claws and her once feminine form was replaced with the monstrous hybrid look of a woman and a rat.

The door closed revealing a small squat dwarf. He had brown hair and a thin human like beard. He stood confused scratching his head as he stared at the table in the center if the room. Kellacun leapt from the counter behind the door. She hit the dwarf in the side and her weight sent them headlong into the room. She lashed her long rat tail into the wooden door knocking it shut as she twisted, her weight pinning the small thin dwarf under her.

"Wait... wait!" the dwarf said with his hands up in front of him defensively.

Kellacun sniffed the blood that was dripping from several wounds her claws made on his neck and arm. "Speak quickly, inquisitor."

The dwarf swallowed hard that she recognized what he was. "You are a wererat?"

Kellacun did not respond.

"Um, obviously," the dwarf giggled nervously, "Are you from that guild that tried to kill the duke a year or two ago?"

Kellacun glanced around the room cautiously. If she knew where she was at, she would just go ahead and kill this fool. But he may be useful.

"Speak your mind."

The dwarf cleared his throat. "My name is Fraitizu. I am a defector from Clan Stoneheart. I was their chief inquisitor and the duke wanted my services after the king moved them from Mountainheart. I was told I would be paid well and I would be able to return to the clan after the war. He lied. I hear whispers that the clan was destroyed. I am locked in this dungeon and must work for scraps of food."

"So you want me to help you escape?" Kellacun asked, rolling her eyes.

"Escape? Who gives an orc's ass. I want the duke on my table!"

Kellacun smiled. "How about you fetch me my gear, and then we discuss the manner and capacity of his death."

Fraitizu smiled. "Your gear is in here. I figured that if I kept it in the storage locker that would pose a problem for you trusting me, and me walking around with a naked woman."

Kellacun stuck her claw under his chin. "And tell me, inquisitor, why am I naked?"

Fraitizu chuckled. "Not for my enjoyment. You can guess that! Though I am sure you are built handsomely for your own race, I find your build a bit revolting."

Kellacun pushed her claw harder into the underside of Fraitizu's chin.

"The duke wanted you tortured. So I administered a sedative to you. A small dose of Jahallawa extract. He clearly did not want you tortured and killed unconscious and I knew that would keep you down for a day or so. I pretended to be perplexed at your unconsciousness and told him I would call when you awoke. Then, I unrestrained you and left you in this room."

Kellacun nodded and eased the pressure from her claw. "Understand that I have no pity for your predicament and that you are merely a means to an end."

Fraitizu giggled. "Honesty? I did not expect that from you. I like it. You know," the dwarf said as he glanced up and down at Kellacun's naked furry form, "You might want to get your gear. While I am disgusted by your natural form, it seems I am finding this one a bit alluring."

Kellacun sat up and allowed Fraitizu to get to his feet. She decided she would kill the disgusting little pest as soon as she could.

"Keep your mouth shut, or I will kill you."

Fraitizu nodded as he fumbled with a small ring of iron keys. After a few seconds, he opened the locker and puller her things from the cabinet.

Kellacun quickly dressed. As she kneeled down and tied her boots, she examined the tear where the worm thing had slashed her. Of all the places she was protected, who would have thought her boots needed to be too?

"Let's get moving."

Fraitizu nodded eagerly and opened the chamber door. The hallway was dark and dank. Deep gray stones lined the walls and old crumbling wooden rafters lined the ceiling. Small roots jutted out from between crumbling mortar. Had she not been able to see in near darkness, she would not have been able to make her way in this lightless hell.

"Why are there not any guards?" Kellacun asked.

Fraitizu glanced up into her face. He was surprised to see her back in her human form. Her change had been quick and quiet.

"I don't know. The last few days, have been odd. The guards were removed and no one has been down here. The door is normally locked, so I can't see what is going on."

Kellacun did not reply. Her thoughts wandered to the empty cells in this dungeon as Fraitizu led her down several halls and up several flights of stairs. He paused at a huge iron door. The door was reinforced and though it was pitted with rust, still seemed incredibly strong. Kellacun kneeled down at the lock and examined it as she pinned her hair up with her silver hairpin.

Fraitizu narrowed his eyes as he noticed the silver burned her hand as she placed the hair pin into her hair.

"Doesn't that hurt?"

Kellacun frowned and glanced up at the odd little dwarf. "Yes."

"Then why use it?"

"This hair pin is personal, dwarf. A man that betrayed

me gave it to me. It was a silver knife then. I took a grinder to it and made the damn thing into a hair pin."

"Oh," Fraitizu said as he twiddled his thumb awkwardly.

Kellacun opened her belt pouch and removed a small cloth wrapping. She gently set it out in front of her on the stone floor. She carefully selected a long metal tool with a curved hook on the end. She inserted the tool into the lock and turned her head to the door.

"So does it hurt your head?" Fraitizu asked.

"What?" Kellacun asked as she glanced up at the dwarf with her brilliant blue eyes.

"I mean, does the hairpin hurt your head. If silver hurts you, it is awfully close."

Kellacun rolled her eyes and turned back to the door. She gathered another tool and inserted it into the lock, keeping the first one in place. "Yes. It stings. I like the pain. It reminds me of how I suffered at the hands of another. That pain reminds me that no one will ever love me more than they love themselves."

Fraitizu turned his head and pursed his lips. *What a crazy bitch,* he thought to himself.

Kellacun smiled out of the corner of her mouth as she heard the resounding click. She carefully replaced her tools and rolled them back up in the dirty cloth before placing it back into her belt pouch.

"Now, this is where we start being quiet," she whispered, "You have two options. You can leave, or you can stay here."

Fraitizu stammered nervously, "What? You said you would get me out of here."

Kellacun lightly opened the door and scanned the hallway before drawing her sword. "I did. You are free. Now, go."

Fraitizu grabbed her arm angrily. "Now you just wait one minute."

Kellacun whirled and stuck the tip of her cutlass deep into the throat of the dwarf. He gurgled in protest and clutched the killing blade. His eyes went wide briefly before the life faded from them. Bright red blood spurted out from the side of the wound and sprayed a fine mist over the dark stone floor. As the dwarf fell to the floor, Kellacun pulled her blade free. She was not sure what the dwarf's crimes were, but he clearly tortured men and woman that were put before him. He was an agent of the duke and therefore she knew she must kill him. The rogue wondered how many innocent victims that inquisitor had before her.

Kellacun made her way down the hall. It was lit with sparse sconces and she quickly recognized the under quarter of the royal housing. It seemed odd to her that the duke would have a prison under his housing quarters, unless he housed prisoners that he did not want anyone knowing he had. Kellacun found her thoughts drifting back to Joshua, the only man she ever loved. She recalled the night he was walking home from the market with her and she found her parents murdered by the elf assassins. Though he lost his arm defending her from one of the assassin's hunters, she always felt like he betrayed her. There were just too many unanswered questions.

Kellacun made her way down the hall and up the stairs. She paused in front of the duke's antechamber. There were no guards. There were always guards there. What was going on? Kellacun made her way down the hallway. It was lined with red colored rug and bright green plant life decorated the corners. Great tapestries hung down from the walls depicting battles from the orc wars to coliseum battles. Kellacun paused in front of one of the coliseum battles. It depicted an orc and a large Kai-Harkian fighting against four ogres and wining. Though clearly a fictitious work, she was somehow move by the emotion in it. The green skin, in contrast with the bronze, fighting side by side stirred her.

Voices roused her from her contemplations. She frantically glanced around. There was no way to go except back the way she came. As she started to flee, she spied the thick wooden rafters above her. She squatted low and with her powerful legs launched herself up just high enough to grab the rafter. She groaned quietly and pulled herself up. She was still a bit weak from the poison, but she quickly perched above the floor. She diligently watched down from the dark rafters as Duke Dolin Blackhawk turned the corner. He was accompanied by two guards and a one armed man.

Joshua! His face hit her like a punch in the face as a tidal wave of emotion flooded into her. She felt her heart melt as she gazed at his features. Though he had aged with time, he was still handsome. She recalled how he held her. How she felt safe in his strong arms.

"I don't care, Joshua. That army is not coming in the city. Period."

"But, Father, something is going on! We have never had such a late season snow. The animals in the forest have been going crazy. And now, the Central Army is perched on the other side of the river," Joshua countered.

"This is nothing more than the dwarves, or the thieves' guild. I quashed both. If there is something coming I will quash it too! Without the king's troopers fouling up my city."

Kellacun felt her love replaced with the fiery white hot heat of hatred. *Quashed the thieves' guild? He murdered them in cold blood. He murdered my parents and he will pay.* Kellacun drew her sword and slid a dagger out from her boot. This was her chance. She had waited for this moment for nearly sixteen years.

As the duke neared, Kellacun dropped from her perch.

"Greetings, Joshua. Dolin."

"What is the meaning of this?" the duke demanded.

The two guards drew their swords and moved in front of the duke.

"Kellacun?" Joshua asked, astonished.

Kellacun casually walked toward the group. "You didn't murder all of the wererats, Duke."

"Ma'am, do not come any closer," the guards warned.

"Joshua, you told me you killed her?"

Kellacun smiled verdantly. Her bright blue eyes flashed silver in the dim light of the hall. "You missed one, Duke."

"Father, run!" Joshua yelled.

Kellacun transformed as she charged forward. She hurled her dagger as she ducked a slash from the first guard and parried the strike from the other. The small blade slammed into the lower back of the duke. He cried out in pain and collapsed on the floor.

Joshua ran over to his father and removed the dagger.

Bright red blood flowed from the wound and covered the cold stone floor. Kellacun stabbed upwards and pierced one guard under his chin. Her thin leather armor turned a strike from the second as she twisted her weight and brought her cutlass into the inner thigh of the second guard. He clutched the wound as blood spurted from his served bloodway. Kellacun regained her composer as she looked down on the mortally wounded guard. He looked up at her in terror. She contemplated killing the man, but she was not here for him. She was here for one purpose, the duke.

Joshua jumped up and drew his sword. "I'll not let you take him, Kellacun."

Kellacun lowered her head and glared at Joshua with her bright blue eyes. She transformed back to her normal form as she stalked forward.

"Stay back. I will kill you," Joshua warned nervously as he stood in front of his wounded father.

"Kill her, Son. Kill her now!" the duke screamed.

Kellacun glanced down at Joshua's severed hand. She recalled how he stood in front of a hunter to protect her. He faced an undefeatable monster to save her. "Tell me, my love. How long after my death did it take for you to *wed another?*"

"Kellacun, you were a monster. I had to put you out of my mind."

"Tell me, Joshua. Tell me why you did not kill me in the alley. Why did you defend me against the hunter?"

Joshua relaxed and put his sword down at his side. "Kellacun, I loved you. Your parents were thieves. They were murders. I had to turn them in."

The words hit Kellacun like a knife in the back. She had spent the last sixteen years suspecting this truth, but to hear it from the mouth of the only man she ever loved was nearly unbearable.

"Your father is a murderer too, Joshua. Now, stand aside and let justice be done."

"I will not let you kill him, Kellacun. I will fight you if I must."

With unnatural speed, Kellacun brought her sword up and stabbed Joshua through the heart. His eyes went wide with horror and disbelief. He tried to bring his own blade up, but his knees buckled and he fell to the floor. He tried to speak, but no words left his lips. Before Joshua took his last breath, Kellacun kneeled down and kissed his lips.

"Goodbye, Joshua."

The duke turned onto his belly and crawled across the stone floor, dragging his useless legs behind him.

"Guards! Help me!"

Kellacun slowly walked over to the wounded duke as he tried to crawl away. She glanced out the window that she once climbed down from when she and Joshua were in love. Without a thought, she brought her cutlass down and severed the duke's head. And, without a whisper, she was out of the window and back into the night. The only friend that ever embraced her.

"Kellacun. The poor girl never had a chance at life. As a teen-ager her entire world was ripped upside down and everyone that was close to her was murdered. And those that were somewhat close, betrayed her. Makes no wonder why she turned into the cold blooded killer she is today.

But what of Delania? She was in the Abyss, a world of deceit and trickery on a scale that Kellacun could never fathom, so how was Delania able to fall in love? The answer is simple.

Personal integrity is like a tree. If you leave a seed out in the winter, on shelf, through a forest fire, there is still a good chance that if you immerse it in water and dirt that the seed will grow. This is Delania. She was never give any nourishment. When she was, she grew fast and strong.

Kellacun was a tree that had been chopped down, cut up, and turned into a fence post. But even then, we all know of some rare cases of fence posts, if not stripped of its bark, that sprouted roots and began to grow. While Kellacun seems to be a cold lifeless rod. I dare say, she still has her bark. Time will tell."

-Lancalion Levendis Lampara-

6

Triniqy's Arrival

Tracy started towards the leeches. It was a fair walk and she normally enjoyed it. But this morning, it was different. The cold west wind seemed portentous and the unusual snow fall was increasing. She pulled her overcoat tighter around her and hurried her pace. She noticed several vultures perched in the trees just outside of town and she could see more hovering overhead.

Tracy ducked into the small building that housed the leech. He was an elderly man that had a small shop in Central City. Tracy smiled warmly at him and hung her jacket on the old iron hook behind the door. She turned and glanced around the room. Normally there was someone in with some kind of ailment, but this morning no one was in.

"Where is everyone, Doctor Freely?" she asked as she pulled her long red hair up and fastened it in a bun behind her head.

The leech was organizing his building, putting bandages and cutting tools away in the cabinets when he responded, "Child, I closed the shop this morning."

"Did Jennifer not come in?"

"She came in, I sent her home. As well I am going to do to you. There is something bad coming, child. You best not be here when it arrives."

Tracy chuckled nervously. "You mean the vultures. No

big deal. They are probably lefty over from the Adoria kill-ing fields. Remember four years ago when they wandered this far east?"

"No, child. This is different. I think the world is going through a great change. I think that change is on us now. I can't explain it, it is just a feeling I get in my old bones. Why don't you go home? Go home to your family and be with them. If it is nothing, then I will see you tomorrow."

Tracy nodded tautly. "What will you do, Doctor? Come with me. There is no need to stay her. Papa is an able man. He can shoo off any bandits if need be. Plus, Travis is old enough to scare off any polecats they may have."

The doctor shook his head forlornly. "Go, Tracy. Don't make me say it again. Get home."

Tracy nodded absently and pulled her coat off the hook. She slid her arms into the thick leather jacket and opened the door. She paused briefly as if to say something to her friend, but elected to obey. She closed the door behind her and was surprised to see that the snow was accumulating quite rapid-ly. Heavy white flakes were falling down and the wind had picked up. The trees were alive with hundreds of vultures. Their silent gazes were deafening as they peered down at her. She hurried back down the path, passing several boys throwing rocks at the vultures. Two lay dead on the ground under the tree. Their black feathers had littered the bright white snow around their avian bodies.

"Wanna' throw some rocks with us, Tracy?" one of the boys called out, "They just sit there! Easy pickins!"

Tracy shook her head and pulled her coat tighter around herself. "Boys, you ought to go home. Something bad is about to happen."

The boys laughed and waved their hands in dismissal. They promptly began to find more rocks under the ever ac-cumulating snow.

As Tracy passed the inn, she could hear a strange buzz-ing in the west. It started first as a distant growl. Yet as she continued home, it became a louder roar! She paused in ter-ror as she glanced west. The entire sky was black. The dark clouds seemed so black that they sucked in light. Fear crept into her like a piercing blade. She could not run, or scream. She could only watch in terror as the black cloud came closer and closer. Tracy gripped her coat so hard her white knuckles started to go numb as the cloud revealed itself. It was no cloud at all, but a wave of crows and vultures. Hundreds of thousands of the animals danced and darted in the sky like a school of fish. There squawking was so loud, it overpowered her senses. Their bodies blotted out the sun and the early morning turned to midnight.

Tracy turned and ran. She ran faster than when she did at the races in Central City. She ran as if her life depended on it. Tears from the cold air ran down her face and she ignored the drip from her nose. Somehow she knew she was running for her life. As her home came into sight, she smelled it. It was a powerful, overwhelming smell. The smell of rotting flesh. As she neared her home it became stronger. How could that be? How could something dead move?

In a single leap, she hurdled the fence in her front yard and sprinted towards the door.

"Momma, Poppa!" she cried out.

It was the movement on the forest line that caught her eye first. It was not much, subtle at first. She slowed a bit and stood in horror as what she saw became apparent. Her blue eyes franticly scanned to the south and the then to the north. From horizon to horizon it was the same. Tens of thousands walking dead bodies shuffled towards her home. They shambled more than marched. They were hard to see in the darkness, but in minutes they would be on her.

Tracy ran into the house. "Travis! Momma, Papa?"

"Here. Quickly child!" Came her father's voice from the other room.

Tracy ran in and saw the living room rug raised up a bit with a small trap door just under it. She could hear the clawing and scraping of wood on the outside of her home. The ravenous sounds of undead monsters and the screams of the townsfolk were lost to her as the trap door closed and locked. She hugged her father close. His warm embrace filled her with security. Fear soon gripped her as she glanced around the room.

"Where is Travis?"

Trinidy slowly rode among his army of walking death atop his Abyssal steed. The dark black fur of his deathly equine seemed to shine in the lightless day. The animal's fiery hooves melted the already snow covered earth with each step and its eyes trailed a bright red hue like smoke from a small fire. The cloud of black vultures and crows blocked the remaining sunlight that his storm cloud did not.

Havrion Trinidy Lampara was a king among the dead. A champion of righteousness wielding an army that did not hurt, did not hunger, did not lust, and did not fear. His lich queens surrounded him, ready to lay waste to any enemy with their limitless magical prowess. Though he happened upon the small community by chance, he relished its destruction. His ghouls were feasting on the bodies of the living as they lay paralyzed from their toxic bites. A fitting end for the wicked.

"My Lord, the shadows report that there is one still living," Marzahna announced.

Trinidy glanced down at her. Even in undeath she stood proud and defiant. Her once brilliant yellow robe was dark and torn. He recalled when he took her. She had stood defiantly against him at Lostom. And, even in all her power, he overcame her. Now she served righteousness. Now she was an agent of good that would snuff out wickedness. She was the scythe that he would use to harvest the black souls from the land.

"My Lord?" she asked in confusion as Trinidy gazed off toward the sacked town.

"Show me," Trinidy answered.

Marzahna turned and made her way through the sea of swarming undead. That surrounded a small shack. She pointed with her crooked decayed finger, "There."

Trinidy narrowed his glowing blue eyes as he spied a small unassuming shack. "Why does this hovel stand against us?" he growled.

"The symbol, My Lord. The symbol on the door prevents us from traveling through it or harming the structure."

Trinidy rode up to the hovel. It was small, even for a shack. It had a chimney of stone that leaked a small trail of smoke and two windows that were shuttered closed. On the door was a scrawled symbol of some sort. It was a tear drop encircled by a sun. The symbol seemed familiar to him. Where had he seen it before?

Trinidy dismounted from his steed and walked up to the door. His ghouls danced around the building with lustful hunger for blood. Their excited nature upset Trinidy as he gazed at the symbol. They seemed to distract him from remembering. They angered him. As if sensing his displeasure the ghouls turned and fled from the home. Thousands of animated undead monsters scattered away from the hovel instantly, leaving a trampled garden and the skeletal remains of those that were run down and eaten.

The death knight traced the symbol with his finger and he felt sorrow. What was this symbol? Why was it important to him? Trinidy reached down and grasped the shiny brass knob with his black crusted gauntleted hand. He paused briefly and turned the handle. As he entered the home he witnessed it was not a home at all, but some sort of leech office. He could see shelves that were filled with bandages and cutting tools. The hearth was alit with a small unassuming fire and sitting calmly in a chair across the room was an elderly man.

"Close the door, sir. You are letting the chill air in," Doctor Freely said.

Trinidy frowned and obeyed. This man did not speak Abyssal. Though his heart mocked him with its wickedness, he could speak words of righteousness.

"Your righteous tongue and magic circles will not save you from the blade of justice."

"Sit," the man commanded and motioned to a chair.

Trinidy glanced down at the chair and then back to the unassuming man. He removed his crusted helm and held it in his gauntleted hand. The hue from his bright blue eyes lit up the dark room. The death knight felt whole here. He felt peaceful.

"I want to tell you a story, Havrion," the man said.

Trinidy glared at the old man, "How do you know of my name?"

Doctor Freely wiped sweat from his brow, "You came through here years ago with your bride. You were leaving Dawson."

Trinidy felt dizzy and placed his gauntleted hand on his head. The black stinging insects and scorpions began to fall from his face. They quivered on the ground and died.

"The woman you traveled with was named Panoleen. She told me of her name and that a day would come when absolute evil would come to my door. She told me that you would be that evil. She taught me her symbol and told me that it would save me and all of mankind from you."

Trinidy glanced down at the dead scorpions and centipedes at his feet. He noticed that the man was not aging and dying like the others did when they were near him. He noticed that the fire remained lit near him, where in the past it went out and the logs froze over.

"Panoleen was my true love. Only a few souls in any given time can experience that."

Doctor Freely nodded. "Yes, Havrion. She told me. Look at what you have done. You have raised an army of abomination. You have murdered thousands and for what?"

Trinidy stood from his chair and placed his helm on his head. "You are correct, sir. I have raised an army of abomination. But, I have not murdered anyone."

"Then what do you call the bodies outside?"

Trinidy drew his sword and stabbed the doctor. The doctor's eyes went wide with shock and surprise as the Abyssal cold from the wicked blood red steel froze him before the wound killed him.

"I call them the same as the body before me. Justified."

Trinidy walked from the hovel and was greeted by the dark cold air. His heavy boots crunched in the white snow.

"What was in there?" Marzahna asked.

"Just another wicked heart."

General Bodrell rode atop his heavily barded steed. His armor shone in the early morning light. Flag bearers rode behind him as the banner of Beykla flapped in the cold western wind. The crimson banner with the tilted crown pierced by a sword fluttered like the tail of an anxious cat. To his right rode Jonathon Klement, the crown's arch-mage. His heavy crimson robes were fastened about him with gold tasseled cords and his saddles were littered with tomes and scroll cases.

"So, what do you think they want to discuss, General?" the arch-mage asked.

General Bodrell frowned and bit his lip. "I will assume they will tell me to pack up my army and leave the fringes of their city."

Jonathon chuckled. "And I can assume to know what our response will be."

"Yes, my old friend, you most certainly do."

As the pair sat at the end of the Dawson River Bridge, they took in its splendor for a last time. It had been crafted dozens of centuries ago. Some say forged by the old arch-mages during the great Dragon Wars.

"So, this bridge is going to make one hell of splash," Jonathan said to break the ambiance of its beauty.

"Yep," the general replied with a half chuckle, "Yes, it will."

As the pair sat in silence again, a small group of armored men approached the other side of the bridge from the city. They wore the golden plate of Beykla and their red flowing capes fluttered in the unusually cool spring wind. The three of them rode side by side onto the bridge and towards the general.

"That's a bit odd," Jonathon said, "The three of them side by side. The duke would most commonly ride in the front and, if I recall Dolin, he would demand it."

Bodrell nodded. "I agree. Perhaps the gods are not shining down on us today."

Jonathon chuckled. "Well, given the reason we are mustered here in the first place, you think they could throw us a bone."

Bodrell nodded. "Here they come, let's see what they have to say."

"Greetings, I am Captain Oswald. Due to unforeseen circumstances, the duke will not be able to make any further meetings."

Jonathon sneered. "Dolin is an arrogant prick!"

"Hold your tongue, Jonathan. The captain does not need to deliver such messages to his duke," Bodrell said, "I guess we will march into his city and tell him ourselves."

Oswald shook his head. "You will not be able to do that, General."

Bodrell narrowed his eyes. "Who will stop me? I am operating under the name of the king and if Central City tries to turn me away, I will treat every man, woman, or child who lifts a blade against me as a treasonous leper and they will be put down."

The captain shook his head slowly from side to side. "No, General. I mean the city is yours. I am here to offer you the duke's sword as freedom of the city."

"And what manner would cause the duke to change his mind so rapidly?" Jonathon asked.

Oswald saluted and handed the duke's blade to Bodrell. "A simple manner, really, The duke is dead."

Bodrell took the sword and glanced over at Jonathon, who wore an equally confused expression.

"So when will you be coming into the city?" Oswald asked.

Bodrell handed the sword to Jonathon. "I will be coming in tomorrow afternoon. There is a storm coming that I expect to be here in a few days. The city has many measures that need to be taken."

Oswald nodded. "I expect there are. I ask to be notified of any movements and information. I am now in position to provide for the welfare of my citizens. It is a burden I do not take lightly, General."

Bodrell nodded. "I will be sure that one of my liaisons keeps you fully abreast of what is going on. Set a command dinner in your civic hall for twilight tomorrow. If you really want to know what we are facing, I will disseminate all that we know."

Oswald nodded and turned back across the bridge. Jonathon turned to Bodrell as they started back to their camps.

"Do you think it a wise move to give him a full day of preparing?" Jonathon asked.

"Of course not. The duke isn't dead. I'm no fool. This is some ruse. We're moving out tonight. Get word to the Darayal. We'll collapse the bridge just after we cross it."

"A wise move, General."

Bodrell nodded, "Dolin Blackhawk cannot be trusted... Even in his death."

"It's so hard to trust someone. A common statement. But, if it were true-you're not really trusting them. The truth is, "trust" is an easy act. It is the building of this trust that is quite difficult. Worrying about being able to trust someone is simply mistrust.

If there were a thousand gold coins in a room and Jude had two options. He could kill me and take it, or allow me to live and not get them. I would not fret or worry. Trusting him would be easy. Now, if I were in the room with Kellacun... Well, let's just say trusting her would be hard. Why? Because of mistrust.

See, trust is easy. Mistrust is what consumes the waking hours of many."

-Lancalion Levendis Lampara-

7

Blackening of the Sallow

"I don't care if you disagree, Ehleeshuh," the old elf growled, "You will obey."

The unicorn stamped her feet on the ground and tossed her head in irritation. She neighed angrily as her deep blue eyes burned into the elder.

"I understand you do not believe Amerix will honor the wishes of Songsinger, but this is not your decision to make. She wishes to be taken back to Apollisian. She knew the dwarf would be coming up the trail when he did. Can you explain how she knew the renegade general would be marching toward a city inhabited by a race that wants him dead? It is not our way to question. We are going into the void tomorrow. This is our last action on Terrigan. A great cleansing will wash over the world and we will return in a hundred years."

Ehleeshuh neighed again and tossed her head a final time before she trotted off into the forest.

"Noverian, I want you to follow her. She has too much fiery discontent in her heart. Make sure her anger towards the dwarf does not lead her away from the light."

The elf nodded as he thumbed his gnarled pine staff, "I am sure she will come to reason, My Lord."

"But what if she does not?" another elf asked.

"Then she will be forced to remain here during the rupture," the old elf said as he wiped his brow.

"Is this rupture for certain, Elder?"

The venerable elf nodded. "We received word from the Minok Vale in the north. They watch the scrolls and have already went into the void. I am afraid there is little to save the realm at this point."

Noverian nodded and lifted his thick green cloak over his head. "You know this decision will taint all our hearts for a time. Turning our backs on the innocents will scorch that in us which has been pure for a thousand years."

The old elf nodded. "I am aware, but that is what must be done. Just as I feel the darkness creeping on my own heart, I know it will not be for long."

"So be it, My King," Noverian said as he rubbed his chest, "I hope the void that will hide us will be big enough to conceal our shame.

Ehleeshuh stomped through the forest. Her heavy hoof falls ripped up the soft vegetation when she smelled a strange odor. She turned her brilliant horned head toward the odor. Her sallow ears strained forward and her deep blue eyes scanned the forest as the light breeze fluttered through her long mane. The leaves rustled and the spring branches tossed, but something was out of place to the equine.

She lowered her head and trotted timidly toward the strange odor. It was sharp but floated under a sweet floating scent. Her nostrils flared in and out as she ducked from tree to tree. After several minutes she came to a small clearing. The smell was much stronger here and the trees seemed pushed away. The scent of fresh dirt from half uprooted trees filled the air. Bright flickering speckles or orange magical energy floated in the air and rested on the leaves of the ground flora.

She dared not step into the clearing. It was clearly not natural, but she felt compelled to linger. She cocked her head to the side and her belly tightened as she whinnied to herself softly as her bright blue eyes peer forward. Knowing that she was staring at something, but not knowing what it was.

"You cannot see me," a raspy voice spoke out from the clearing.

Ehleeshuh glanced around. She could tell the voice was coming from the clearing, but she could see nothing. She did not see any footprints or any sign that there was someone there. She wanted to run. She could tell she was in danger. She could feel it in every strand of her pure white hair, but still she stood still with her bright blue eyes locked onto the area the voice originated from

"We have a common enemy. His name is Amerix Alistair Stormhammer."

Ehleeshuh tossed her head at the mention of the wicked renegade general.

"He is going to partner with a Beyklan by the name of Lancalion. The man has a succubus traveling with him in disguise in attempt to lure the righteous from his god. You do not have to take my word this is truth. Follow Amerix. He will stand with Lancalion against the Abyss Walker and his army. Standing beside him will be a warrior of justice, Apollisian. The true owner of Songsinger. He and his temptress will lure him away from the light. They must be stopped. Kill Lancalion, or his succubus, and you will be able to save Apollisian."

Ehleeshuh narrowed her bright blue eyes. She shook her head in doubt and snorted loudly.

"Your elf friends want this Abyss Walker to scour the land. That is why they flee. They want the old ways back. They want to reclaim what the humans have taken from them. You are wise. You know this. That is why you are here."

Ehleeshuh took a couple of steps into the clearing. She could feel the power of the magical aura wash over her. She could feel its embrace, like that of a lover.

"Ehleeshuh, they call you? Know this. To prove the lot of the Fey, they have sent one to follow you and kill you. He will be cloaked with magic and is coming to kill you now. The fey have never had a reason to come to you protected by such magic. Why do so now, if they were not trying to end your life? You are in a trying time, Ehleeshuh. You can stand where others flee or you can lift your neck to the butcher's blade."

Ehleeshuh blinked as the voice faded and the ambience of the clearing drifted away with the glittering magical dust that rested on the leaves and grass. In moments, only the half uprooted trees gave any indication that the speaker was ever there.

The proud equine turned and trotted back to the road. She was planning on following the dwarf regardless. She had taken a dozen steps when she smelled him. Noverian was behind her. He was following her, just like the voice had said. She had a link with the Fey and he was a fool to try to deceive her.

Noverian moved slowly and quietly through the forest. He had several weaves about him to muffle sound and one that made him invisible. The bright red weaves still shined in his peripheral and he wondered how anyone used illusion magic with any success.

He did not like spying on Ehleeshuh, and he was sure the equine would be angry with him if she found out. She paused at a clearing and he was unable to advance further. He suspected that she sensed him so he did not move until she moved on.

Ehleeshuh felt the words of the voice at the clearing ring true. It was playing out just as he had described. She narrowed her blue eyes and focused her thoughts on the elf's inner heart. She lowered her head and turned toward the elf's location. She stamped her hooves into the soft earth in anger as the tendrils touched on a dark black spot in the elf's heart. She lowered her head and charged through the underbrush. Her powerful equine form slid gracefully amongst the trees.

Noverian sighed in frustration. The unicorn had seen him and she was surely angry. It was not until he felt her tendrils probing his soul that he realized what had happened. Fearfully, he stood up from his brush hiding spot.

"Ehleeshuh, we all have the taint," he yelled as he stood in the forest and waved his arms over his head.

Ehleeshuh ignored his words. He was clearly stalking

her, he was armed, and his heart reeked of wickedness.

Noverian's eyes went wide when he realized that the unicorn was not going to stop. He turned and ran into the forest, ducking behind large thick trees as he ran.

Ehleeshuh exploded into a fine white powdery mist and quickly reformed on the other side of the large tree Noverian had run behind. Her powerful hooves closed the distance rapidly. Soon, the wicked elf would pay for his treachery.

Noverian could hear the unicorn's hooves pound the soft earth. He ducked behind a large oak and continued to run. If he could make it to the river, he would be safe.

Ehleeshuh erupted in a fine white mist a second time and reformed in time to ram her thick powerful horn through the back of the fleeing elf. She felt his ribs splinter from her piercing horn and his spine snapped from the powerful force of her skull. The elf was thrown forward from the blow as Ehleeshuh continued her charge. She purposely brought down her heavy ivory hooves and crushed the elf's small fragile skull. In her rage she continued to stomp until the elf was an unrecognizable mass of pulped flesh. Bright red splotches of blood covered her legs and underbelly as she stood panting in the cool spring air. She had done it. She had killed the only person that knew of her plan to stop the wicked dwarf and his demon friends. She had lost nearly two days and the fiend would be reaching Central City soon. She had little time to waste.

Ehleeshuh took one last glance at the twisted body of the mangled elf. She felt a small bit of remorse at having to kill him, but he allowed himself to become blackened by wickedness. With a toss of her head, the proud equine galloped to the north. She had a long journey ahead of her.

Rupert dismissed the bright red illusion weaves that had concealed him in the clearing. He was unsure if Kellacun would be able to pull off her task to kill the boy, or his woman. The tired old lich felt that the unicorn had the best chance. His plans were coming together smoothly. He waved his rotting arms awkwardly and began to channel a powerful abjuration weave. Its bright orange radiance lit up the forest and cast an orange hue on the thick flora. With a flash, he stepped through his gate and returned to his keep.

Amerix made his way along the dirt road to Central City. It was becoming increasingly populated with farm houses and other tradesman. He had narrowly avoided a fairly large contingent of Beyklan soldiers that started to set up some sort of blockade on the south road. He was not sure of their intentions, but it appeared as if they were attempting to monitor traffic to and from Central City. The Kai-Harkian from the bar had given him a fine cloak to wear, but it would do little to hide his race in the daylight. The old general kept his cowl down and clutched Songsinger in the green bundle.

You are making good time, Son of Durion.

"Shut up, you!" Amerix growled back at Songsinger.

We will need to hurry. Look to the north.

Amerix lifted his head from the cowl and glanced north. The road opened up into a large grass clearing. Set atop a wide gentle sloping hill was Central City. It had grown since he had seen it last. Gently, green grass waved in the northern breeze and the gray slate walls of the buildings seemed to tower above the horizon. The great Dawson River Bridge spanned from the east and met the thick forest tree line on the other side of the river gorge. "What? I see the stinking city. I ain't going in 'til dark. Ye think I got some contempt fer ye. Wait 'til them bastard Beyklans see me."

Not the city, Son of Durion. Farther to the north.

Amerix frowned and creased his brow as his old blue eyes scanned to the north. "All I see is a dark storm cloud."

Yes, we must arrive before the storm does, Son of Durion.

"Stop calling me that, ye blasted hunk of junk," Amerix snarled as he shook the bundle.

Amerix stood for several seconds waiting for the sword to reply, but it did not. He smiled at the silence and entered the clearing. It was late afternoon and he hoped to enter the city at nightfall. All he had to do was meet with Apollisian, find the whelp, and get out of there.

Androdius scraped his thick black claw against the thin green magical veil that sealed him in the great swamp. The visits from the red mother piqued his interest in the prophecy and he knew that it was rapidly coming true. The powerful black dragon flexed his leg muscles and leapt into the air. He extended his mighty wings and let them catch air. He thrust them down and launched his heavy body high above the swamp fog. His bright yellow eyes scanned the lush marsh tree tops that poked through the billowing fog that perpetually covered the great swamp. After a few more powerful thrusts that wafted the fog revealing the lush swamp floor, he glided to the south, away from his dark cave lair. It had been many years since he visited the alter of his keeper. He wondered if the other greats hated their keeper as much as he hated his.

Androdius spied the small unassuming temple sitting on a tiny rock spire that just protruded above the swamp. The great black tilted his mighty wings and glided over to the temple. He turned his body and crashed into the spire. The force of the blow sent tiny shards of rocks and moss into the air. Androdius flexed his powerful muscles and climbed to the top of the temple. His thick black claws scratched and pierced the magnificent dome.

"Where are you, Lukerey?" he growled, "Our time is coming!"

A small form began to materialize on the dome in front of Androdius. It was an unassuming form that appeared a cross between a halfling and an elf. It was almost four foot tall and as it began to materialize, the shape became clearly female. She had short brown hair that was littered with bouncing curls. She wore a silk tunic and breeches that were blue and adorned in silver.

"Yes," the goddess said.

Androdius filled his lungs with air and exhaled his horrible acidic breath. Great gouts of green mist and spittle covered the dome and the forest below. His head shook from side to side as he covered the swamp in his ghastly cloud. Moments went by before the cloud cleared, revealing a forest that was half dissolved. A quiet sizzle of melting foliage filled the air.

Lukerey giggled to herself and wiped her shoulder, as if her incorporeal form had been touched by the beasts breath.

"Laugh, fool! The Abyss Walker has come. Soon he will rupture the veil of worlds and we will be released."

Lukerey smiled and cocked her head to the side. "Silly snake, you're too late. The crown has been breached. You and you're kind have nothing to win."

Androdius raised his head and arched his neck. He glanced down at Lukerey with his bright yellow eyes. "Do not play me for a fool, goddess. You may have the mortals tricked into believing you are a man, but I am not fooled so easily."

Lukerey pretended to dance on the rock dome. "I have many forms. I chose a masculine one for a few thousand years and everyone thinks me a man."

"Crown or no crown, we will have vengeance," Androdius growled and slammed his fist through the rock dome he sat upon.

"So angry, all the time," Lukerey replied, "The King of Gods has been banished and the crown is broken. We all have fled Merioulus. Even if the Abyss Walker ruptures the veil, what will you defeat? What will you capture? An empty city of nothing."

Androdius flicked his tail like an angry cat. "The Abyss Walker is not what you think. You fools believe it is the walking monster that Bykalicus created."

"Well, what is it then, fool snake? Surely you do not know."

Androdius chuckled a throaty laugh. "I'll not spoil it for you. You will see."

Lukerey frowned. "You will fail, snake. Your kind is too weak to rule."

Androdius launched himself into the air with his powerful legs. "We shall see, won't we."

Apollisian spied a large contingent of Beyklan soldiers along the road. They were setting up defensive settings along the road, facing west. They were lightly armored, which told Apollisian that they planned to be able to move quickly. It appeared as if each soldier had a mount that was well taken care of.

As they neared the soldiers, two rode out to great them. They were armed with heavy spears that were based in a stanchion in front of the rider's leg.

"What are they doing?" Steiny asked.

"They are turning away travelers."

Ian nodded at Apollisian's observations, "But look at how they are positioned. Riders distributed deep into the forest. It would seem to me they are also trying to keep travelers from fleeing."

Alexis examined the tree line as far as she could see, "He is right, Apollisian. They have archers set in the tree tops."

Apollisian glanced at her. "How can you tell?"

"The trees have horizontal positioning in their branches. Nothing in nature sits horizontal."

"Greetings traveler," one guard called out, "Might I interest you in returning the way you have come. Though it looks as if you have ridden many days, there is a siege coming from the west."

Apollisian frowned. "You know of this threat?"

"Yes, My Lord. We have been dispatched to meet it here and crush it. General Bodrell will enter the city tomorrow."

"See Alexis," Apollisian said as he turned to regard her, "It has nothing to do with the boy."

Alexis crossed her arms under her breast and fumed. "I still think it does. You don't see what I see when I look into his eyes."

The guard glanced at both briefly. "I don't know what you know, but maybe you ought to go see the general."

Apollisian nodded. "General Bodrell?"

"Yes, he will be stationed at the city civic building.

Just know that if you pass us, you may not return until after the battle."

"Figures," Steiny mumbled under his breath.

Apollisian nodded and waved the others by. He reined his horse as the carriage moved by.

"If I may be so bold, sir," the guard asked.

Apollisian smiled. "You may."

"Are you Apollisian Bargoe? The Hero of the Torrent and defender of Central City?"

"I am Apollisian Bargoe, but none of the other titles..."

The guard smiled and he seemed to relax as if a great weight had been lifted from his shoulders. "It is great to know a champion of your repute will be fighting alongside of us. Perhaps we will defeat this foe after all."

Apollisian smiled as warmly as he could. "Of course. You should never have any doubt. Why do you think I have returned?"

The guard smiled as Apollisian rode past. "Henry! Henry, do you know who that was!?"

"A parent has one job. That is to teach their children how to grow up to survive in the world. One may argue that establishing norms and values that are important to them is what should be done.

However, these desires will form along the way regardless. If you teach your children that murdering results in the will of the people taking their own life, then they most likely will not commit the gruesome act. Seldom do people obey the law out of a sense of right and wrong. It is because of the potential penalty.

No, raise your children to become fruitful adults and the rest will fall into place."

-Lancalion Levendis Lampara-

8
Old King and the Greyshalk

King Minostak made his way up the long hill to Petrovisk's hut. He was tired and weary from travel. His muscles ached and he needed rest, but he forced himself onward. Petrovisk was outside chopping wood. His long arms wielded the axe efficiently, making the weapon look tiny in his grasp. He straightened and sniffed the air. His dark blue nose flared in and out as he picked up the king's scent. His graying head whirled to see the king starting up his hill. The tall greyshalk stuck his axe in the wood he was chopping and placed his clawed hands behind his back and stretched his back.

"Greetings, My King."

Minostak rubbed his weary head. "May I come in for some brief rest and some food?"

Petrovisk placed his arm around the weary king, noting the dried blood on his weapon and on his shield. Noting the odd blade fastened in the shield's edge he asked, "Encounter a bit of trouble on your pursuit of a new land?"

The king ducked under the tent flap and signed as the warm are hit him. He gently placed his morning star against the tent wall and plopped down on a fur bag cushion. "Times are grave."

Angelique dished some hot stew from the pot hanging over the fire. She handed the wooden bowl the king and bowed slightly.

"How so?" Petrovisk asked, "No luck finding new land? Perhaps we should go into the mountains like the tribes of old?"

The king gripped the wooden bowl with both hands and sipped the warm soup. "No, it is much more grave. The humans have massed their entire army to stand against this foe and it will not be enough."

Angelique gasped quietly and excused herself. Peter stiffened. "Then we should stand with them. From your descriptions this foe does not differentiate race, only life and unlife."

The king stiffened. "This is why I came to you. Many of the chief's do not feel the way you do. I could challenge them for standing against me, but I do not have time. I have put forth a call to all the tribes to stand with me against this foe. We are meeting tomorrow in the golden field."

Peter nodded. "You have the support of me and my family."

The king nodded and smiled as he took another sip of the fine soup. "I look to have a good three thousand warriors."

Peter nodded. "And how are we to tell the humans that we are there to fight with them. And will they care?"

"I think they know the depth of the task they face. They will certainly care," Minostak said as he chewed a bright orange tuber from the soup, "But letting them know will be the tricky spot. Grayspot, the shaman, says he can make my voice known to the humans, but not theirs to ours. I have learned that a white fur dangled on a stick is a message of peace to the humans. We will march with that fur waving. We will tell them we are there to help. I hope that will be enough."

"And if it isn't?" Petrovisk asked.

"Then we will stand alone to the north of their city and do what we can."

Petrovisk nodded. "It will be a great honor to lay down my life, and the life of my family to fight by your side."

The king smiled and tilted his head back briefly before falling asleep. Angelique returned to the tent. "The girls are getting ready. Katrinal is pouting. She wants to go with us."

Petrovisk bit his lower lip with his thick yellow tusk. "Tell her to armor up and that she better hope she remembers her lessons. This is a foe that will surely kill all of us."

Angelique grabbed Petrovisk by the side of his furry face and kissed him. "I love you. You are a great father to allow us to fight as a family."

Petrovisk rolled his eyes. "Did I have a choice? Knowing Katrinal, she would have snuck away at first night and you would have been unbearable until she got with us."

Angelique smiled. "It's true, but at least you know it."

Bodrell sighed heavily in the dark tent. He forbade the use of torches or lanterns as the army began to prepare to move into the city. He strapped on his greaves and slid his sword into its scabbard. He gave himself a final once over in the mirror and frowned at his indistinguishable reflection before he stepped into the cool night air.

"We are ready, sir," the arch-mage said, "It appears your soldiers are as well. Reports are in from all units that we are ready to march.

"Send the word," Bodrell commanded as he mounted his horse and started toward the road.

As he rode through the forest, he marveled at the empty tents and other equipment that they would normally never abandon. Soup pans were still hanging above the cold fire beds, creating a ghostly presence in the massive camp. The general wondered how many souls would haunt this place? Perhaps his would be among them.

The general entered the forest road and smiled at the force that was lined up in formation. It was probably the largest army commanded by one man in the nation's history. Perhaps even greater than any nation in man's history. How would he be remembered?

The general gave the order and trumpets blared in the black of night. The sounds of hundreds of horse hooves landing against the hard stone of the Dawson River Bridge pained the general. This would be the last time anyone was able to gaze on the greatness of the bridge. This was clearly the end of an era and the beginning of another.

"Jonathon."

"Yes, General?" the arch-mage answered.

"I will stand by the bridge once we cross. In the meantime, I want you to tell the colonels to get their men in defensive positions to the west of the city. Send out riders to recall the north and south regiments that were set to keep travelers in. Tell them to burn any bodies of those that tried to break ranks and were put down. We do not want any of our own rising up to stand against us."

"Yes, Sir. Where shall we muster the men?"

"Use the coliseum. Take a few engineers and a cart of weapons that were to be used for the civilians. Place a blade outside of each cell. Have the engineers rig some sort of system to release the prisoners once the undead attack. We will need every arm that can stand against our foe."

"What about guards working in the coliseum?"

"Break them up and integrate them into different companies. I don't want them banding together," Bodrell answered coldly.

"It will be done, Sir. But, don't you fear the prisoners turning against our men?"

"No, they will be too busy fighting for their lives."

Jonathan nodded. "Will that be all, Sir?"

"No, I want your wizards to set up a station in the city civic building with me. Tell Oswald that I will have breakfast with him and explain what is going on. When you have completed this, return to me and we will drop the bridge."

"It will be done as you command, General."

The general sat atop his horse as it swished its tail back and forth. He gazed at the astonished looks the night walkers and street folk as his army marched in. It was an impressive sight to behold. The creak of thousands of suits of armor and leather filled the night air. Their footfalls pounded the cobblestone streets and echoed into the night alerting dogs and eliciting lanterns from rooftop domiciles. What surprised the young general was that the duke had not come out to complain to him, or threaten him. He stood by the bridge as his army literally exercised the freedom of the city privilege. Perhaps the duke was dead after all.

"Where shall we post?"

The general looked down and gazed on the fiery red varmin of Tylergaiden. The Darayal Legionnaire stood fearless and emotionless before him. The mere sight of him evoked courage and confidence in the general.

"Most of the men are posting in the coliseum, but you may post your men where you like."

"I will post my *elves* in a suitable area. Thank you, General."

Bodrell bit his lip and ignored the emphasis placed on the word elves. As the legionnaire marched off with his companies, he surmised that calling them soldiers might have been more appropriate. He quickly cursed himself for even thinking of catering to the elf's sense of superiority. That was why the races could never get along. They took pride on self-imposed identifying titles.

The general was soon roused from his thoughts when Jonathon emerged from the crowd of legionnaires in the street. He moved quickly and gracefully. His loose fitting robes fluttered in the cold north wind that foretold the undead were not far away.

"All is set, General. The legionnaires will be staying in different spots in the city."

Bodrell nodded. "So are we ready to drop this then?"

Jonathan nodded and walked to the edge of the bridge. It stood quiet, almost accepting, as if it knew its end was coming, "It is a shame to drop her."

The general nodded solemnly. "Aye, she was built under the kings of old. She was a gateway to the west. A symbol of Beyklan power and expansion."

"She also stands as a gateway to the east. To the heart of Beykla. To our king and crown. Should we fail, the bridge will be a crutch to our enemies."

Bodrell motioned his hand forward. "Drop it, Jonathon."

The arch-mage nodded and began to swirl his hands

around rapidly. Great gouts of blue energy formed in front of him as hundreds of evocation weaves whipped around him. The arch-mage masterfully weaved them into thick balls of electrical energy that floated in front of him as he weaved more and more. After a short few moments, he rocketed his hands forward, shooting bright blue bolts of lightning from his hands. In a jagged flash that lit the night sky, they struck the blasting points. Bits of rock and stone shot out from the bridge. The mighty gateway lurched and shook. The great towers that spanned the center crumbled under their own weight and came crashing onto the center of the bridge. A great cracking sound of crumbling stone exploded from the base of the bridge and in moments the entire structure fell away into the night and splashed into the mighty Dawson River below.

Bodrell rubbed his head to remove the static build-up from the powerful blast that Jonathon released. He was excited and anxious to see that power as it tore into the undead. He felt good that they had wizards. It would be a great advantage that he would have over their rotting enemies.

The trotting of hooves on the cobblestone street roused the general from his thoughts. He turned to see a man on horseback. He was dressed in small cloths and looked as if he was recently awakened.

"General Bodrell?" the man asked.

Bodrell nodded. "Yes, what can I help you with?"

"Captain Oswald requests your immediate presence in the civic hall."

Jonathon arched an eyebrow at the general with a wry smile.

Bodrell sifted his weight in his saddle. "Tell him I will be there shortly with a full briefing and that I would like some tea and warm bread. It is going to be a long night."

The messenger nodded and turned his horse. The fading pound of the animal's hooves echoed in the silent night.

"General, did you know the city began constructing a small stone wall around its borders last week?"

Bodrell frowned as he spurned his horse forward toward the civic building. "Oh? I did not know this."

"Yes, though it will not be completed by the siege, it will funnel the undead where we wish them to go. Why try to go through a wall when you can go around it?"

Bodrell nodded. "This is good. Tomorrow we will have the men place some pit traps and oil in these areas."

Jonathon smiled. "A few well-placed blasts of fire from my wizards will tear their numbers apart."

"We just may win the day yet, Jonathon."

Edge growled and lowered his head. Vlargcar awoke and rubbed his bright blue eyes. He grabbed the powerful war dog across the muzzle with his giant hand, "Shhhhh! It's sleepy time."

The dog growled again and glanced at Vlargcar and then back down the small corridor that lead to the mouth of his cell.

"You shush," Vlargcar said again, "I need sleep. You get to sit all day in here. I might have to go fight."

The dog relaxed a bit but kept a tense eye at the door of the giant orc's cell. Vlargcar closed his eyes and began to drift to sleep when Edge started growling again. His deep guttural growl was menacing.

"Ugh. What has you worked up?" the orc asked as he sat up from his hard wooden cot. He rubbed his head and stretched his thick muscled arms, "I go see."

Vlargcar got up and smacked his lips together as he made his way to the door of his cell. Edge followed behind him, growling. When he got to his door, he could see several men dressed in brass colored scale mail armor with red silk flowing capes. They had several other men that were rigging some sort of contraption above the doors to all of the jail cells. Vlargcar glanced down at Edge and then back to the guards. "You could hear them, huh Edge?"

The dog glanced up at the orc and then back to the door and nervously wagged his tail.

"You are a smart dog. But nothing to worry about. They are just guards fixing the doors. Let's go back to sleep."

Edge uneasily followed Vlargcar back to bed. The big orc wrapped his thick arms around the dog and cuddled him as they fell back asleep.

Jude awoke to a pounding at his door. He did not move and slowly opened his eyes to a small indistinguishable slit. He could make out several shapes that were affixing something to his door. They hammered and banged so loudly Jude, figured there was no sense in pretending to be asleep. He sat up and was surprised that the men did not jump in fear. He hopped down from his cot and walked right up to the cell door. The men did not even flinch. They were dressed in brass colored scale mail and had red flowing capes. There were two other men with them that were affixing some sort of a mechanical contraption on the exterior of the door.

"What are you doing?" Jude asked.

The unarmored men did not reply and kept diligent at their task. One of the guards looked up, but did not seem afraid, like the coliseum guards were. "There is an army coming this way..."

"What kind of an army?" Jude interrupted.

The guard did not seem angry at the interruption. "A big one. The cells are being rigged. When the army hits, you are to pick up the sword we leave you and join the battle."

Jude chuckled. "And what if I decided to fight with the invading army?"

The guard smiled. "In order to do that, you will have to die."

Jude frowned. "I am no simpleton. Do not speak to me in riddles. I am Jude, gladiator champion."

"Ah. So that is what this bronze sword emblem means on the outside of your door," the soldier replied.

"Sir, we passed another one of those a while back. The cell we heard the dog growling in," one of the engineers said.

"Yes, that is my co-champion, Vlargcar," Jude replied, "Tell me about this invading force? Who would dare? The dwarves again?"

"No, the dwarves were defeated by king Theobold before his death."

"The king is dead?" Jude asked surprisingly.

The soldier frowned. "I am sorry. I am not here to catch you up on current events. The army coming is led by the Abyss Walker. He commands thousands of undead, like himself, and we are making our stand here."

Jude briefly marveled at how civil the soldier was with him, before the title Abyss Walker hit him. His thoughts immediately went to Lance. "No need to be sorry. A friend of mine was once accused of being the Abyss Walker. His name is Lance. Is the leader of the army named that?"

The solider shrugged. "Who knows. Just be ready to fight for your very life."

Jude smiled. "I do that nearly twice a week."

The soldier half smiled and set down a small sword just out of reach of Jude.

"What is that for?" Jude asked.

"When the undead hit the city, the doors will all be raised at once. Grab the sword and go find a garrison to meet up with."

Jude chuckled. "I would be better served with my armor from the war room. As well would the other champion."

The soldier shook his head. "I am not familiar with this building so this will have to do."

"I know where that is, Sergeant," one of the guards said, "Would you like me to go get their stuff?"

The soldier eyed Jude for a moment. "Is the other champion as big as you?"

"Bigger," Jude replied.

The sergeant bit on his lip for a moment. "How will my man know what stuff is yours?"

Jude smiled. "Our stuff will be marked with our names. It is in a wooden locker in the war room against the far wall. I have a great sword and chain shirt. Vlargcar fights with the two swords and the studded leather."

The soldier nodded and hurried off.

"Good luck to you. I suspect the army will hit us tomorrow night. The undead are not formidable soldiers, but stabbing will not kill them. They must be mechanically broken down."

"You mean like cutting their legs or heads off?" Jude asked.

"That is precisely what I am saying," the sergeant replied.

As the engineers finished and started to the next door the sergeant paused. "I am stationed on the wall section just west of the coliseum. You seem a decent man, despite your crimes. I would be honored if you and your friend stood with me."

Jude nodded. "I will tell my friend about you and we will come to your wall. But, my friend is different. Do not be alarmed by him."

The sergeant smiled. "As long as he is a living breathing man, he is welcome on my wall."

Jude smiled and turned to his bunk as the men moved on to the next cell. He chuckled at the sergeant's assumption that Vlargcar was a man. Boy, was he in for a rude surprise.

Azcarnicus sat on his fiery throne of brass. His bright red skin was ablaze with a hellish fire that thickened around his torso to form a molten loin cloth. His head was wreathed with a crown of flames and his deep black horns protruded from his temples and ran alongside his head to jut out far in front of him, like an elephants tusks. The fallen King of the Gods marveled at how his body changed with each passing day, as the essence of the Fire God flowed through him. Balls of molten rock floated in front of him, twisting and turning in the air, dripping thick globules of magma onto the chamber floor. The once God King gazed into the orbs. Images from the realms shined back at him. Rupert, the elves, and Trinidy.

Azcarnicus smiled. He recalled the faithful paladin, turned by a woman's curve. The fool man had allowed himself to fall in love with Panoleen, the fallen Goddess of Mercy. Azcarnicus had found it a fitting punishment for the foolish man to spend eternity in the Abyss, but this new form. This walking death seemed a more befitting torture to an unlawful worshipper. He had amassed an army of other walking dead and was about to kill the Abyss Walker for him. It would seem the arch-demon was enacting their plan perfectly.

Azcarnicus waved his finger and brought forth a ball of magma towards him. He twirled it in the air and growled in frustration. The once mighty God King tried to scry on the arch-demon, but he could not. It bothered Azcarnicus that he had to rely on the arch-demon to uphold his end of the bargain. That was something that demons were not known for. Ever since Rah Cordan created all of the demons, they have been a lying, deceiving, backstabbing lot.

Azcarnicus stood from his throne and walked through the molten marbled archway. The four balls of magma floated behind him as he marched down the long hallway. When he neared the end, he made his way through a second, more magnificent archway and out into the realm of fire. His palace floated high above an ocean of magma. Great chains of magical weaves held the citadel aloft. As he stood admiring his new realm, Azcarnicus summoned one of the floating magmatic orbs. He twirled his finger until an image appeared. It was of a deep red and black armored worm. It was segmented with thick black plates. Its upper torso was that of a humanoid. It had two thin, but muscular arms and a serpent head. It wore a deep red helm that was adorned with spines that were shaped like wisps of fire. It wielded a long spear on one hand and a small shield in the other.

"Shanorian," the God King spoke into the orb.

The creature turned and regarded the air, as if he were looking in an orb himself. "Yes, My Master."

"How soon will we be ready to reclaim Merioulus?"

The serpent creature smiled revealing a maw of sharp black teeth. "We will soon be ready. The army will crush any celestial defenders that stand in our way, My Master. But, what of the Abyss Walker? What if the arch-demon's puppet fails? If the boy understands his true power, he might be able to defeat the death knight."

Azcarnicus nodded as he rubbed his fiery chin. "I have considered that. Along with the expectation the arch-demon will try to betray us. Therefore, I have summoned one of the arch-devils I sent to the realms. They have amassed small armies themselves and will gate these armies into the battle. I do not see how the death knight and my three arch-devils can fall to the Abyss Walker."

"And what will you do once the boy succumbs?"

Azcarnicus smiled. "I will fill the arch-demon with the power of Flunt to overthrow Rha Cordan. Our armies will march on Merioulus while his defeat the Keeper of the Wicked. I will rule this realm, reclaim my throne, and the throne of the Abyss!"

The fiery serpent frowned. "My Master, how will you rule the Abyss?"

Azcarnicus chuckled. "The power that I will infuse the arch-demon with will force him to bend to my will. He will be king, but a puppet to my whims. Now, return to your duties. The time of our reckoning will come and we will need every single one of our numbers."

"Quadry, wake up."

The tired elf opened his eyes and stretched. "What is it?"

Silas ran to the window of the inn and pointed outside into the dark street. "Look."

Quadry sat up quickly and hurried to the window. His keen elven eyes adjusted to the night and revealed thousands of armored men marching into the city. "What do you make of that?"

Silas shrugged. "My guess is that our time to find Alexis and Apollisian is running out."

"Agreed! As much as I enjoyed watching that orc fight last night, we should have spent it looking for them."

Silas nodded and closed the curtain. "First thing in the morning we are going to have to go to the leaders of the city for their assistance."

Quadry lumbered back to his bed. "What are we going to do if we don't find them tomorrow?"

Silas shrugged. "I don't know, but we need to make a

choice if we don't find them. Stand with the other legion-naires… or head back to the king."

Quadry nodded as he snuggled under the blankets. "Well, let's hope we find them tomorrow and save ourselves from the decision."

"Many youths do not have the luxury of having two parents. Their father was run off, or their mother died during the birth of a sibling. Whatever the reason, life is hard.

Too many times the remaining parent understands the need for the other one. But, they error. They try to fill both needs. This does not work.

Apollisian grew up without a father. His father had ran off, enchanted by a woman he claimed was a goddess. His mother was wise. She understood that she could never be his father. She understood that all she could be was the best mother she could. Mother and father are as different as black and white. If you mix them, all you get is grey.

Had his mother not understood this truth, I wonder how the world would have been affected. What would have happened had he not crossed swords with Amerix. What would have happened had he not inspired the Minok Nation to stand against Trinidy?

Funny. As parents guide their children, they are undoubtedly guiding the future. Too bad the drunkards and whores fail to realize this truth within their own children."

-Lancalion Levendis Lampara-

9

The Calm Before the Storm

Petrovisk and his family marched down from the thickly wooded hill. The journey from the mountain peaks had been fairly easy and the bright orange glow form the eastern sky announced the coming sun. He had hoped that there would have been more of a showing from his kin. As it stood, barely a thousand greyshalk were mustered and he doubted many more would arrive. Though this was a massive gathering for the furred folk, he had hoped for more.

"Go and find where we are to be striding," Petrovisk said, "I will meet with the king. I am sure we are to leave soon. I awakened him long before the sun announced itself and I am sure they are ready to stride soon."

Angelique nodded and motioned for the girls to follow as Peterovisk made his way toward the large hut that surely belonged to Minostak. The cool spring air blew from the west and ruffled his thick fur. The old warrior was a bit surprised how cold the air was. It was normally much warmer in the valley this time of year.

"The air is a bit cold, eh?" King Minostak announced as he came out form his tent.

Petrovisk nodded and glanced around at his kin. He narrowed his old eyes and shook his head slightly. "A poor showing."

Minostak nodded as he surveyed his kin. "Yes, I was

hoping for more. It seems the tribe's chiefs have more influence than I expected. I can see our entire tribe breaking if we survive this foe."

Petrovisk growled low and the hair on the back of his shoulder rose. "I will stand with you and cut the pompous jackals down like the Kriel they are!"

Minostak chuckled as Petrovisk mentioned the Kriel. He was but a pup when their cousins united against the Beyklans. Their coward-like spotted hides were ousted by a human woman near Frishian Wood. Had the humans faced greyshalk, they would have had to cut every one of their numbers down. Though, it did strike the king as odd that his people were now going to rise and stand with the Beyklans when just a few short decades ago, they were bitter enemies.

"How will we approach the Beyklans? You mentioned white skins held aloft by a stick. Do we all carry one?"

Minostak chewed on his lower lip. "We do not have the time to hunt that many snow leopards. Instead, I have broken our kin down into ten groups of ten. Each will have their own frider skin."

Petrovisk nodded. "And who is to approach the Beyklans when we arrive? Surely they will see us coming and worry."

Minostak smiled exposing a wide mouth of yellow teeth. "I figure you and I will approach them. If they do not accept our frider skins, think of the glory to stand against so many."

Petrovisk smiled distantly and imagined the site of he and his king, back to back, fighting against the Beyklans.

Amerix pulled his cloak tight around his neck. The thick cowl would hide his face, but it would not hide his stature. He was hoping that his height would disperse suspicions that he was a dwarf. The warm glow of the eastern sun was beginning to crest the horizon as he topped the small hill on the southern road. The renegade narrowed his old steel blue eyes and gazed upon Central City. He had planned to enter the town at dusk, but his cloak was warm and his old bones were tired. The ancient dwarf elected to sleep an hour or two that turned into six.

As he neared the city, it was much different than he remembered. Great wall sections were constructed on the outside and were teaming with soldiers and workers. It appeared as if they had been working all night. Several patrols of soldiers wearing brass colored armor and long flowing red silk capes wandered the roads and the fields around the city. The old dwarf tried his best to maneuver toward the city limits without meeting a group, but his stubby little legs did not move fast enough and he soon found himself coming face to face with one of the patrols.

"Turn away, citizen," the guard called out, "Lest you be kept in the city. By order of General Bodrell, no one is allowed to leave."

Amerix did not glance up. He watched the soldier's feet for sign of an attack. If they were to try to harm him, they would shift their feet. He had no idea what they were saying and if they tried to stop him, he would have to cut them down. This would surely attract the attention of other groups, which he would then have to cut down too. Of course this would attract even more attention. The old general sighed. He would have to kill the entire town just to return one sword and find the whelp. The thought did not cause the renegade general much grief, since he had tried to do that once before.

"Sir, are you deaf?" the sergeant called out, "If you continue into town, you will not be allowed to leave."

Amerix slid his hand to his one of his axes as he walked past. He considered saying something. But, the two languages he spoke would most likely enrage the soldiers. Dwarven would give him away, and orc wouldn't be much better. Seraneen used to speak elven. She used to speak several phrases to him. He never learned what they were, but he had better say something. If the guards stopped him, it would be a battle for sure.

"I love you, my rage filled muffin," the old dwarf said with his best attempt to mimic his late wife's phrase.

The sergeant paused as he started to reach for Amerix's

cloak. "What did he say?"

The other guards frowned.

"I think it was elven."

The sergeant turned to one of the other soldiers as Amerix hurried toward town. "Jeffrey, you speak elven. What did he say?"

Jeffrey shrugged his shoulders. "I'm not real sure, Sergeant. I think he said he loves mad muffins, or something like that."

The other soldiers stifled their snickers as the sergeant shook his head. "We don't have time for foolery. He was warned. If he tries to leave the city, he will be rebuffed, or slain like the others."

Amerix glanced over his shoulder as he started up the long sloped road into the southern quarter of the city. The patrol moved on and did not follow him. The old general chuckled to himself and pondered what he had actually told them before feeling a familiar empty feeling that was now occupied by the memory of his wife and child.

Amerix entered town and was surprised to see so many soldiers. It was as if the entire Beyklan army was camped in the city limits. Very few citizens were moving about and it seemed if the city would burst if another person walked in. Finding a particular soldier in a city full of them was going to be near impossible. Maybe if he found the whelp first, his task might be easier.

Amerix kept his head low and made his way through the bustling city streets. The soldiers paid him little attention and the scarce locals that happened to be out seemed terrified and never lingered. Though the old general had been in human cities before in his long life of travels, he still did not speak their language and was unfamiliar with their customs. He made his way to the north and ducked into an alley.

Go to the north, Son of Durion. You will find him there, the honeyed voice of Songsinger echoed in in his head.

Amerix growled, "Shut up, ye stupid sword."

Apollisian will be arriving soon. He will be coming from the north.

Amerix shook the green bundle. "Listen, ye blasted

sword. I liked it better when ye were broke. Or at least when ye made that shrill hum."

That noise warns the wielder when they are surrounded by wickedness.

"Ha!" Amerix taunted, "That ain't true. Ye made that sound all the time I carried ye from the Torrent into the under mountain. I wasn't around no evil."

You carried me.

Amerix narrowed his steel blue eyes. "So? Are ye trying to tell me I am evil."

No, you were.

Amerix chuckled. "I was? Yea, right. What do ye know, ye stupid sword. Anyway, ye broke after the battle. Water shut ye down or something?"

I wasn't broke, Son of Durion, Songsinger answered, *You were no longer evil.*

Amerix grabbed his belly and laughed as he fell back against the wall of the alley. "Me, evil? Bah!"

Wickedness often blames the character of greater men for their woes, Amerix. You blamed innocents for the deaths of your family. You extracted vengeance for your pain with their blood.

Amerix stopped laughing and removed the sword from the green cloth. He stared at the brilliant blade and slowly turned it in the morning light. "So, if I am some monster, why do ye not make noise now, sword?"

I only warn my wielder of current wickedness. You are no longer wicked, Amerix Alistair Stormhammer.

The old general took a deep breath. "Say what ye will sword, if I had to do it over again, the Beyklans would still be dead."

Of course. You cannot make a different choice other than the one your fate will have you make. You had to make that choice to get you here.

Amerix shook his head. "No fate controls me, sword. I control me. I could bash ye against the wall right now. Would that be yer fate? To be broken on some alley wall?"

Yes, you could do that. But that is not my fate.

Amerix chuckled as he tucked the sword back into the green cloth the elf had given him, "So what is yer fate, sword?"

I will save the world for a short time before it is destroyed by its own wickedness.

Amerix shook his head and attached the bundle to his pack, "Well, I'm glad yer fate is so pleasant, sword."

It may seem unpleasant to you, Son of Durion. But, it is paradise compared to the fate of the Ecnal.

The cold wind whipped from the northwest and Alexis pulled her cloak tight against her body. The morning sun had washed away the deep blue night sky revealing a much different city line from the last time she had made this journey.

"Apollisian," she called out, "Are they building walls?"

The paladin trotted his horse alongside hers and rubbed the sleep from his eyes. "It would appear that they are building wall partitions. In fact, they are nearly finished."

"Why would they do that?" she asked.

Ian cleared his throat. "A common tactic of communities rushed for war."

Apollisian nodded. "He is right. If a community does not have time to construct a complete wall, they build partitions. The invading force will not try to break them down so the walls do not need to be strong."

Alexis frowned as they neared the city. "But if they can run around them, what is the point of having them?"

Apollisian watched with earnest as he studied the partitions. "Well, my sweets. If you were to be attacked, wouldn't you like to dictate the path the attacking force took."

Alexis frowned. "I have not studied human siege tactics, but I can assume that the defenders would dig pits and drop hot oil in these locations."

Ian smiled. "She learns fast, Pauly."

As the group rode through the large partitions Apollisian marveled at the number of Beyklan soldiers that manned them. To have such a number on the walls would indicate a force of about thirty thousand in the city limits. Central City could not support that many troops for long.

"They know the monster and his army are coming."

A few of the troops glanced down at Apollisian and the carriage but they did not wave. One of the sergeants made eye contact with Apollisian and nodded gravely. Ian watched the exchange. "They know he is coming, Pauly. And I think they know the extent at what comes with him."

Steiny opened his eyes as the wagon jostled him. He stretched and lurched as the carriage passed under a huge stone partition. The bricks were as large as a man and it was topped with dozens of scary soldiers.

"Are we here?" he quipped.

The wagon driver nodded quietly as Steiny gazed in wonderment at the new structures. "What are those for?"

Fehzban came from the carriage and sat next to the half-ling. "Those are defensive stanchions."

"What are they for?" Steiny asked.

"They are for guiding the enemy troops into places you want them to go. Like pits, collapsing tunnels, burning oil... That kind of thing," Fehzban answered.

As they rode into the city, it was much different than before. The streets were teaming with soldiers that were carrying out various tasks. The coliseum looked to be shut down to the public as there was a constant flow to and from of armored Beyklans. The group rode up to a large three story wooden building. There was a stable attached, but it seemed bare. Ian glanced up at the sign and read it aloud, "Inn of the Welcome Wench. That sounds like a pleasant establishment."

"Do as you wish, Ian. But, my crew is not here to debunk young girls," Apollisian said as he dismounted his horse.

Alexis shot Ian angry glance.

"What?" Ian said as he tossed up his arms defensively, "I was just saying."

"Do you think halfling women work here?" Steiny asked with a chuckle.

"None that are willing to listen to your incessant whin-ing," Alexis said as she gathered the horses and lead them to the stables.

The wagon master dismounted and collected his coin from Delania. She emerged from the wagon wearing her robe of the blue sept. It was a remarkable outfit that marked her immediately for some sort of nobility. She handled a small leather case that carried her small stuffs as Lance emerged from the carriage wearing his cadacka. The cold northern wind blew his black hair about his face. Much had grown back since his time with the witches, but it was still somewhat short.

"Lance," Apollisian called out, "We are going to see the magistrate here in town. It would be nice if you would secure lodging here at this inn."

Lance glanced at Delania who hugged his arm warmly. "How many rooms?"

Apollisian glanced at Steiny, Alexis, and then to Ian before responding, "Three for us and how many you require."

Lance nodded and entered the inn. Delania was in tow and Fehzban was close behind. The common room was bare. The tables had been moved over to the wall and the legs were removed. Several of the tables had been hammered to the wall, covering the bottom floor windows.

"Hello?" Lance called out.

A man came from the a small door behind the bar. He had a large hammer in his hand and a large wooden box of thick nails. "We're closed."

Fehzban pointed to the tables covering the windows. "We can help you with your defenses if you can offer us a room."

The man turned white and lost color in his face. He set his nails down on the corner of the counter.

"Get that murdering bastard out of my inn, or I will kill him where he stands," he said shaking the hammer at Fehzban.

Delania channeled a thick blue weave of evocation and hurled it at the bar keeper. The bright energy struck him in the chest and hurled him back against the wall. His leg struck the bar and splintered the wood as his lifeless body fell behind the bar. Thick smoke rolled up from the charred hole in his chest and the room begin to fill with the smell of charred flesh.

"Holy smokes!" Fehzban shouted.

"Whoa!" Lance shouted as he ran to the man's lifeless form. "What did you do that for?!"

Fehzban glanced at Delania and slid a few steps back from her.

Delania pointed to Fehzban, "He threatened to kill him. He is our friend, right?"

"Yea, but his kind attacked this city a year or so back. The whole city is not going to like him!" Lance answered as he checked the body. "Dang it, Delania. He's dead."

Fehzban shook his head. "I don't think I am safe here."

Delania arched her pointed eyebrow at the dwarf. "As opposed to the front lines in front of the wave of death? I think the undead will not treat you as good."

Lance shook his head. "Delania, you can't kill people. This is not Aten."

"He was going to try to hurt the dwarf," she pleaded.

Lance frowned. "If he had tried, then we could have intervened. He was probably just angry."

"Now what?" Fehzban asked. "Apollisian will not likely approve of the dead man."

Delania folded her arms under her breasts. "So. Who cares? He is not our keeper."

Lance shook his head. "We have an army of undead bearing down on us. Killing people, our only allies, is not a good idea. I don't care if Apollisian approves or not. I don't approve and it has to stop."

Fehzban glanced back at the two of them and quietly moved back to the far wall.

Delania tightened her fists. "Who are you to tell me anything, spawn?"

Lance frowned. "Spawn? You used to say that in Aten. What does that mean?"

"It means that you are in no position to tell me anything. If someone threatens you, or our friends, then I will end them," Delania said focusing on the word, friend. It was an odd word for her.

"But, he didn't threaten."

"Yes, he did. He said to get him out of the inn, or he

would kill him," she said, "And that is good enough for me. I would not let anyone try to harm you. I love you."

Lance softened. "You act as if you are not even from this world. I love you too, but to kill a man for an angry threat?"

Delania narrowed her eyes. "What do you mean, threat?"

Fehzban watched the woman carefully. Something was wrong about her, but he could not put his finger on it.

"A threat. You know, when I am angry and say things I don't mean," Lance replied as he glanced down at the dead body.

"How do you know if someone is threating?" she asked.

"Threatening," Fehzban corrected.

Delania glanced over at the dwarf. "What?"

"Never mind him," Lance said as he motioned to the dwarf, "Look, he may have been serious. But, I don't think so. You have to learn to determine before you act."

Delania bit her lip and mumbled under her breath. "Humans are so weird."

"You're human, aren't you?" Fehzban asked moving toward the door of the inn.

"What was that?" Lance asked as he looked up from behind the counter, "I am trying to figure out what to do with this body."

"Nothing," Delania said with a smile and then turned with a murderous look to the dwarf, "I am from Aten. We are above humans."

Fehzban did not reply.

Lance came back from the kitchen. He wiped a small trickle of sweat from his forehead. "I found a locker down stairs. It had old brooms and table parts. I put the body in there. It will smell after a bit, but I don't think Apollisian will notice by tomorrow."

Fehzban did not say anything and Delania smiled as she examined the table tops that had been nailed to the window, "That's fine, my love. This should make a suitable dwelling to defend. The undead will have a hard time getting in. They don't use tools effectively and we can rain spells down on them from the roof."

Lance nodded. "Shouldn't we get to the front lines? We

can do more damage to them there and retreat back here once the lines break. I heard Apollisian talking about that as we rode in."

Fehzban glanced at Delania cautiously. There was something sinister about her. "I served under General Amerix Stormhammer. Besides his vile soul, he was a great tactician. If we are to defend this structure, there are certain defenses we will want to implement."

Lance nodded. "Great. Devise some plans and we will get to it. Apollisian will be back soon and if we have the materials ready, we can use his knowledge on war. He is a holy warrior after all."

General Bodrell sat in the magistrate chair under the great dome of the civic building. He mulled over various large scrolls that were too big for the oak desk. Blots of ink were carefully corked and dry quills littered the floor around the desk. Several armored soldiers stood impatiently as the general mulled over the reports. Caption Oswald Thorrin sat in one of the hard wooden benches that lined the great chamber and rested his outstretched arm on the back of it.

"I could use more assistance, Oswald!" Bodrell growled in frustration.

"You proved you know everything, General. You dropped a bridge that stood for over a thousand years, you declared martial law, and have killed or arrested citizens that have tried to leave the city. I might as well consider you an occupying force."

Bodrell slammed his fist down on the desk and pointed his finger at the captain. "I do not need this, Oswald. Your duke has been assassinated, your city is in turmoil, and the only person that is qualified to run the city is the fat noble, Doogan Raymer. Stephanis knows why he is even here in the first damn place."

Oswald leaned back as he sat on the hard bench. He crossed his arms and his legs and smirked. "The king is not going to be happy to find you have imposed martial law on one of his nobles. That is assuming he is capable to rule. Maybe the nobles are pulling the strings of his crown."

Bodrell gritted his teeth together. "You are walking on dangerous ground flapping your fool tongue like that."

"I am not saying anything that has not been thought by nearly every Beyklan."

Bodrell relaxed a bit. "Oswald, a kingdom is run by the foundation and belief of its citizens in its king. Thoughts like that can undermine his crown before he grows enough to wear it."

Oswald signed. "And that has nothing to do with our situation here. I simply do not believe that this army of walking dead is as vast as you say."

"It is probably larger than all of the armies of Beykla combined," Apollisian said as he boldly walked into the chamber.

"Who is this?" Bodrell demanded angrily.

The guards started moving toward Apollisian with Alexis and Ian in tow.

"I am Apollisian Bargoe of Westvon Keep. Champion of Justice and Defender of Light."

"Ha!" Oswald barked, "No one uses the powers of the gods anymore, they have abandoned us."

Apollisian clopped Oswald on the back of the head as he walked by. The metal gauntlet hand made a pop on Oswald's unprotected head. "Sit up when you are in the presence of men greater than yourself."

Oswald rubbed his head and jumped to his feet. "You dare accost me? I shall have you in chains."

Bodrell smiled. "I assume you are here to claim sovereignty of this city, Apollisian."

Oswald put his hands on his hips keeping a wary eye on the elf and the gruff middle aged warrior. "I don't see how you can do that. Who are you again?"

Bodrell smiled. "He is your replacement. As a holy warrior of Stephanis, he will be claiming sovereignty over this city due to an impending act of war."

"Yes, I am here for just that," Apollisian said, "I will not make the same mistake I made last time with the dwarven threat. I am claiming charge now. Where is the duke?"

Bodrell pointed at Oswald. "The duke was assassinated a few nights ago."

"Suspiciously," Oswald added.

Apollisian turned to Bodrell. "So you are in charge in his stead?"

Oswald smiled. "I am."

"Then you are relieved and dismissed to your quarters," Apollisian answered.

"I am not going anywhere," Oswald said defiantly as he crossed his arms over his chest.

"General, as commander of Central City, my first order of business is for your soldiers to remove Oswald."

Bodrell smiled wide and gestured to his men. "I was hoping you would say that. If I did it that would be the final nail in my coffin as an occupying force!"

Oswald yelled and screamed promises of arrest and execution as he was violently escorted from the chambers. His angry shouts echoed distantly down the hall. Apollisian glanced back at the fading shouts and exhaled slowly. "Okay, General, what do you know?"

Bodrell motioned for Apollisian to sit as he filled two goblets. "Our runners have had a difficult time. The army is moving at an unprecedented pace. They don't need to rest or even sleep. Our wizards have attempted to scry on them when they can, but the Abyss Walker blocks them somehow. We suspect they number around fifteen thousand, maybe more."

Apollisian nodded. "I think more."

"You have seen them?" Bodrell asked with earnest as he handed Apollisian and Alexis a goblet before pulling two more from an old chest next to his table.

"We were nearly overtaken by their ghouls. They can run as fast as a man, and they never tire. It seems once we began to outdistance them they backed off. They won't trail too far from the main force. Their tactics are nearly non-existent, but the fact they remain together either tells me they are run by a tactful leader, or magic forces them to remain close together."

Bodrell nodded silently as he poured two more goblets.

Apollisian shifted his weight on the wooden bench. "General, I am not as versed in mass war as you. I offer the city to you. Use me and my friends where you can, but the lives of the entire kingdom, maybe more, will rest on whether we can defeat this army."

Ian nodded as Bodrell handed him a goblet. "General, my name is Sir Ian Silverman. I was a knight in Lostom. This army sacked it in moments. They have many different units that I think we should explain and prepare for."

Bodrell sipped his wine. "Siege weapons?"

"No, not like that," Apollisian answered.

Ian grimaced. "More dangerous. See, the fast movers are able to paralyze their victims with a single cut from their claws, or from their bites. But ahead of them is a contention of shadow like figures. They don't have real bodies. I do not know how to fight them. They can pass through solid stone and their touch is as chilling as the Abyss itself. When they defeated my duke, they sent the shadows in first, followed by the fleet footed ghouls. The walking dead were like peasant conscriptions. They are our least fear."

Bodrell scribed everything down quickly. "Can you guess their numbers?"

Ian squinted and shook his head from side to side. "Hard saying, General. I would guess several thousand shadows and probably twice that in ghouls. The rest will be the walking dead. Maybe twenty thousand of those. "

His words cut into the general's spirits. Those numbers alone would be difficult to defeat, let alone with the power of the shadows and ghouls.

The general started to ask another question when a messenger erupted into the room.

"General!" the messenger said excitedly, "You are needed, quickly."

Everyone in the room stiffened. Had the undead arrived already? "What is it? Are they here?"

"Um-no, Sir. Not exactly. But something is here. A large force to the north. They appear to be dangerous, but they are waving several white flags and are no longer advancing."

Apollisian frowned. "What is it? Undead?"

The messenger cleared his throat uneasily. "No, Sir, greyshalks."

"Greyshalks" Alexis said suspiciously.

"Yes, My Lady. About a thousand of them."

The general shook his head as he grabbed his helmet. "This day just keeps getting better and better."

Petrovisk towered among his kin as they stood in groups outside the human city. Though time had washed away his soft brown fur and replaced it with scraggly silver streaks, he was still a monster among monsters. The light wind blew his thick fur cape as his hawk like eyes scanned the horizon.

"Do you think they will send someone out?"

The king glanced up at his hulking friend before staring back at the massive city. "They have not dispatched soldiers yet, so I think this is a good sign."

Pertovisk took the city in for all of its glory. "Why do they only have sections of walls?"

Minostak bit his bottom lip. "I am not sure. Seems silly to me. But have you ever seen them fight one another? Too much structure in their own ranks and no structure between warriors. It's like the only honor is among the leaders and they don't fight!"

Petrovisk growled as a small contingent of horsemen rode out from the city. They wore armor and had a flag bearer behind them.

"Easy, Petrovisk," the king said as he motioned for one of the frider wavers to approach him, "I think this is a good sign. Surely the do not think this small group can stand against us."

Petrovisk pointed to the flag bearer. "Why don't they have a frider? Their banner is red, like blood-like war."

Minostak nodded. "I think our frider means peace for both," he said as the frider waver arrived next to him.

Petrovisk looked down at the young warrior. He was powerful, like many greyshalks, but he wondered if he was powerful enough. To carry a frider should be reserved for the best warriors.

The king motioned for Petrovisk to follow as he, the frider bearer, and the shaman walked out to meet the Beyklans. Peter glanced over to Angelique and his daughters one final time before heading out with his king.

Apollisian gripped his reins tight as he rode out with Bodrell, Alexis, and Ian. He tried to summon the power of Stephanis to see if the greyshalks had dark hearts, but the empty hollow feeling was all that answered.

"Are you sure this is wise, Apollisian?" Ian asked as they trotted from behind one of the huge stone partitions and into the north field.

"They wave the banner of peace," he said, "A banner that is not accustomed to their folk."

Ian nodded. "But during the orc wars, they fought alongside of the green skinned demons and the kriel."

"Not exactly," Bodrell replied, "The greyshalks defended their territory from us. The kriel joined the ranks of the orc hordes. We had to fight them to capture Grimolikin Hill. The kriel were using it to stage raids on our supply lines."

Alexis chuckled. "You all talk as if you were there."

All three smiled uneasily. "Yes, My Lady Overmoon. I can imagine you do recall the events."

"Not as you describe them, or to the detail. Our culture does not recognize victories or give titles to battles."

"What about the Quiegen?" Ian asked.

Alexis nodded. "Of course there are exceptions. But that battle is known as the Battle of Quigen, but merely as Quigen. Which you may know means sacrifice in our language. The title was given to honor the dead and their sacrifice, not glorify the battle or its combatants."

"Well it looks like we won't be fighting them at this moment after all, they are sending out a chief and a peace bearer."

"Be mindful of a trick, General. If they have studied enough to learn the significance of a white flag, then they have studied enough to use that as a trap to lure us in," Ian warned.

Petrovisk gripped his kerstap tightly as the Beyklans approached. He was not sure which one was the leader, but all of the men were heavily armored. The third seemed not to fit. He had less of a presence. More of a feral look about him. Petrovisk decided he liked him the most. His bright yellow hair marked him different.

The shaman adjusted his many leather straps, rare furs, and feathers. "The time comes soon, Minostak."

The king nodded. "Make sure it works."

"I will, King. I have brought bark tablets. The dead walker has blocked us from communicating with Larunthus, but his word is still strong in the old tablets."

The shaman drew out an old piece of thick bark from his weathered leather satchel. He read the words aloud and sprinkled white powder in the air as he read. Petrovisk growled as the bright magical energy swirled and popped above the bark.

"Easy, Petrovisk," the king said, "I dislike magic as well, but the shaman have always helped our people."

Petrovisk did not argue, though he wanted too. If they helped half as much as they thought they did, he and his family would not have lost Grimolikin Hill and had to move to the western mountains.

The shaman finished his chant and looked pleased with his self. "It is done, King. The humans should be able to understand us, but we won't be able to understand them."

Petrovisk mumbled under his breath as the Beyklans rode up.

"Greetings. I am King Minostak. I do not mean you any harm. You will able to understand me, but I will not be able to understand you."

Bodrell frowned. "What is he saying? Either of you speak greyshalk?"

Apollisian frowned. "I speak a little orc from my days at the academy. Should I try that."

The king frowned and looked at the shaman. "They speak our tongue?"

The shaman looked confused and started examining his pouch.

"We have come with a frider banner to show peace. We, too, wish to battle the dead walker that threatens the land."

Ian rubbed his forehead. "This is insane. I am pretty sure they are not planning on fighting us, but no one knows how to talk to them?"

Alexis shot him an angry glare.

Minostak stepped forward. "Of course we are not here to fight you. We are here to stand against you. Apart, we are few. But together, we are many."

"King, they can't understand us. We can understand them. Cleary the shaman's spell worked backwards."

Minostak shot an angry glare at the shaman who sulked his shoulders low and looked away. "This is not good. How will we tell them we want to join their stand?"

"Why here?" Apollisian asked in his best attempt of the orc language.

Minostak frowned. "Is that orc?"

Petrovisk nodded and stepped forward. His heavy ker-stap was nearly twice the height of Apollisian. "I speak this. We are here to aid in your fight with the walking dead."

Apollisian smiled. "He speaks orc. He says they are here to help. Not sure what else he said."

Petrovisk frowned. The Beyklan showed his teeth to him. Had he said something wrong?

"Careful, Petrovisk. He is displeased. He bears his teeth," Minostak warned.

Petrovisk nodded. "We want to join your ranks. My king offers our blood to you. To do as you wish."

Apollisian frowned. "He says he wants to join our blood with his?"

Ian nodded. "I get it. They want to fight with us. Join our ranks."

Bodrell nodded. "Their size and strength would be a great asset. It will take some time to integrate them. Tell the warrior that I see he has ten flags. I want to break their numbers down into equal groups with a flag. Their leader can fight with me if he wishes."

Before Apollisian responded, Petrovisk broke in, "I can understand your chief. We agree."

Minostak nodded. "Yes, tell them that will be acceptable. That we feel we must stand together to defend the land."

Petrovisk motioned to Minostak. "My king agrees and is eager to stand alongside you and die as warriors."

Apollisian turned to Bodrell. "They wish to join us for sure. How difficult do you think it will be to get the troops to accept them into their ranks?"

"Considering the circumstances, I don't think it will be too difficult. The real problem will be communicating with them once they are among our ranks," Bodrell said, "Tell them to follow us. We will take them just inside of the north side of the city. I will set the wizards to task creating something that will allow us to speak with them and I will begin assigned them a partition to fight from."

Apollisian smiled wide. "Welcome to Central City. We shall stand as brothers."

Bodrell motioned them to follow. King Minostak walked alongside of Bodrell as Petrovisk walked alongside of Apollisian. The two looked each other up and down once before meeting each other's gaze. Both felt a feeling of admiration for the other. As the group marched back towards Central City, the greyshalk army marched behind them. The west wind picked up and sent an icy chill through their ranks. Apollisian glanced behind them at the darkening gray clouds to the west and he knew they did not have much time.

"They came like a storm from the pits of the abyss. The undead apparitions marched on us like the dropping of an executioner's guillotine. There was no place for us to go. No place to run, and there was no place to hide. We had one chance and that was to stand and fight. We armed the citizen's, we armed the women, we armed the children. The horrors the dying faced is beyond imagine. And even as I write these words, they come for me. Their incessant clawing, scratching, and gnawing at my wooden door. They do not tire, they do not hunger, and they do not fear. I know my hours are numbered. I know that soon I will be cut down as they devour my living flesh. And soon after my death, I know I will rise up to join their ranks.

I am not sure how many souls we lost. I saw many a hero fall. Even the champions that stood so valiantly against the onslaught of the dwarven horde had casualties among them. This is truly a dark day on earth. The Abyss Walker has come. He has come for us all."

-Author Unknown-
(Piece of parchment found in the
basement of the Central City ruins)

10
Preparations for the Stand

"It's happening, Hector."

The aging King of Nalir glanced down into the bowl of blood as an image began to take shape on its syrupy surface.

"Is that Central City?"

Kalen frowned. "I believe so. They must know Trinidy is coming. They never had wall partitions before."

Hector smiled gleefully and ran his hands together. "So the link is still functioning? The Ecnal is in Central City, yes?"

Kalen nodded and rubbed his smooth narrow chin. "Yes, he has to be. But, he must be gaining in power."

Hector's smile quickly faded. "What? How so?"

Kalen pointed at the image with his slender manicured finger. "He has united a sizable force of greyshalks to stand with him."

"Greyshalks? Why would they stand with him?"

"Perhaps they feel his power, My King."

Kalen and Hector's attention jerked to the chamber door as a young woman walked in.

"Father, I…"

Hector snarled, "Girl, your father is not in here! I am engaged with important matters. Look for him elsewhere!"

The girl nodded and ducked back from the chamber.

"Now, why would they stand with him?" Hector asked.

Kalen felt his blood boil. Father? Hector had a daughter?

And an attractive one at that. How could this be? How was he able to hide the girl all this time? This complicated his take over.

"Kalen?" the king growled in annoyance.

"Sorry, My King," the elf answered, "There could be several explanations. But I don't think it matters. Trinidy has grown ten times as strong as when we first released him."

"Let's look in on his army," Hector suggested.

Kalen shook his head. "I have tried. He has grown so much in power that he has managed to block attempts to scry on him. This is surely to stop his enemies from looking in."

"So how are we going to watch the battle?" Hector asked.

Kalen smiled a wicked smile. "I have embedded several anchor weaves in the city. Trinidy's scry shield prohibits an intrusion, but he should not be able to stop an existing link."

Hector glanced down at the bowl. "I want a larger bowl for the battle. Kill whatever you need to get it done, but by the time the battle begins, I want a huge image."

Kalen nodded. "Yes, Hector."

"Lance!" Delania called out as she looked from one of the inn's second story windows.

Lance hurried over to the window. An army of greyshalks were being marched through the cobblestone streets. Their russet fur gleamed in the late morning sun as streetwalkers moved far away from them in awe. Their hulking seven foot frames cast long shadows on the west walls as the army was escorted south through the city towards the coliseum. Apollisian, Overmoon, Ian, and some other armored fellow led the procession.

"What do you suppose they are?" Delania asked.

"Greyshalks," Fehzban answered from behind them, "And most of the Pyberian tribe, I would say."

Delania turned to Fehzban. "You know what they are?"

"You don't?" Lance asked suspiciously, "I know you are

from Aten, but greyshalks are everywhere."

Delania waved her hand in dismissal. "They have their own god, that's why. Probably Larunthus."

"What does their god have to do with it?" Lance asked earnestly. "I am sure there are tribes in the forests of Aten."

Delania waved her hand in dismissal. "It doesn't matter. I spent all of my time in the tower doing my studies. They are here, they look like they can fight fairly well, and they are not walking dead."

Fehzban rubbed the short beard growing on his chin. There was defiantly something hidden with this woman.

Petrovisk marveled as he walked down the stone path between the buildings. Never had he seen a human village from the inside. They had shaped and twisted the very stone of the earth into amazing towers and blocks. The earth was lined with small smooth creek stones that he surmised kept their wagons and ponies from getting bogged down in the mud. And the number of them! Petrovisk guessed there were more humans in this village than there was in his entire tribe.

"Look at all of them," he muttered to the king.

The king was wide-eyed as he glanced up at the tops of the mighty structures. "Yea, makes you wonder how they are not able to conquer the world if they can do such things. Their shamans must be powerful indeed."

The pair followed Apollisian wide-eyed as Bodrell rode off to the east. They gave little thought to him as they wondered what it would be like to live in such a village. Apollisian led the army south until he reached the coliseum. Its extensive towering floors and fine mason craftsmanship were far beyond the greyshalks simple comprehension. Only when the processions halted did Petrovisk and Minostak rouse themselves from their doldrums. Apollisian dismounted his horse and walked up to Petrovisk. The knight had many golden amulets in his hand. They had a large earthy colored center stone and were affixed to a thick iron chain.

Apollisian handed one of the amulets to Petrovisk and one to Minostak. He motioned for them to place them over their heads. Minostak placed his on first and then urged a reluctant Petrovisk to do the same. The aged greyshalk timidly slid the amulet over his and then glanced to his king. "What do they do?"

"They allow us to understand one another," Apollisian said with a warm smile.

Minostak rubbed his clawed fingers over his amulet and stepped forward, "You can hear me?"

Apollisian nodded. "I could always hear you, but now we can understand one another. The general's wizards have constructed sparse few of these. They created them to speak with the Darayal Legionnaires."

Petrovisk snarled, "I fought the Darayal in the old days. They killed many of my vinrs."

Ian squirmed in his saddle. "This might not be a match made in Merioulus, Apollisian."

Petrovisk stiffened his neck. "Of course it is. They are valiant warriors that gave my vinr honorable deaths. I would be grateful to fight alongside of them."

Minostak turned to the other greyshalks. "We are to fight alongside the Darayal!" he shouted raising his mighty morning star into the air.

In unison, the greyshalks stretched their necks and howled into the air. Petrovisk turned and drew his mighty kerstap and howled with them.

When the howling died down Apollisian began again, "We will give one to you, Petrovisk and one to you, King Minostak. We will also give you ten others to distribute to your leaders. That will be about one per hundred men. Communication will be vital during this conflict, so I urge you to give it to one of your soldiers that will be in command. If that man…," Apollisian cleared his throat, "Soldier falls, be sure that someone else puts the amulet on."

Petrovisk nodded as a cold west wind ripped down the cobblestone street. He rubbed his old muscled arms and glanced to the west. He could not see the undead, but he could smell their stench on the west wind.

"They are coming."

Minostak nodded and began barking orders to his leaders to come get their amulets.

Bodrell rode up on his horse as the amulets were being distributed. "The amulets work. The elves have distributed them."

Apollisian nodded. "They work here as well. Be sure to tell your arch-mage that his wizards are worth their weight in gold."

"Tell him yourself," the general said as he motioned to Jon.

Apollisian smiled warmly. "Great job, Sir. They may help us win the day."

Jon smiled knowingly. "Just wait 'til the battle starts. My wizards have many more talents than creating pretty baubles."

The general pulled his heavy cloak around him. "That west wind is cold. Reports from the western partitions is that a storm is coming. They can see the dark clouds in the west. It's strange, how these storms are coming so late in the spring."

Apollisian mounted his horse as the greyshalks divided and began to move towards their perspective partitions. "I don't think the storm is natural, General. I think the undead leader is making it himself."

Jon narrowed his eyes. "He is controlling the weather?"

"Well, not all the weather, but it is my belief that he has somehow created a perpetual snowstorm that follows his army."

Jon took a deep breath. "This Abyss Walker is much more powerful than we had anticipated."

Amerix slipped deeper into the alleys of Central City. Like smaller cavern passages in the under mountain, he navigated the main streets with them. Amerix rubbed his silver streaked beard as he paused to rest on the wooden doors of an old store cellar that was attached to an abandoned building.

"Okay, sword. What's up. I done seen furry folk, elves, and humans all in the same town."

What makes you so sure something is amiss, Son of Durion.

"Don't play yer blasted games with me, sword. I'll toss ye in this darn cellar and you can sit there till some fool finds ye. Then ye can torment them with yer riddles."

Perhaps the cellar might be a great place for us both, Son of Durion. You can get some rest before you meet with Apollisian.

Amerix groaned as he stood. He easily hoisted the decrepit doors and slid under them into the small dark staircase. "I could use a fair nap, sword. Ye seeing a bed in here or something?"

This was an old domicile of a rogue hero. There should be suitable furnishings for you.

Amerix pushed open a creaky door at the bottom of the steps. There was a singular room that was completely round. A small stone ledge lined the entire room. Various baskets and pottery were still in place. There was a cooking hearth, but no fireplace. There was a wooden bed on the far wall and a hammock affixed to the cellars ceiling. The old dwarf leaned Songsinger against the bed and sat down on it. It was soft and the wool blankets felt cozy and warm. Amerix felt his eyes grow heavy. When was the last time he had slept? The renegade general laid down with his armor still on. The cool pillow felt good against his head. He considered removing his boots but quickly fell asleep.

Apollisian rode through the city and watched the greyshalk as they broke down into groups and made their way toward their assigned partitions. There was something about the way that old tall one looked at him that bothered Apollisian. But as they faded from view, his thoughts turned to the inn.

"What's wrong?" Alexis asked.

"Nothing, my love."

Alexis cocked her head. "I don't believe you."

"The large greyshalk looked at me funny."

Alexis frowned. "Funny like how?"

"Like he knew something about me, or like he could see inside of me."

Alexis smiled. "There is no need for any worries. If he can see inside of you, he will see a man of the utmost honor and virtue."

Apollisian smiled half-heartedly. "That may very well be true. But, when it comes down to it, I am just a man. I bleed, I lust... I am not perfect."

Alexis guided her horse close to his and leaned over to him. Her almond eyes gazed deep into his bright blue orb. "And that is why I love you, Apollisian Bargo."

Apollisian placed his gauntleted hand behind her neck and guided her lips to his. He relished the sweet taste of her and he inhaled her breath as she exhaled. He wanted to take her in, to be one with her. He wanted to dance in Merioulus with her for eternity.

As the kiss ended, her eyes danced across Apollisian's face. "I love you so much, Apollisian. I hate we must make this stand. But when this is through, we will leave this place. Our time together is too short to spend another day in the service of others."

Apollisian smiled and gently stroked her cheek. "My love, as long as we are fighting for innocents, it is a day well spent."

"No," Alexis argued, "My love, you have done enough. Promise me that when this is over, you will hang up your shield that protects others. Let's take up our sword and take what is ours! Our time together."

Apollisian sighed as he gazed her angelic face. "My love, if it will please you, we could move to an old wooden box and live the rest of our lives there. As long as I have you, I have everything."

Alexis smiled and wiped a tear from her eye. "We are near the inn. Let's get this job done. I grow weary of waiting for our future."

Apollisian smiled as he dismounted in front of the Inn

of the Welcome Wench. The windows seemed to be boarded up extremely well.

"Alexis, they have done a remarkable job. This building could serve as a defensive area. It is sound, large, and can house many soldiers. If the undead make it passed the first wall, we could meet here."

The wry elf nodded as she entered. "Come on, you can marvel it the integrity of the structure from the inside."

"It is a well-built building," Fehzban said as the pair entered the common room. "Delania used her magic to meld the wooden table tops into the wood from the wall."

"Where are they?" Alexis asked.

"They are upstairs checking on the other floors. That woman has an eye for defense. There is more to her than we see."

"How so?" Apollisian asked.

"She says odd things. Slip ups. She doesn't know our world like she should," Fehzban said as he nervously glanced at the stairs, "She called me a spawn."

"Spawn? I think I heard her mention that on the trail. What does that mean?" Apollisian asked.

"I don't know, but I think it is an outer realm term," Fehzban answered.

"Outer realm? Like another world?" Alexis asked as she began to take inventory of the wine and other spirits.

"I was thinking of the Abyss," the dwarf said nervously.

"The Abyss?" Apollisian said doubtfully, "Are you suggesting she is a demon?"

Fehzban motioned for Apollisian to keep his voice down. "Think about it. You studied at the academy. All of your types have. They say when the Abyss Walker comes he will open a gate to the Abyss and much of its evil will escape to the realms of dwarves."

Apollisian frowned. "If she were a demon, she would have attacked me on sight."

Fehzban shook his head. "Not if she were a succubus. They are the most cunning of all demons. They have no ego, no pride. They only care about chaos and seduction."

Alexis popped the top on a cask of spirits. "She can stand

up and challenge the Shark God for all I care. She has been a great help fighting the Abyss Walker and as long as she continues to do so, I could care less."

Steiny pushed open the kitchen door behind Alexis. "I have the beef roasting in the stew pot and the tubers will be ready soon too."

"Be mindful of her then, Fehzban. Report anything you see to me. But as it stands, we are ill equipped to investigate unlikely complaints against a proven ally," Apollisian said as he started to remove his armor. "I need a bath before this battle."

"Gonna be a cold one," Steiny said, "It's starting to snow."

"Just great," Silas said as he glanced out of the window of the upper coliseum suite, "It's starting to snow."

Quadry mumbled to himself and pulled the covers from the bed tighter.

Silas frowned. "Oh, piss and moan. So we didn't find Alexis. We are here, the legion is here, what more could we hope for?"

Quadry sat up from the bed. "I would have liked to find Alexis and taken her to her father. I would have liked to have been able to complete the task we were set upon...*By our king!*"

Silas sighed. "I know, but if she isn't here, what can we do?"

"We do as we are. We stand against our enemies with our brothers," Quadry said dejectedly.

Silas still stared out of the window. "That's odd."

Quadry slid out from the bed and began to place his boots on. "What's odd?"

"Remember that huge greyshalk that we fought by the cross roads?"

Quadry slid his other foot into his boot. "Yea."

"Well, I think I see him now marching with the human general to one of them partitions."

Quadry jumped up and ran to the window. "Where?"

Silas pointed to the far west partition that seemed to spearhead the western wall. "There."

"Huh. What are the odds of him being among the greyshalk that came to defend the Beyklans?" Quadry said as his eyes drifted to the western skyline, "Oh my! Look how dark it is getting."

Silas glanced to the west. "That is no snow storm like I have ever seen."

Quadry nodded as he felt terror creep into his body. The hair on the back of his neck stood on end and his fingers and toes began to tremble. "We're not going to make it, Silas."

Silas nodded distantly. "I don't think so either."

"I oft recall the shining day that you were brought into this world. I held you in my arms and gazed into the eyes of my baby boy. I could see such passion and mercy in your striking jade orbs.

I watched you grow into a fine young man. You had an aptitude for the arcane arts like your mother. I wanted to teach you the sword, the way of the steel, but I knew you were not suited for it. You mother chided me when I would try to mold you. She always spoke of your future and how you would one day rescue the heavens.

The day I was murdered, I hung from our tree by my neck for nearly a minute before I drifted into a world of darkness. I heard your mother scream as she died and I felt a hatred for our killers grow inside of me. I carried that hatred into the depths of the Abyss.

I now stand poised to wipe evil from the face of this world. I stand to bring the wicked to bear before me under the millstone of righteousness. You stand to defend the very evil that I have so worked to scour from the face of this land.

Though I admire your strength, your skill, and your power, I will not allow you to defend the very wickedness that has brought me endless torment. I am the walking resonance of justice and I will not be denied. If you and your brother choose to stand against me, then you will fall.

Of all your knowledge, know this, my son. I brought you into this world, and if I must... I will take you out of it."

-Havrion Trinidy Lampara-

11
Those Who Stand with Me

The snow came down like millions of tiny puffs of cotton. The velvety flakes covered the grass, replacing the sea of green with a blanket of white. Soldiers armed with crossbows, swords, and long pikes stood guard over several wizards who stood atop of each partition that were fifty yards from one another. Soldiers stood ready in their heavy mail. Greyshalks lined their ranks, as well did the Darayal Legionnaires. The defenders of Central City stood defiantly before an army that they could not yet see. But, the thickening snowfall announced its inevitable coming.

"Today is the day that we stand against what our father's fathers have feared. Today we stand against the Abyss Walker!" Sargoth shouted to the soldiers standing in front of the hidden pits between each partition.

"I fought in the battle of Stoneheart Mountain. I faced the wrath of the great white dragon! And now, I stand before you to face this foe. I am not afraid of dying. And I will not be raised up as one of their own. I will not fall to their black magic," he shouted as his voice trailed off.

A single black vulture landed on one of the partitions, only to be quickly struck down by one of the soldiers. Its lifeless body fell to the earth and landed in the thick snow in a puff of black feathers. Its bright red blood and black body was in stark contrast to the ashen blanket that surrounded it. Sargoth felt terror creep up from his belly as he gazed at the lifeless vulture. How could they win when life was so easily extinguished? How could the living prevail against such a foe?

"Gods save us," a soldier mumbled.

Sargoth turned to the west to see a cloud that was as black as the night. Its odd dark billowing clouds advanced on them like a wave washing over the clouds. As it neared, he could tell it was not clouds at all, but millions of black birds of prey and scavengers flocked together like a school of fish in the ocean. The flock was so thick it blocked out the sun and the day was as night. The soldiers were deathly quiet. Nearly twenty five thousand bodies stood around or in Central City and no sound was heard, save for the beating wings of the birds that danced and circled overhead. Sargoth forced his eyes away from the birds and gazed to the west. As far as he could see from the north and to the south, the forest line was teaming with movement. The undead had arrived. Death was upon them.

"Why do they not advance, Jonathon?" Bodrell asked from his tower atop of the Coliseum.

The arch-mage stared for a moment before he pointed to the northwest tree line, "Their leader advances. It appears he has some civility to him. He comes mounted on a horse right out of a nightmare. To his right and left are two women in tattered yellow robes. They bear twisted staffs teaming with magical energies."

Bodrell nodded and grabbed his helm from the polished oak stand next to him. "Messenger!" he called out sternly.

"Yes, General."

"Send for Apollisian and his men. Send for Orantal, and send for Minostak. Our great leaders will go out and meet this foe."

"Yes, General!" the messenger replied as he hurried down the stone stairs from the coliseum watch tower.

"Perhaps he can be reasoned with. If he comes out to us, he wants something," Bodrell said to Jonathon.

"Do you want me to go with you, General?" Jonathan asked worriedly.

"No, Jonathon. You stay here. If the monster strikes me down, I need someone the men trust to lead them. Someone of power."

"But, General. You will need someone trained in the powers of the arcane. Someone powerful."

Bodrell waved his hand n dismissal as he started down the stone stairs. "I will have Apollisian bring his boy wizard and his woman, Delania. He claims the boy has the power to heal, when no one else in the realms can. I suspect that he may be tied to this somehow."

Jonathon nodded. "As you wish, General."

Bodrell hurried down the stairs and into the dark corridors of the coliseum. He glanced at the rigging that the engineers had created to allow the prisoner's to leave their cells and take up arms. He hurried past dozens of worried looks from his own men and into the street where his horse was waiting. He mounted his steed and made his way to the north, toward the Inn on the Welcome Wench.

"General Bordrell is coming up the street, Apollisian," Steiny called out from the open front door of the inn. He had gathered their horses.

Lance glanced at Delania nervously and then back to Apollisian. "I don't know if me going is such a good idea. I'm not that great of a wizard."

Apollisian waved his hand in dismal. "Well you and Delania are the best I have… So let's get going."

Alexis grabbed her bow and double checked her chain armor straps before heading out of the door with the others.

"Greetings, Apollisian," the general called out, "It seems the leader of this army wants to meet our fine champions."

Apollisian nodded as he and the others mounted up.

"Perhaps he can be bargained with. This could go in our favor."

"Where are the other leaders?" Bodrell asked.

Apollisian shrugged. "They sent messengers informing me that they had no interest meeting the undead general for anything other than cutting his rotting head from his body."

"Probably just as well," Apollisian said, "That would make bargaining with him a bit more difficult."

Delania shook her head as she gathered up her long black hair into a bun. "You cannot bargain with the dead, Apollisian. They hate life. They hate you. This is most likely a trap designed to kill your friends. However, if it is, we will destroy this fool leader and end this threat once and for all."

Alexis trembled and leaned over her saddle and whispered in Apollisian's ear, "I am afraid, Apollisian. I can't lose you now."

Apollisian smiled. "No need to worry, my love. Even death cannot stop me from loving you."

Alexis wiped a tear from her eye as she pulled away from his embrace. She glanced at Lance, Delania, and Bodrell as they rode up the cobblestone street. She looked back at Apollisian. Her life, her love. She exhaled softly, "Death has no terror when compared to a life without you."

Apollisian smiled and rubbed her cheek. "Come on, my love. The others are leaving without me."

Alexis sighed and smiled as he rode to catch up. She turned her horse to her partition on the western front.

The group rode out passed the north portcullis and turned into the northwest field. The heavy snow had piled up a three inch blanket on the earth as the sea of eerie birds danced about overhead. As they neared the undead general, his hatred rippled from him like light from a lantern in the dead of night. He was fully plated in what was once immaculate armor. It bore several skulls for buckles and rusted iron spikes jutted out from his shoulders like a shroud of metallic spines. Black soot and rust covered his mail. His face was rotted and twisted and his eyes glowed a bright blue. Smoke-like energy drifted out from his helm. Scorpions, centipedes, and other stinging insects crawled all over his face, skirting in his eyes sockets, his mouth, and his nose. The undead champion carried a large shield that bore the skull of some unknown serpent whose eyes shined as well. He rode atop a nightmarish war horse that had glowing blue eyes. The animal's hooves were ablaze with a deep blue Abyssal flame. The snow froze where the horse stepped, leaving a slick sheen of ice behind the death knight. To his right and left were two women. Their bodies were equally rotted and their dirty yellow robes were tattered and torn. They wielded thick, gnarled, wooden staves that glowed with a similar blue energy that dripped black snake like wisps. The wisps twisted and turned down the haft of the staff and dissipated just above the women's hands.

"mih rof emoc evah I dna arapmal ydinirt noirvah si eman ym," the undead general said as he pointed to Lance.

"What did he say?" Bodrell asked.

Delania felt her blood boil and rage creep inside of her, "He says he wants your children. If you give them to him he will leave."

"Our children?" Apollisian asked.

"He came for our children?" Bodrell mumbled to himself.

Delania silently spun several threads of white magical strands and encircled Lance's head.

"What do you want from him?" Delania asked the death knight.

"He is the right that I am to wrong. He is the core of wickedness that plagues this world."

"I am not evil," Lance answered the death knight, "My whole life people have tried to harm me. I watched my father hang from a tree until he was dead. I watched my mother die in my own home."

Trinidy frowned in familiarity and he rubbed his own neck as Lance continued.

"I have been imprisoned by a race for a crime they assumed I would commit. I was sent to a land and made a slave. I have watched innocents die and I have bled to save them, yet you tell me I am a wrong that needs to be righted?" Lance growled, "What gives you and your twisted army the sick belief that I am something wrong. Look at yourself, and your evil soldiers. You are an entity that is a bane on the earth."

Delania looked at Lance in surprise. She could see the magical energy rising to the surface. She could see the air rippling around him in his power. Never had she seen such strength save for the mighty demons that were sometimes indwelt by the dark gods they served.

"You are in the company of a succubus. A demon from the Abyss that forged my torment. A being of ultimate evil, yet you question your own wickedness? Whatever whore birthed you into existence should be ravaged by dripping phallics from the lowest demons and the disgusting creature that fathered you should be cursed for eternity," Trinidy answered back.

Lance clenched his fist. "You are a puppet, monster!" he said as he waved his hand, revealing the thick black magical tendril that led from his heart to the Death Knight's.

"You can see it, can't you?"

Delania crept to the back of the group. She remembered this man. His name was Havrion Trinidy Lampara. He was the husband of the fallen goddess, Panoleen. His child was feared to become the Abyss Walker. A monster that would bring about the destruction of the mortal world.

"I have been tasked by my god to right that which is wrong. You are that wrong," Trinidy answered, "Give yourself to me. Bow down and stretch your neck to my blade and I will depart from this spot. I will dismiss my army and save these wicked souls you desire to protect."

"No!" Delania yelled.

"So, you dare to speak on his behalf, Delania? Is this how you run from Bykalicus? Or did you finally lie down before his lust?"

"What is going on, you two. What is he saying?" Apollisian asked worriedly.

Lance shook his fist in rage. "You speak to me, monster. Not to her. We will not submit to your commands. In my mother's name, Panoleen, I will not sit idly by while you slaughter anymore innocents. I will not submit to you, because I will destroy you."

Trinidy shook his head. "Your mother's name is Panoleen?"

Lance nodded. "And my father's name is Trinidy, and he would not bow down to your tyranny."

The undead knight coughed and shook. The bright blue energy from his eyes dimmed and the scorpions fell dead from his face. He grabbed his saddle to keep from falling and his steed shifted her weight to steady him.

"That means your name is Lancalion Levendis Lampara," Trinidy growled as he righted himself. His blue eyes shining brighter than before.

Delania turned to Bodrell and Apollisian. "He claims that since we will not give up the children, then he will kill us and take them. We should go now."

Bodrell nodded. "Lance, leave him. The sword of the righteous will deal with him."

"How do you know my name?" Lance asked.

"Because my name is Havrion Trinidy Lampara. I am your father. My god predicted your fall from goodness. Submit to justice, my son. And there may be redemption for your soul."

"Lance, leave him!" Delania shouted.

Trinidy ignored her and continued, "Lance, I oft recall the shining day that you were brought into this world. I held you in my arms and gazed into the eyes of my baby boy. I could see such passion and mercy in your striking jade orbs."

Lance felt tears stream down his face as Trinidy continued.

"I watched you grow into a fine young man. You had an aptitude for the arcane arts like your mother. I wanted to teach you the sword, the way of the steel, but I knew you were not suited for it. You mother chided me when I would try to mold you. She always spoke of your future and how you would one day rescue the heavens. The day I was murdered, I hung from our tree by my neck for nearly a minute before I drifted into a world of darkness. I heard your mother scream as she died and I felt a hatred for our killers grow inside of me. I carried that hatred into the depths of the Abyss."

"You think I did not cry? I was a boy! A boy!" Lance screamed, "But, now I am a man. They have turned you into a monster! Look at yourself, Father! I cannot allow you to kill these people. They are innocent!"

Trinidy continued without pause, "I now stand poised to wipe evil from the face of this world. I stand to bring the wicked to bear before me under the millstone of righteousness. You stand to defend the very evil that I have so worked to scour from the face of this land."

"Evil? You are the evil one, Father. Let go of your hatred! Look what it has caused!" Lance said as he gestured back to the thousands of undead that waited at the tree line, "How many innocents scream from their graves for justice against you?!"

Trinidy ignored his pleas and continued, "Though I admire your strength, your skill, and your power, I will not allow you to defend the very wickedness that has brought me endless torment. I am the walking resonance of justice and I will not be denied. If you and your brother choose to stand against me, then you will fall. Of all your knowledge, know this, my son. I brought you into this world, and if I must... I will take you out of it!" Trinidy said as he turned his nightmarish horse and started back towards his army.

"Brother? What brother? I don't have a brother!" Lance shouted back as Delania grabbed the reins of his horse to try to turn him. "Don't turn your back to me, you son of a bitch!"

Trinidy solemnly rode back to his army and did not respond.

"You're not my father! You're a beast that I will put down!" Lance screamed as he summoned gathered weaves from the clouds above him.

"Run!" Delania shouted as she began to weave a globe in front of Lance.

Lance ignored the strain and brought hundreds of weaves together. Sweat beaded up on his brow as he hurled a blast of lightening from his fingertips. He ignored the mass of bright blue flowing weaves that rocketed around him like magnetic waves.

Trinidy turned and raised his shield as the electric blast crashed into him. His arm recoiled from the blow and the eyes of the skull began to glow a bright green. As quickly as the lightened struck the death knight's shield, the two liches straightened their staffs and let loose a fury of black necromantic balls of energy. Lance extended his hand and severed the first two in half. They fell harmlessly to the side as the other two came in too fast for him to sever. He brought his arms up feebly and prepared for the energy to take him when the bright blue transparent globe surrounded him. The necromantic spheres hit the globe and dissipated in a flash of deep violet.

"Enough!" Trinidy shouted to the liches, "He has made his decision. We will meet him on the battlefield."

The undead women glanced up at their master with their dead white eyes. They did not respond, but their posture relaxed as they turned and followed Trinidy. They kept a wary eye on Lance as they hurried back across the grassy plain.

Delania rushed to Lance, "Come on, Lance."

"What is that fool boy doing?? Bodrell growled, "Apollisian, take the others and hurry back! I think the battle is about to begin sooner than we thought!"

"What was that?" a soldier asked as he pointed to the northwest field.

Sargoth glanced around the edge of the stone partition. He could see several flashes of light that danced across the black sky. The sun had all but been blocked by the waves of birds and he could not make up much more than shadows.

"It has begun!" Sargoth shouted, "Ready arms!"

It was at that moment that the field darkened. A wave of shadowy figures began to sweep across the plains. From horizon to horizon, the wall of shadow silently approached like the executioner's axe-like death itself.

"Combat. It is an easy word. It often is glorified by those who have never experienced it. Many fantasize about the glory and adulation being a combat veteran brings. Yet, they discard the real description of it from those who have experienced it. As if the truth of how ugly it really is detracts from their sick fantasies.

I am one that has been there. Trust me, there is nothing glorious about it. The truth that sticks out with me about combat, though there are many, is that the first time is easy. You don't realize the levity of what you are about to do. Everyone going into combat the first time will be brave.

It is your second time that your true metal is tested. Anyone can eat a hot pepper if they have no experience on how hot it is. The real question of inner character is this: Can they eat a second one?"

-Lancalion Levendis Lampara-

12

The Breaking of the Lines

"Fire!" the partition sergeant shouted.

Scores of fiery arrows rocketed through the back sky and landed harmlessly in the field.

"The arrows went right through them!" Petrovisk growled.

The sergeant turned to their partition mage. "Signal the other towers. The wizards have to deal with these."

The wizard nodded and grabbed a thin wooden pole that had a long narrow blue flag on the end. He waved it back and forth several times. Trumpets and waves of the same flag soon echoed down the partition line.

The other wizards began channeling bright blue balls of energy and hurled them into the rapidly approaching wave of man-like shadows. As the magic projectiles struck the shadows, they twisted and popped into ash and smoke before dissipating into nothingness.

"Were not getting all of 'em!" the sergeant shouted before leaning over the partition wall, "Sargoth, ready your men, they will be on us soon."

Sargoth nodded uneasily. Weapons of steel and stone seemed to pass through these monsters. He hoped his father's enchanted blade could kill them. The shadows had already reached some of the southern towers and he could hear the men scream in agony.

Petrovisk glanced down at the southern partitions. He

could see that a few of the soldier's blades harmed the shadows, but many others had no effect. He drew his mighty kerstap and examined it. The king of the old days had awarded the fine weapon to him. He bet its magic was stronger than the death knight's.

"Peter, what are you doing?"

Petrovisk turned to see the sergeant staring at him angrily. "I am going to help those men."

"No, you are needed up here to guard the wizards," the sergeant called out as the shadows reached their partition.

Peter glanced down as the men futilely tried to defeat a foe that their weapons could not affect. Only Sargoth seemed to be able to harm them.

"You do it!" Petrovisk snarled as he leapt over the edge of the partition and dropped thirty feet below.

He landed hard and his old knees erupted in fire. Twenty years ago, he made leaps twice that size. It did not take the shadows long to swarm to him, their long wispy claw-like hands reached for him. Petrovisk swung his sword in long powerful strikes. His kerstap began to glow white hot and the shadows writhed silently as it cut them into nothingness.

A cold pain erupted in Petrovisk's back, and then another. He turned and sliced apart the shadows that had hit him, only to feel the cold again from the other side. With each strike, he felt weaker and paler. Though he was destroying scores of their numbers, they swarmed him like rapid lions.

Sargoth lunged in and took his back. "Back to back!" he shouted.

Peter turned and focused his attacks on the shadows in front of him. With his back no longer exposed, he and Sargoth were able to stand firm as blasts of magical energy from the wizards above rained down on them.

"Protect them!" the sergeant screamed from above, "Ignore the second wave! If these shadows kill our ground troops, we are doomed!"

The wizards glanced to the west. They could see thousands of pale putrid bodies across the field that were beginning to advance. They ran as fast as a man can sprint and they doubled the number of the shadows. Great clods of dirt and snow kicked up behind their clawed charge as the monsters raced across the plain.

As the spells rained down, the shadows abandoned their attack and vanished into the inner parts of the city. Some took alleys, others passed right through the walls of the buildings. A trumpet soon sounded to the north, signaling the release of the coliseum prisoners. They were each given a weapon. The sergeant doubted the prisoner's would be of much aid and would most likely flee the city. Before he could give the idea much thought, the sergeant looked to the west. The sheer size of the second wave seemed to be as large as his enter force.

"Rha have mercy on us."

Vlargcar lay on his rack with one hand folded behind his head. The other was in front of his face while his index finger worked vigorously inside of his nose. The mighty orc squinted and made faces until he managed to dislodge what he was looking for. He held the massive lump of green gooey substance in front of his face.

"I got you, boogar. You made me sneeze, but now I got you," he said triumphantly.

Edge growled low and hopped down from the bunk. His muscled bugled as he kept his head low, sniffing the air.

Vlargcar sat up and flicked the gooey substance on the cold stone floor of his cell, "What is it, Edge?"

The powerful war dog glanced back at Vlargcar and then returned his iron like gaze to their cell door.

Vlargcar hopped up from his rack and made his way next to his friend. He timidly peered around the corner of his cell and gazed at the iron door that kept him locked in, "What do you see?"

Suddenly the cell door popped open and Jude stepped from around the corner. He was dressed in his native Kai-Harkian breastplate and had his great sword strapped to his back. Just like when they fought the ogres. Edge stopped growling and wagged his tail. He licked his chops submissively and trotted up to Jude.

"What are you doing with your sword and stuff?" Vlargcar asked.

Jude reached down in front of the door and tossed in Vlargcar's chain shirt and swords. He sighed as he tried to decipher the orc's words. Jude had managed to learn a bit of dwarven, and even some orc, while in the coliseum, but he still didn't know what the hell Vlargcar was saying half of the time. And, it did not help that Vlargcar often mixed the two languages.

"There is no time. Get your shit on and let's go."

Vlargcar smiled when he saw his armor and swords. He quickly donned them and followed Jude into the hallway. Prisoners were exiting their cells and grabbing the weapons that had been laid out in front of their doors. Many of them seemed eager and happy. Vlargcar rubbed his forehead and shrugged. "Why is everyone getting out?"

Jude shook head. "Don't worry about it Vlargcar. Follow me. We need to get to the western lines. There is a sergeant there that is expecting us."

Vlargcar frowned and followed Jude. He had no idea what the hell he was saying, but the Kai-Harkian seemed excited. Vlargcar trusted him, so he decided to follow. Besides, Edge seemed eager to bite someone and Vlargcar did not want him biting any of the other prisoners.

Wake up, Son of Durion. The sands of time have run out, the honeyed voice echoed in Amerix's head.

The old general opened his eyes abruptly and scanned the dark room. Reality quickly fell on him. He sat up and wiped his face with his hand.

The Abyss Walker is here. Your time of rest is at an end.

Amerix growled and stood from the bed. He stretched his weary old bones. Sleeping in his armor had made him a bit stiff.

You must hurry, Son of Durion.

"Quit yer damn bitchin, sword," Amerix growled, "Durion almighty ye whine worse than a woman."

I was a woman, Son of Durion.

Amerix shook his head as he snatched up Songsinger and slid the weapon over his shoulder. "I couldn't tell."

Songsinger did not reply as Amerix started up the old cellar stairs. The old renegade pushed open the rickety doors and peered out into the alley. Bits of snow fell between the cracks of the door. He could hear crying and wailing coming from the streets. "What in the blue blazes is going on?"

The Abyss Walker is upon us, Son of Durion. Despair and death follow him.

"Blah, blah, blah. Don't ye ever shut up, sword?"

You asked, Son of Durion.

Amerix growled under his breath and made his way to the thoroughfare. Citizens cowered in the streets on their hands and knees. Others prayed and wailed. In the middle of the cobblestone roadway was a small wooden cart that contained dozens of old rusted swords and other weapons. Amerix tossed off his cloak and looked to the sky that was black with crows, buzzards, and other scavenger birds. Their sheer numbers seemed to block the sun as they eerily danced and dived in the air.

"That's a lot of birds, sword."

Yes, they follow the undead.

Amerix dusted a bit of snow off of his brilliantly sculpted shoulder plates, "And what of the snow, sword? It follows the undead too?"

The undead king created it, as it was foreseen, to protect his rotting minions from the natural decaying process.

Amerix shook his head. "Great."

You have two choices, Son of Durion. Find the Abyss Walker and return me to Apollisian, or we can combat the devils of the Azkarnicus Triad.

"Aza who!?"

The fallen God King, Azkarnicus. He created three devil lords and they are arriving soon.

"What the hell is a devil lord? In fact, ye know what,

sword. I don't give an orc's ass. Ye walked me into this shit. I am gonna get rid of ye as soon as I can," Amerix said, "Ye tell me how to find that human champion so I can be done with ye."

If all you care for is your own safety, Son of Durion, then you are lost.

"Yer right. I couldn't tell ye which way was which in this Durion forsaken city," Amerix said as he glanced down the many roadways. He removed his horned helm and turned his wrinkled old ear to the west, "I hear the sweet sound of men dying this way."

Those are the sounds of your allies as their souls are ripped from their living bodies.

"Allies?" Amerix snorted. "Ain't no Beyklan me ally."

Who were the enemies of Clan Stormhammer?

Amerix placed his helm back on his head as he started to the west. "Inside or out?"

Either.

Amerix pursed his lips. "Well, I sure didn't like the Malletmoors."

And when Berylys-Quieness attacked your home city, did you stand against them, or with them?

"Bery-who!?" Amerix asked. "Ye mean that great white dragon?"

Yes.

"How in the bloody blue blazes do ye know about that?" Amerix bellowed.

I know much, Son of Durion. I am older than the mountains.

Amerix caught the flash of a dark shape in the alley. He whipped his head around as his old eyes scanned the edges of the dark street. "We got company, sword."

Shadows.

"Yes, I saw something in the shadows," Amerix growled as he started towards the alley.

No, you saw a shadow. They are sinister undead apparitions that were previously wiped from the face of Terrigan. The power that created it is ancient.

A scream echoed out from the far alley. Amerix turned to see a man scrambling into the street. Two shadow figures silently clawed and grabbed him. The man punched and kicked, but his hands passed right through them. He screamed and writhed in the cobblestone roadway. He arched his back in pain before he died. The shadows looked up from their victim and started towards the general.

"Come get you some," Amerix muttered under his breath. He gripped his twin axes tightly and narrowed his hawk like eyes.

Unless your weapons are enchanted, they will be useless against these foes, Son of Durion.

Amerix ignored Songsinger and stalked forward. The shadows ignored the other fleeing townsfolk and rushed toward the renegade general.

Amerix ducked a clawed strike and brought his right axe into the dark shadowy form. The form hissed as the enchanted axe passed through it. The shadow trembled and shook as it rapidly dissipated into smoke and ash.

The second shadow lunged in. Its clawed incorporeal hand hit Amerix's breastplate and bent down as the magic from the enchanted mail repelled the undead monster's strike. Before it could react, Amerix brought his other axe down and cleaved the shadowy apparition in two. Amerix paused briefly as the undead beast convulsed on the street and crumbed into a pile of black ash and smoke that was in stark contrast to the white snow covered street. "That wasn't so bad."

If your armor was not enchanted the shadows would reach into your body and slowly rip out pieces of your soul. It would only take a few seconds for them to completely devour you.

Amerix chuckled as he started back down the street. "Good thing my armor is enchanted. It ain't no issue, is it sword?"

Your arrogance will be the death of you, Son of Durion.

Amerix chuckled as he continued towards the west, "That's what I'm counting on, sword. That's what I'm counting on."

Kellacun ducked low in the snow covered alley. The largest dwarf she had ever seen had emerged from Soranna's old cellar dwelling. He was covered in a cloak and was nearly five and a half feet tall. The dwarf paused in front of the cellar and began to talk to himself. Kellacun waited for a several seconds before the dwarf wandered off towards the main street.

Careful the dwarf had not seen her, Kellacun hurried over to the cellar doors. She hoisted them up and went down inside. Much of Soranna's property had been taken. The old sorceress likely moved, but it was possible that she had passed. Kellacun had spent to long away from the city. After escaping the dungeons, she had been assisting Kalen.

The assassin quickly rummaged through old boxes, looking for anything she might use. She stumbled across some old books and filtered through them. Most were old books on prophecy written in the ancient language. Kellacun tossed those books on the bed and pilfered through another box. She found an old artists rendition of Soranna and her parents. Kellacun fought back a tear. Even after all these years, she missed them. Kellacun tossed the portrait back in the box and plopped on the bed. No word from Kalen. He should have sent for her by now. The army was set up and the siege was to begin soon.

Kellacun checked over her enchanted armor. It had served her well for many years. Perhaps Kalen knew about the siege. Perhaps he intended for her to be caught in it. After all, she was the only person that knew of his crime against the throne of Aten. Kellacun sighed and slid a lock of her long black hair behind her ear. It mattered little. What did matter was why this dwarf was back in Central City of all places.

The assassin hopped up from the bed and made her way from the cellar. She followed the tracks in the snow and kept a watchful eye on the cloud of birds overhead. Their unnatural gathering filled her with terrible fear. She ducked in and around the alleys, following the dwarf as he made his way west. He seemed uninterested in the cloud of birds and unconcerned if the locals noticed him.

Kellacun watched for several seconds as the dwarf paused to talk to himself. She started to step out of the shadows when something caught her eye to the alley north of her. Though the streets were dark, she could make out a shadow like figure that passed through the stone wall of the alley. The dwarf saw it too. Kellacun felt fear rise up her spine. Goosebumps rose on her sallow skin and the hair on the back of her neck stood up. She sniffed the air and caught an unnaturally strong odor of rotting flesh blowing in from the west. Nothing was making sense to her.

Erupting from the south alley was a man with two shapes on him. They looked like the shadow figure that she had just seen in the alley just up from her. The shapes ripped and pulled at the man as he ran into the street screaming. He flailed about until the shadows had killed him. Kellacun silently drew her enchanted sword. If there were two of these things, there were more.

The assassin watched as the shadows rushed across the street at the dwarf. He tossed off his cloak and squared off with the monsters. He was clad in some sort of brilliantly crafted plate mail. He wore a thick helm with ram horns on either side. He had a radiant sword strapped to his back and held two vicious looking axes. As the two shadows rushed in, the dwarf cut them down easily. The dwarf began to talk to himself again as a third erupted from the north alley. Kellacun leapt from behind the crate and rushed across the street in the snow.

An enemy of my enemy is my friend, Kellacun thought to herself.

Amerix felt a deep cold rip through his body. He arched his back in pain and whirled his axe around in a quick slash. His weapon struck air as he felt his strength wane. The old general slashed his second axe at the dark shadow that lingered in front of him as it clawed and slashed its incorporeal claws at his neck. But before his weapon could hit its mark, a shimmering silver blade pierced the undead apparition from the back. It silently shrieked and convulsed into a fading cloud of ash, revealing an unusual human woman.

She wore a sleek black leather outfit. It was covered in thick leather plates that covered her shoulders and arms, though the leather armor appeared to be sleek enough not hinder her movement. She was a few inches taller than Amerix and her long shimmering black hair seemed to fade into the darkness around her. Amerix felt his strength regaining as he met the deep blue gaze of the imposing woman. The two stood in the dark street amid screams and shrieks from alleys and buildings.

"I guess I ought to say thanks," Amerix muttered.

"Not needed. I don't think these shadow monsters show me much favor," Kellacun answered in the dwarven tongue. She had learned a dozen languages in her travels to make her opponents easier marks.

Her name is Kellacun, Son of Durion. She has seen much in her life. Her heart has nearly been consumed by the dark. Much like your heart when we met.

"Met?" Amerix growled, "I never met ye, ye stupid sword. Ye just started talking one day."

Kellacun stepped back and narrowed her eyes. The dwarf appeared to be talking to his sword.

"Uh," she stammered, "My name is…"

"Kellacun," Amerix interrupted, "I know already. The sword told me."

Kellacun started to reply but was cut off.

"Let's get moving. I ain't got all day to stand here in the street chatting."

Kellacun watched as the dwarf mumbled to himself and started to the west. She glanced back to the dark alleys before trotting through the snow towards the massive dwarf.

"Has there ever been a point in your life that there was a fork that you did not recognize? A moment, that when reflected upon, revealed two vastly different paths that were unseen at the moment it was chosen?

I recall the meeting with the undead prison that blackened my father's soul. It twisted the good left in him into a corrupted monster bent on the destruction of all beings. He allowed his disgust for life to permeate and grow. Killing pleased him, but soon it left a larger hole that could never be filled.

He felt he was giving me a chance to surrender. A chance to do the right thing in his rotted fetid eyes. I answered with violence. I oft ponder that day. How would things have went had I given him such an ultimatum? Would the phrase; "father I love you," had any effect on his tormented mind?

I will never know. I do know the scars that path placed upon me and the deaths of heroes that resulted. Trinidy had become an unyielding agent of evil. The gods tried to stamp out evil once before. And even they failed. No, Trinidy is not a tormented soul. He is the manifestation of wickedness that dwells in us all. The difference is, goodly men are able to contain it. They are able to keep it locked away. What must be recognized is that there is always a situation in which this evil can escape. I wish I had learned this truth before the evil in me had slinked its way up from my deepest recesses.

Yes, I did succumb to darkness for a time. But had I not, I might never have learned it was hiding there."

-Lancalion Levendis Lampara-

☙13☙

Devils and Demons

A bright orange flash lit up the dark alley. The thick weave of abjuration cackled and popped until a large oval portal formed. Amyrillion, the Devil of Betrayal and Pain, stepped into the snow covered alley. She glanced around and examined her surroundings. The deviless could hear the distant shrieks of pain and death. She smiled coolly and placed her black lacquered hand on the alley wall. She marveled briefly at her lithe hand against the brick before she channeled a bright orange weave of abjuration into the wall. The thin orange magical weave embedded itself into the stone and began to glow. Amyrillion watched the magic's brightness fade away before she turned to the street. It was dark and snow covered. Shadow's filtered about, oblivious to her presence. The deviless continued embedding the orbs of Abjuration throughout the alleys as she made her way to the west. Amyrillion smiled as two other bright flashes of orange abjuration announced the arrival of Mortigalus and Donathuku. They would kill the son of Panoleen and please their master.

Petrovisk gripped his heavy curved kerstap with both

hands. The color began to come back to his skin and the pale touch of death began to fade from his tight lips. "The shadows flee to the inner city."

Sargoth nodded. "Yes, but we will have to deal with them later."

Petrovisk pushed off of the wall and glanced to the west at the charging wave of rotting flesh that began to bear down on them. He tightened his old muscles and held his kerstap over his head. His fingers flexed as the curved blade pointed high into the black sky.

"Svell!" he shouted as the blade began to glow a fiery blue flame.

The Beyklan soldiers glanced at the awe-inspiring sight of the great greyshalk and his glowing weapon held above his head. Their faces turned from that of fear to one of grim determination.

Petrovisk narrowed his hawk-like eyes as the ghouls streaked across the battlefield. He growled low and smiled sadistically.

"Don't forget the pits!" Sargoth called out, "Let them fall into their oily depths before we engage. Let their rotted bodies burn the pits full and cross on the ashes of their comrades before we cut them down! Make them earn the right to set foot on our great city's soil, and then cut them down for the privilege!"

Jude hurried down the dark coliseum corridor. He paused several times before making a decision on which way to go. Prisoners were running in all directions. Some were screaming while others were cheering. Jude ignored them as he made his way to Copel's chamber. He reached down to open the thick wooden door, but it was locked. He shoved his shoulder into the door violently and the wooden portal shattered as it was forced open. Bits of splintered wood fell on the stone floor as the barbarian forced his way in.

Copel stood in his small antechamber that had once

housed Jude. The old rickety desk that they played cards on was scooted to the side and the portly former champion was fastening his chin strap on his helm.

"Come to slay me like you promised?"

Jude ignored him and moved the thick double doors at the far chamber. "No."

"Well...," Copel's words trailed off as Vlargcar stepped into the room. He had to duck under the doorway and his thick mohawk brushed under the ceiling of the antechamber. His dark green shoulders seemed to engulf the room.

"Vlargcar is with you, Jude?"

Jude did not answer Copel as he examined the double doors. "This will not hold our enemy. We must find another place to make our stand."

Vlargcar scratched his chin. "Want me to test it?"

Jude arched an eyebrow at the massive orc. "Sure. But, I was making reference to the shadows that are rumored to be in this monster's army."

Vlargcar smiled and rammed his shoulders into the double doors. They crumbled easily under the might of the seven foot orc. Pieces of stone cracked and fell from the door frame as dust and debris fell from the ceiling. Vlargcar brushed off his shoulders and glanced up the ramp that led to the city street.

"There is snow, Jude. And birds. Lots of birds."

Jude ignored Copel and stepped onto the ramp. He could see the snow covered streets and the swirling cloud of black birds that blocked out the sun. It was as if it was sundown. The streets had an eerie calm about them and occasional screams and shrieks of death echoed in the distance.

Copel stepped out from his chamber clad in his chain armor and great sword. He still walked with his limp, and despite his advanced age, he appeared a worthy warrior, "Gods save us."

"The gods have abandoned us," Jude said, "You want saved? Save yourself. The orc and I are going to the front lines to the west. You can go where you wish."

"Why not just flee?" Copel asked, "Why risk your life?"

"To even ask that question shows that you would not

understand my answer."

Vlargcar ignored the pair and waked up the covered ramp and stepped into the snow. The streets were barren and dark. He could hear an occasional scream or shriek that echoed from all directions.

"Jude, why is it dark?"

Jude waved his hand in dismissal at the aged gladiator keeper and jogged up the ramp. He glanced around at the snow and then up to the swarm of black birds that swooped and dived, blocking out the sun.

"There is foul magic afoot, Vlargcar. Stick close to me."

Vlargcar nodded as followed behind his new friend. They jogged at a good pace through the city. Their heavy boots crunched the new fallen snow as they made their way west. The silent buildings seemed to loom down on the escapees making the avenues seem more haunted than deserted. The pair rushed west towards the sounds of battle when two silhouettes caught their eye. Jude turned to see a woman dressed in dark leather armor. She wore some sort of skin tight suit under her leather plates and her long black hair flowed in the wind as she ran. When Jude's eyes fell on the mountain of a dwarf next to her, his heart sank. He stared into the cold eyes of the ruthless killer, Amerix Stormhammer.

"Vlargcar, this dwarf is going to take all of our skill to kill."

Vlargcar's ears perked when he heard Jude say dwarf. He paused and turned to the east. There he saw the most wonderful sight. Amerix had returned! The dwarf had a new suit of mail that looked as if the god of the under mountain had crafted it himself. "Broh-tah!

Amerix paused and narrowed his old eyes. He could see a large human to the west and a somewhat short ogre, "Bare yer steel, woman. We got a Beyklan and an ogre coming."

That's no ogre, Son of Durion.

Kellacun drew her sword and widened her stance. "Why is an ogre attacking the city? And how did he get past the soldiers?"

Amerix lowered his axes.

"That's no ogre! That's Vlargcar!" Amerix shouted as he

ran towards the orc.

Jude relaxed a bit when Amerix called out the orc's name. Amerix was the 'brohe-tah' that had saved him those years back? Then who was the woman?

Vlargcar ran up to Amerix and tightened his fist. He started to swing and remembered that was not how to great a friend. He extended his right hand instead. "I missed you, Broh-tah."

Amerix felt tears well up in his old eyes and his nose began to burn. "I missed ye too, boy. Ye sure got big," Amerix said as he knocked the orc's hand away and hugged his waist.

Vlargcar was unsure what to do but the embrace made him feel warm inside, so he patted Amerix's helmet. "Why you no come for me, Brohe-tah?"

Amerix wiped the wetness from his eyes and glared at it angrily before softening his gaze when he looked up at the blue eyes of his only friend. "I had to find me first, or I would have never come."

Vlargcar bit his lower lip. "Good thing you didn't have to find me first, I was much harder. They had me in there," Vlargcar said as he pointed to the top of the coliseum that jutted above the other rooftops in the south. "I fought every day. Just like you showed me. Got real good too. I use two swords at once now. The big ones, like Jude uses with two hands."

Amerix glanced over at Jude who was standing behind the orc. "Ye look familiar to me, Beyklan."

Jude frowned. He couldn't make out too much of what Amerix was saying. "I only learned a little dwarven from the orc."

Amerix waved his hand in dismissal "Bah. Matters little. Come on boy! There is some fightin' to be had and it will be a pleasure to do so next to ye."

Introduce the woman, Son of Durion.

Amerix stopped abruptly, "What?"

The other's looked on with confusion.

Kellacun folded her arms under her breasts. "He is talking to the sword again."

Amerix snorted, "Why would I do that?"

Because it is what you are supposed to do, Son of Durion.

Amerix shook his head. "Before we go, this here is Kellacun. She wants to kill whatever it is to the west too."

Jude nodded his head to her, and she nodded back. He glanced at the renegade general that seemed a bit confused.

"Undead," Kellacun spoke out.

"What?" Amerix said.

Kellacun cleared her throat. "We are fighting undead. They are bearing down on the city," she said before repeating it in dwarven for Amerix, "My employer sent me here to kill a woman and the duke of Central City. He was supposed to send me a portal to escape. Clearly he hopes to have my death here. I aim to disappoint him."

"How does he know there are undead attacking?" Jude asked.

"Because he works for the King of Nalir that sent them."

Jude frowned. "Why on earth would the King of Nalir send an army of undead? How could he?"

"There is much I do not know in the ways of magic. But I do know they summoned a ferocious monster from the bowls of the Abyss. He is some sort of undead king that has raised the army to hunt down a Beyklan boy believed to be part of some old ancient prophecy."

"Bah, you guys talk too much," Amerix growled, "Come' on boy."

Vlargcar glanced back at the two and grabbed Amerix by the shoulder, "No, I think we should wait, Brohe-tah. They are talking good things. Plus, many swords are greater than few."

Amerix glanced up in astonishment that soon turned into a warm smile. "I did a good job teaching ye, boy."

Vlargcar smiled and nodded.

Jude rubbed his chin. "This must be the monster that attacked the elven vale. He knew Lance was there too. He must have some sort of magical link to him. That means if he is attacking here, then Lance must be here too!"

"I don't know this Lance, but Kalen did mention that there was a demon woman running with the boy. That she needed killed, or she would help the boy fulfill the prophecy," Kellacun said as they hurried towards the west.

Jude nodded. "Yes, she no doubt masked herself as a human. Lance is my best friend. We must get to him in time. Did your employer say how we would identify the demon?"

Kellacun hurried her pace to match the great strides of the large man as Amerix and Vlargcar followed. "Yes, he said she would be wearing a special type of necklace."

Apollisian burst through the door of the inn. Steiny whirled around and choked on a piece of bread as he sat on the bar.

"Holy Smidft!

"Where's Alexis?!"

Steiny felt the color drain from his face as he pointed to the stairs. "On va woof," he said as he slowly started chewing again.

Apollisian rushed up their stairs in his armor, taking two at a time. Lance and Delania came in behind him.

Steiny swallowed his bread and quickly tucked it in his pocket. "What's going on?"

Lance studied the door, ignoring the halfling.

Delania went behind the bar and began filling a small sack with provisions and breads. "The fight has started. They sent shadows first. They will be here soon."

Steiny hopped down from the bar and dusted the crumbs from his hands. "What are we to do?"

Lance channeled thick heavy brown weaves into the door and the wall. The wood hardened and started to turn gray.

"No, twist your hand," Delania said

Lance frowned and twisted his hand slightly. He watched in wonder at how such a subtle movement altered the weaves. They changed into a spiral much like an inverted cyclone. The weaves soon enveloped the door and extended throughout the room. Lance could feel every board in the inn, every wood fiber, every nail, every window.

"Um, worrying here," Steiny said nervously.

"Now, do you feel the entire structure?" Delania asked

Lance nodded.

"Now, widen your hands and tie it off. Do it quickly."

Lance obeyed. He widened his hands, making a small eye in the tip of the cyclonic weave that erupted from his fingers. He could feel the entire inn open up, like he had found a secret door inside of a piece of paper.

Delania came up behind Lance and put her arms around him. She closed her eyes and focused a straight line weave. It spun in the opposite direction as Lance's cyclonic spell. The weave turned bright blue and expanded until it matched the inside of Lance's brown weaves.

Lance felt sweat drip down his cheek as he strained to hold the ever growing spell. "Delania, ...I ...I can't hold it much more."

"Shut up and do it."

Lance nodded. The pain in his arms felt like he had been holding them outstretched for hours. His fingers were numb and he was not sure if he was even controlling the weaves, or they simply were acting on their own.

"Okay, let it go."

Lance reluctantly released the weaves. He watched in amazement as they rocketed into the wall like the sapling of a triggered snare. In moments, the walls turned dull gray and hardened into stone. The inn shook and trembled as the stone expanded and grated on itself. He wiped the sweat from his brow and leaned against the bar.

"Are you sure this will keep the shadows out?

"Yes. We have turned this inn into Abyssal Stone."

"What's that?" Steiny asked as he gingerly ran his fingers across the cold stone.

Delania smiled and placed her and on Lance's shoulder. "It is stone from the Abyss. It contains certain properties that block incorporeal movements. The only way in or out is through the use of a gate or portal."

Lance held his head in his hands as he felt his strength returning. "That took a lot out of me."

"You are doing great, my love. Never have I seen someone so inexperienced yield power as you have. There is something about you. I think the gods themselves have a play in your fates."

Lance looked up sternly. His normally warm green eyes seemed dark and cold, "No one controls my fate, but me."

Delania smiled disarmingly and kissed his cheek. "Of course."

Apollisian barreled down the stone stairs with a half-smile on his face. "By the gods, I think you have done it!"

Delania smiled warmly. "Great. This should hold. Shadows cannot climb stairs or ladders. They can only climb anything that is related to the ground. Cliffs, for example, but not walls. The ghouls and other undead monsters have no such restrictions. Second, the shadows cannot pass through Abyssal Stone. I think it is important that we climb to the roof and destroy as many as we can with our spells."

Apollisian nodded. "Alexis is on the roof. She will use her bow. It is enchanted and should aid us. My question is, how will we aid others if they cannot get in?"

Delania smiled. "I have embedded a weave within the stone. Another great point about Abyssal Stone. It channels magic easily, like a rod conducts lightning."

"And that means?" Apollisian said pointedly.

"Well, I created a life-force channel. Using Lance's life force, I have made it possible for anything that is alive, or has a soul, to be able to pass through the stone as if it were not there. They will pass through it like a hand through a waterfall."

Apollisian walked over to the wall. He extended his hand and pushed it into the wall. His hand passed easily, but his gauntlet resisted and pushed tight up on his wrist. "I see a problem."

Delania frowned. She was a demon in the Abyss. They did not normally wear clothes. This was clearly a miscalculation on her part. It would seem that anyone that ran through the wall would leave their clothes, weapons, armor behind on the ground. "Well, I did not anticipate it working like that, but clearly a live naked refugee is better than a clothed dead one."

Apollisian nodded. "I can't disagree with that."

Lance hopped up from his chair. "Okay, Delania. Let's get to the roof with Overmoon."

Delania nodded and followed Lance up the stairs. Apollisian glanced over at Steiny who was stuffing his pockets with bread and cheese.

"What?" Steiny asked, "And where is Ian?"

Apollisian motioned to the stairs and started up them. "Ian went to the front lines with General Bodrell. Get to the roof as soon as you are finished here. Just in case the spell does not hold out the shadows like Delania and the boy think it will."

Steiny glanced at the cold stone shaped walls and the color drained from his face. He hurried up the stairs behind the weary warrior.

Trinidy watched his shadows as they penetrated the front lines of the humans. He could feel the magical pull, commanding him to enter the city. To kill his son. The undead general fought the insatiable lure as he surveyed his creations end the wickedness of man.

"What are you waiting for, Trinidy. The right that must be wronged is in there somewhere," his steed called out to him.

Trinidy narrowed his cold blue glowing eyes. Black centipedes skittered excitedly from his eye socket to his nose. His steed did not know that Lance was the wrong he was to right. It did not know that the magical pull that brought him to this day was linked with his son.

"Yes, he is in there. Our servants have the city on all sides. It is unlikely that he will escape."

"But what if he does?" Nefertora answered, hoping that the questioning did not reveal her true nature.

"Then we will chase him longer."

"Lord Trinidy!" one of the liches called out, "The shadows have suffered heavy losses. The city has many wizards."

Trinidy turned his rotting head and glanced down at the

lich. One of his finest creations. "Then send the ghouls."

"Yes, My Lord."

Trinidy turned to watch the battle play out. The shadows had no purpose except to kill as many as they could as they penetrated the inner city. The ghouls would pay more attention to the soldiers that thought to stand against him. After the ghouls, he would send his walking dead into the mix. He would lead them personally.

Petrovisk sliced and chopped rotted corpses into small pieces of ichor as the wave forced him back. His human comrades were dropping by the dozens under the swell of undead. The flaming pits quickly filled with ghouls and the others charged over their burning bodies. The heat from the fires melted the surrounding snow and the soldiers began to slip in the muck. The undead turned every loss into a victory.

"Fall back!" Captain Trimlee shouted as the towers continued to rain down blasts of magic and fiery arrows.

Petrovisk glanced at the towers for a final time as the soldiers pulled back between the western buildings of Central City. He knew the men atop of the towers were doomed. The mighty greyshalk cut down another ghoul and roared. His arms extended and he tossed his head back. He roared for the fight, for his comrades and for the men on the towers.

"Do not fret, my brothers! This is only the beginning! Our enemy will feel more of our wrath!"

Soldiers, stark with fear, ignored the words of the giant greyshalk as many turned and ran from the front lines. Petrovisk backed himself into an alley with a score of other soldiers. He stood at the front, cutting and slashing the ghouls that came before him. Time after time he would witness a soldier fall from a single scratch only to be drug off and eaten alive. The old warrior felt his muscles burn from his labored swings and his fingers were a bit number from the many scratches and bites he had endured.

The ghouls pressed forward. Their pale white eyes and

purple taunt skin clambered over one another to get to the front. They had no fear, no worries. It was as if hate itself drove them forward. Hate for the very life they could never again possess.

"Hold!"

Petrovisk turned to see a man atop a horse pushing his way to the front. He was dressed in plate armor and, after a second glance, Petrovisk recognized him. General Bodrell.

"Get off your pony, General!" Petrovisk growled. "It has little armor and the ghouls will cut it from under you in seconds."

Bodrell dismounted and grabbed his shield. He slipped it on and made his way towards the front as several men fought over the horse to run away.

Petrovisk ignored the numbness growing in his left leg and fought on. "Could use your shield arm to my right!"

Bodrell brought his sword down into the shoulder of a ghoul as he stepped up next to Petrovisk. It did not cry, shriek, or moan. It simply fell to his feet as rotted fetid black blood erupted from the wound in its neck.

"How did they get so deep?"

Petrovisk took another hit on his shoulder as he brought his kerstap down, severing the ghoul in two as he answered, "They came in by the thousands. Not like men, they came in running with no fear."

"Gods! NO!" echoed a voice behind them.

Bodrell and Petrovisk stole a glance behind them as the ghouls had broken the ranks in the alley next to them. Several were dangling off of Bodrell's fleeing mount and two deserting soldiers. The wave of ghouls had attacked the back side of the alley, sealing the men inside.

"Up. We must get up, Petrovisk."

Petrovisk gleaned up to the roof to his right. He flexed his powerful legs and leapt to the second floor window sill. He dropped his kerstap but managed to pull his massive frame into the window. He removed his rope and started to dangle it down to the general when he saw him fall under a mass of ghouls. The second it had taken him to leap up, the entire forty men of the western alley had fallen. Petrovisk watched a few fleeting seconds as the general's body was torn apart by the ravaging ghouls. He felt anger for the first time in a battle. His comrades were not honored by the enemy. Their sacrifices were lost to those that did not survive to remember them. The mighty greyshalk wanted to leap down and cut as many as his foes as he could. But to what end? They would not admire his bravery. They would sing no songs of their victory and his heroic leap. This was truly an enemy from the Abyss.

Petrovisk turned from the window sill and heard noises coming from outside of the room. He hastily made his way to the hallway. It was an odd constructed cave. It had portraits hanging on the walls and soft colored furs on the floor. At the far end there was a stair case going up and one going down. He could see several ghouls trying to fit through a downstairs window at the same time. Petrovisk moved to the stairs and watched the ghouls whip into a frenzy when they could see him. One ghoul managed to sever his arm at the elbow on the broken glass, but came rushing up to meet its hulking enemy without fear. Petrovisk reached for his kerstap, but it was not there. He groaned and shook his head at his damnable luck as he hurled a stone punch into the ghoul's face. The mighty warrior felt the ghoul's skull crunch under his knuckles sending out an array of black blood and ichor in all directions. The ghoul fell to the floor and twitched as it slowly slid down the stairs, only to be replaced by two more that had scampered though the window. The door began to shake as the mass of undead began to claw their way through. Petrovisk sighed and started up the second flight of stairs. His mighty strides took two at a time. The ghouls snarled as they started the stairwell behind him.

Petrovisk reached the top of the third flight. There were no more stairs for him to climb. He was in a hallway that was lined with plain wooden doors to either side. There was a window capping each hallway. The old warrior glanced down the stairs and saw the ghouls rounding the second flight. He looked out into the streets at the hundreds of ghouls that were running rampant in between the buildings. Petrovisk stepped from the window ledge. His claws scrapped against the stone as he stretched to reach the roof. His fingers secured his grip as he reached up with his second hand, careful not to fall backwards into the ghoul filled streets. Petrovisk flexed his legs and leaped. His powerful arms pulled him to the roof. He glanced down at the window as the ghouls tried to follow him. Several fell from the window and their bodies made sickly thuds as they hit the cobblestone street. Black syrupy ichor leaked out from their injured bodies and covered the streets where they fell.

Petrovisk wiped a bit of sweat from his hair covered brow and rested on the flat roof of the building. The dark clouds and massive swirling birds overhead seemed to roll and pitch like a storm at sea. The old warrior moved to the north side of the building and glanced down. The ghouls had thinned in the alley, but echoing screams and shouts from towns folks told the story of where they really went. Petrovisk took a deep breath and made his way to the west wall. He felt his heart sink as he gazed out among what once seemed like a stout defense. The undead swarmed around the towers. Several of them no longer had any live warriors on top. Others, the slain defenders had risen up after their death and they wandered around the battlement in a grizzly undeath march. Only a handful of towers had anyone alive on them, and those were fighting fiercely to stay alive. Petrovisk glanced back into the city and then back to the towers. It did not seem like many defenders were left. He wondered if his family was part of the army, or part of the undead.

"What led to the massacre of Central City at the hands of Trinidy's army? Or even the dwarves, for that matter. Did they really need to sacrifice the thousands of townsfolk? Was there not a better way to protect them?

Why do city leaders protect themselves under the guise of protecting others? The leaders of Beykla were worried about themselves. They were worried that the Abyss Walker would come for them. No one worried about the innocent lives of Central City.

Leaders are put in place to provide for the people. Their position exists solely for others, and not to themselves.

I am not saddened that the Abyss Walker destroyed most known civilizations. I am saddened for the innocents that suffered because of it."

-Lancalion Levendis Lampara-

ᴖ14ᴖ
The Stand and the Fall

Tylergaiden ran his hands through his long sweaty red hair. His bloody, blistered fingers stroked his many symas and wondered what his king would award for this battle. He was nearly out of arrows and the ghouls didn't seem to mind when he shot them. He stared out distantly into the sea of undead that had crashed into the ranks below. The fronts had long since fallen back into the city and the towers were slowly being overrun. Silas merged from the stairs of the battlement. He was bloody and limping. He seemed to be dragging his leg. "They've gotten through. Leska save us, they have gotten through."

"Where is Quadry?"

Silas fell to the stone battlement. "Seal the door, there isn't much time."

"Where is Quadry, Silas?"

The weak elf rolled to his back. "I can't feel my legs and my mouth is going numb."

Tylergaiden grabbed Silas's tunic. "Where is he?"

Silas let tears roll down the side of his rapidly numbing cheeks. "He ith with dem."

"What do you mean, *with* them?

"He ith dead."

Tylergaiden ran over the edge and saw the undead fighting with one another to scamper in the lower battlement door. He rushed over to the stairs and witnessed the ghouls devouring screaming soldiers as a few tried to fight their way to the staircase. The soldiers begged and screamed for help as several ghouls scampered up the stairs towards him.

The elf notched several arrows as one of the wizards slammed the door shut and slid the metal bar across the hatch, locking it in place.

"What are you doing?" Tylergaiden asked.

"There is no saving them. We must hold the top as long as possible."

The Darayal Legionnaire bit his lower lip as anger rushed through him. "It will only be a matter of time before they manage to claw through the door."

The wizard nodded as the color left his face. "I agree. So let's maximize our time and take as many of the rotted bastards with us."

Amerix and the group made their way through the city streets. Shouts and screams from the west revealed the undead had broken the lines. It was only a matter of time before the city was overrun.

"What is that!?" Kellacun shouted as she pointed to the east.

The group turned to see a twelve foot tall monster. It had giant crab like pinchers for hands and its skin was a bright red. It was covered with dark ebony horns and spines. The monster had several white shafted arrows embedded in its fore arms and head as it tried to make its way towards a towering stone building. There was an elf standing on the roof blasting arrow after arrow into the giant monster.

Jude pointed. "That looks like the elf Lance and I traveled with. She was the one that tricked us!"

"How can ye be sure?" Amerix asked, hoping that the champion he fought was inside.

"I can't be sure. But she used white ash arrows, just like the elf on that roof," Jude answered.

Go, Son of Durion. Apollisian is in the inn. He is in danger.

The crack of a whip broke through the air. Amerix turned to see a black whip wrap around Jude's neck. The huge swordsman was hosted from his feet and hurled backwards through the air. Stepping from behind one of the buildings to the north was another monstrosity. This one was as tall as the other. However, it was morbidly obese. The monster had red skin that was covered in bulbous pustules. Its head was covered in spines and horns as well, but they were twisted and sickly looking.

"No!" Vlargcar shouted. The massive orc drew his swords and charged towards the beast.

Kellacun glanced back at Amerix. "We should go help Jude."

"No, ye go. I must find Apollisian. I will catch up."

Kellacun started to leave and turned back. "Can you beat that other thing by yourself?"

Amerix didn't answer as his short stubby legs carried him off to east.

"What in the Nine Hells is that!?" Alexis asked as she pointed to a massive monster charging through the streets.

Apollisian ran over to the edge of the building. He could not believe his eyes. Never had he seen a monster so large. It was even larger than an ogre. It had thick plated crab pinchers for hands. Its skin was red and the beast had a muscular body if a human. It ran on hinged legs, like a goat, with a cloven hoof, yet the beast had no fur.

Delania rushed over and began channeling a spell, "Whatever it is, shoot it!"

The monster lowered its shoulder and smashed through buildings like a bull would run through a briar patch. Large bits of debris exploded from the collisions and rained down on the snowy earth. Alexis fired arrow after arrow into the charging behemoth. They lodged deep into the monster's hide. It raised its clawed hands to protect it face as it charged.

Delania let loose a powerful blast if evocation. The sky opened up as hundreds of azure fireballs rained down on the monster as it ran. The balls of energy exploded into buildings, sending rocks and bits of wood through the air. The blasts that hit the monster seemed to glance off. Some left small black singe marks, but appeared to have no effect on the beast.

Lance stepped forward and began to channel thick brown weaves. When the beast saw Lance, it roared with fury and hurried its charge.

"Aquanus. Amyrillion!"

"It's gonna hit the building!" Apollisian called out.

Lance shot out his hands as the light wind whipped his cadacka around his body. The thick brown transmutation weaves shot into the snowy earth leaving a thick rope of earthen energy still in the young wizards grasp. As the huge devil stepped into the threads, its foot sunk, as if he had stepped into a large patch of mud. Lance twisted his body and jerked the earthen thread. The alley mud turned to stone, hardening around the arch-devil's foot. Hs body tumbled head long into the side of the inn. The building shuddered as the beast crashed through the lower walls.

Alexis dropped her bow and fell against the edge of rooftop wall. The structure groaned and cracked. Lance and Delania stumbled to the far side as the roof collapsed under them.

All was silent. Alexis lay under a layer of rocks and stone. "Apollisian," she called out weakly.

Apollisian sat up. His armor was severally dented and he was bleeding in several places, but he forced himself to sit up. He scrambled over to Alexis and ignored the pain in his chest. "Where are you?"

Alexis struggled to lift her arm above the debris. "Under here."

Apollisian tossed down his shield. The thick metal plate clanged as is skidded over the mound of rocks and stone. He reached down and groaned as he rolled a large rock from Alexis. "Are you injured?"

Alexis struggled to climb out from under the rock as

Apollisian helped her. "I think so. My leg is mangled pretty bad. It may be broken."

Apollisian placed her arm over his shoulder and assisted her in climbing down from the pile of debris. The pile began to lurch and the stones groaned as the arch-devil began to claw its way out.

Apollisian and Alexis hurried from under the remaining standing portions of the collapsed stone inn.

"What about the others?" Alexis asked through gritted teeth.

Apollisian glanced back. He could see the massive arch-devil slowly climbing from the rubble. "We must get you to safety first."

The pair hobbled their way across the snow covered ally and into a building to the east. It was a large structure that appeared to house citizens in apartment flats. Now, their bodies lined the hallways. They lay positioned in twisted agonizing poses of death.

Apollisian moved to the far end and gently eased Alexis to the floor. "Let's look at your leg."

Alexis looked away as Apollisian removed her thick leather leg armor. Her almond eyes fell upon one of the dead. The body was a teenage girl. Her face was twisted and contorted in one of pain and horror.

"What do you think killed these people?"

Apollisian tossed the blood soaked leather leg plate to the floor. "Shadows, I would guess. The ghouls haven't broken the front lines."

Alexis looked back to her leg. She could see a long gash and several scraps, but other than that, she seemed okay.

"Is it broken?"

"I don't think so. But, we need to keep moving."

The pair was startled when the door they had just came through erupted in splintered wood and debris as the devil's claw tore through it. Apollisian grabbed Alexis by the arm and hoisted her up over his shoulder. She started to protest, but the pain in her leg held her tongue. They burst through the east door and darted into the alley. Bits of stone and wooden debris began to rain down as the arch devil tore through the west wall.

"Keep going!" Alexis shouted.

Apollisian glanced over his shoulder to see the massive monster ripping through the building as though it were soft clay. Rocks and debris rained down on them as they hurried to the end of the corridor. Apollisian lowered his shoulder and burst through the door. The wooden frame collapsed under his weight. He fell headlong into the alley on the other side. Alexis tumbled roughly to the ground as Apollisian fell into the alley.

The tired paladin shot to his feet quickly. He started towards Alexis when the heavy arch-devil's claw ripped through the building and hit him in the chest. The paladin was hurled back through the air. He thudded on the hard cobblestone alley and skidded to a stop. The arch-devil pushed his way through the rest of the wall. Alexis was unable to stand, but lifted her arms to shield her head from the falling debris.

The wall from the east side collapsed and fell on Apollisian. The crushing weight of the wood and debris pinned his legs to the cold alley floor.

"What have we here?" a husky feminine voice called out.

Alexis turned to see a woman with dark black hair and bright red skin. She was over six foot tall and had no clothing. Her long bat tail twitched behind her nervously. She had two thin horns that protruded from her forehead and two bat wings neatly tucked behind her.

Apollisian struggled to pull himself free from the debris. He could taste the copper blood in his mouth and he could feel its warm trickle down the side of his face. "Apollisian!" Alexis pleaded.

"I cannot get to you. Fight! Fight like you have never fought before."

Alexis struggled to her feet as the devil woman approached.

"You think you can oppose me? I am Amyrillion, the Devil of Pain, Betrayal, and Torture."

Alexis drew her thin short sword. "Stuff it, bitch. I am Alexis Alexandria Overmoon. I am not going to fight you; I am going to kill you."

The large arch-devil watched the two women for a second. He turned towards Apollisian pinned in the debris. One quick claw snap and the trapped man would be dead and he could watch the show.

Kellacun drew her twin swords and rushed in towards the corpulent behemoth. Its skin was covered with masses of boils that rose and burst in seconds, only to be replaced by another a few inches from the first. Jude had been laid low with a powerful blow that had pinned him between the monster's fist and the building next to him. The handsome bronze skinned man had surely broken many of his ribs. The thought of his injury seemed to anger her.

Vlargcar slashed a deep slice in the devil's leg while Edge shook his powerful head and ripped at the other one. The monster twisted in pain and punched down. The agile orc was able to avoid the blow as it hit the cobblestone street sending a shower of rocks into the snow around him. Kellacun transformed and leaped into the air. Her powerful hybrid form seemed to hover over the battle. She turned her swords inward and the assassin plunged them deep into the devil. The monster arched his back in pain. Vlargcar stabbed in with his swords. Kellacun was surprised to see the tips of the orc's weapons as they pierced all the way through the devil's portly body. The devil writhed and flailed. Kellacun pulled her swords free and leapt from his back and landed deftly on the snowy cobblestone floor. Vlargcar growled ferociously and twisted his blades while they were still in the arch-devil. The thick swords curdled the devil's flesh. The monster howled in pain and snatched Vlargcar by his neck.

Jude jumped to his feet and laid a deep slash down the devil's back. The heavy sword cut through the flesh revealing bright red bone that exuded waves of heat in the cold snowy air. Vlargcar let loose of his blades and fought the vice like grip, but even his mighty strength was no match for that of the devil. Kellacun transformed back and circled the monster as it grabbed Jude by the neck as well. She was stronger and faster and more agile in her rat form, but she was faster and wielded her swords better in her natural state. The dark haired mistress of the night watched helplessly as the arch-devil hoisted Jude and Vlargcar in the air. She could see the life being choked from her new companions. The monster did not suffer from wounds to his body like normal creatures. He did not bleed, and other than pain, showed no sign of concern for his injuries. He did not slow, nor tire. Kellacun knew that if she did not free the two men, that the devil would soon claim their lives.

Kellacun sprang to action. She dived in and sliced low. Her keen blades laid a deep gash on the back hamstring of her large foe. The devil whirled and swung the orc's body around like a club. Kellacun leapt over the strike and in one fell motion, she transformed into her rat form as she brought her enchanted blades down. The thin swords neatly sliced through the forearms of the arch-devil. Jude and Vlargcar fell to the snow and quickly wrenched themselves free from the severed hands. Mortigalus arched his back and howled in pain. He stared at his bloody nubs in anger. Kellacun stabbed the fat devil in his thigh. Her blades sunk to the hilt. Jude quickly picked up his great sword from the thickening snow. The arch-devil fell to his knees in pain. But before he could strike out at the young assassin, Jude brought his sword down and cleaved the monster's head in two. Great globules of gore erupted from the wound, but before they hit the snow, the entire arch-devil's body crumbled to ash. Only the heavy panting and breathing of the three newfound companions sounded in the quiet snowfall.

"Sacrifice. Why were so many sacrificed to Trinidy's wrath? To me sacrifice is something that someone gives up. Something they owned, or was theirs to lose. But why do we so often call lives given to war a sacrifice?

If the soldiers stood on their own accord to defend righteousness, or innocence, that is a sacrifice. But the innocents that bled the snow red in Central City, they had no choice. The ones that fled were cut down and the ones that stayed to fight had no chance.

See, they did not give up their lives because of their choosing. Yet, the greyshalks, the elves... They made a great sacrifice. The heroes that once stood beside me that lost their lives fighting the undead horde. That was sacrifice.

The poor common soldier that was slain because his king ordered him to fight, the citizen that was not allowed to flee the city and had his flesh devoured by Trinidy's ghouls... These were not sacrifices.

You see, most lives lost to war are not sacrifices at all. These lives were not sacrificed. No, they were wasted.

-Lancalion Levendis Lampara-

ᴄ❦15❦ᴄ
A Family Affair

Katrinal ducked low under the stone archway and paused to admire the craftsmanship it took to create it. Humans had such strange dwellings. She wondered how they moved them from valley to valley. The young greyshalk gripped her donjurik tightly as she stepped into the market that she could best compare to a small stone valley.

Grogan scratched his head. "What do you suppose this is?"

"Shhhh!"

Grogan groaned and shook his head. His long ears bounced gently. Had he known what a feral Katrinal was, he would never have agreed to go with her.

Screams from the distance alerted both of them.

"Why is it so deserted here, Katrinal?

"Cause of the fighting to the west."

Grogan gripped his thumebar tightly. The powerful heavy club seemed to make him feel more secur, "So when do we meet up with your father? I can't wait to meet him."

Katrinal rolled her eyes. Everyone wanted to meet the great Petrovisk. "Why? He is just a grouchy old feral."

Grogan smiled as he followed Katrinal into the market. "He is not just a grouchy old feral. He is one of the mightiest greyshalks to ever live."

"Katrinal!" Angelique shouted, "Why are you here!? Grogan!? Is that you?"

Grogan relaxed as Angelique, Cathena, and Cheural stepped from a crumbled shack.

"Yes. Katrinal told us how you wanted us to come late. Great tactic, Matre Angelique."

"Grogan, you half-witted kip!"

Grogan motioned his hands in confusion. "What? Katrinal and I did not encounter any resistance getting into the city. Your plan worked brilliantly."

"My plan!? Grogan, you fool. Had I wanted Katrinal here, why would we have sent her to you?"

Grogan frowned in confusion. "Because Petrovisk admired my skill with a thumebar."

Cheural and Cathena covered their mouths as they giggled.

Angelique shot Katrinal an angry glare. The young greyshalk only smiled victoriously. "What, mother? Every kip needs to feel they are worth something. So I complimented his thumebar skills."

Grogan frowned. "You mean Petrovisk didn't request me?"

Angelique shook her head in disgust. "And if the western line had not been broken, I would send you back with the lying little swirler. We are cooking. Petrovisk and some of the others will be returning here soon. I aim to have some fresh meat for them. You two climb to the roof and alert us to any danger."

Katrinal easily scampered up the water spout to the flat snowy roof. She could not see too far to the west. There were gouts of great black smoke.

"Looks like the lines are intact. Well, mostly."

Grogan clumsily made his way to the roof. He stood and dusted some of the snow from his dark brown fur. "So you tricked me, huh?"

Katrinal kept her gaze to the west. "What do you care? You get to meet the mighty Petrovisk."

Grogan crunched through the snow on the roof and stood next to her. He strained his eyes to see what he could from the western lines. "You have a point."

Katrinal glanced up at Grogan. "You really don't fancy me at all, do you?"

Grogan placed his clawed hand on her shoulder. "It's

nothing personal, Katrinal. I just don't prefer matres as mates."

Katrinal chuckled. "What do you mean? What else is there to prefer?"

Grogan smiled and shook his head. "I don't think I am suited to be a mate for anyone."

Katrinal glared and stared off to the west. It was on thing to trick and reject Grogan, but how dare he not want her. The thought almost made her want him as a mate simply on principle.

Ian struggled to free himself from the rubble. He was certain his sword hand was broken and the blow to his head made his eyes cross. He was vaguely aware of the huge devil running off to the east but he had no idea why.

"You okay?" Steiny asked.

Ian lifted his bloodied head and saw the little halfling. "I think so."

Steiny helped pull the man from the rubble.

"We got to get moving. Lance and Delania have made their way to the east. The western lines have broken and the undead are slowly filtering into the city."

Ian struggled to his feet. His leg was badly mangled and he couldn't walk. Fresh blood streamed down his armor.

"I can't make it anywhere, little one. You had better catch up with your friends. I am going to have to ride."

Steiny scrunched his nose at the thought of riding again. He didn't think his sore bottom could handle another minute in a saddle.

"Okay, we are going to meet at the Blue Dragon Inn, across from City Hall."

Ian nodded and winced as he hopped from the debris and into the snow covered street. He watched as Steiny's stubby little legs carried him from the rubble and into the alleys. The swordsman hobbled to the stables across the street. He quickly saddled Knots. The old warhorse whinnied deeply when he came in.

"That's right, old friend. I ain't leaving you to the undead. This battle is lost and I am not leaving you here to be eaten,"

Ian struggled to climb into the saddle and winced as he tossed his bloody leg over and placed it in the stirrups. Knots's ears flickered and he pawed the hard stable floor.

"I know, it sucks to leave our companions, but you are more important to me than they are."

Ian ducked under the low doorway and rode Knots into the snowy street. He turned north and rode towards the edge of the city.

Tylergaiden quickly packed the snow from the battlement roof into a large pile next to him. He ignored the ravenous clawing of the ghouls, even as the young wizard began to hurl blasts of bright blue energy into them. Once he was finished with the snow, the legionnaire took all the arrows from his quivers and stuck them into the pile at an angle pointing backwards. Once he finished, he sat on the corner ledge of the battlement and positioned his bow sideways in front of him. With a deep breath, he began to meticulously pull an arrow from the snow, notch it and fire. The motion was rapid and fluid. Arrow after arrow struck home, lodging deep into the skulls of the attacking zombies and ghouls.

The tiring wizard backed to the opposite corner. He was covered in sweat and had drawn his small sword. "My God, I am really going to die."

Tylergaiden fired another arrow just as the ghouls broke down half of the door. "No you won't! Now fire more spells."

The wizard slowly and solemnly looked back at the iron resolved ranger. His voice was soft and quiet. "I can't. I don't have anymore."

The ghouls burst through the door. Bits of wood shot into the air. Tylergaiden launched his arrows faster and faster. He ignored the screams of the wizard as the poor man was eaten alive. The Darayal Legionnaire fired arrow after arrow. The bodies of the undead began to form a barrier between him and the charging others. The red haired legionnaire fired his last arrow and he quickly stood. He severed his bow string and grabbed the middle of the thick weapon. His razor sharp kumas would have to cut down the rest. But to his surprise, the ghouls did not advance, they just growled and snarled. The elf glanced over the edge of the battlement and to his surprise the undead were no longer fighting the west line. The battlements were all lost. Undead stood atop everyone. The elf looked east and he could see the army falling back, but they were not pursued by the undead. The monsters seemed to be halting and regrouping to secure the ground they had taken.

Tylergaiden stepped towards the ghouls as a figure emerged from the battlement door. It was a wicked monstrosity. It bore thick pate armor that was rusted and corroded. The beast's eyes had a deep blue glow that shined off of the glossy black bugs that crawled from his eye sockets to his nose and mouth. The monster had a thick powerful sword. The weapon's blade was made of some steel that was blood red and the air around it was so cold that ice crystals formed and snowed down from its tip.

Tyerlgaiden scrunched his nose and bit his lip. "You are the Abyss Walker."

Trinidy smiled. "You are able to speak my tongue."

Tylergaiden gripped his bow. "I have been alive for over eight hundred years, monster. I have learned to speak the many languages of my enemies."

Trinidy nodded. "You are the last fighting member of the western front. Your numbers have been cut in half. Your brother elves have fallen to my blade. For surviving, I will offer you chance to be spared. Join my ranks as one of my generals."

Tylergaiden lowered is head. "I accept."

Trinidy smiled at the unexpected reply. He stepped forward towards the elf, but to his surprise, the elf slashed in. The death knight struck out with his shield as he parried the slash with his sword. The thick metal struck Tylergaiden in the face. Trinidy slashed down and severed the elf's arm at the elbow. The legionnaire's wound froze from the Abyssal cold of the blade. He dropped to his knees and held the frozen numb. Trinidy sheathed his sword and grabbed the elf by the throat. Tylergaiden quickly regained his thoughts and fought to escape, but the powerful iron grip of the death knight kept him locked in place.

Trinidy watched in satisfaction as the elf quickly aged before his eyes. Tylergaiden's red hair was quickly replaced with silver. His skin wrinkled and sagged. His eyes drooped and his muscles atrophied. In seconds, the legionnaire was near death from old age.

Trinidy tossed Tylergaiden to his ghouls on the rooftop. "Devour him. Burt start at his hands and feet and work your way up."

Tyergaiden's old feeble screams echoed in Trinidy's ears as the rotted death knight marched down the battlement and back to his army.

Amerix burst through the shattered remnants of the hallway and door. He looked to his left and spied the human champion pinned under rocky debris from the smashed building. The large devil was advancing toward the downed man. To his right, the blasted elf was squaring off against a much taller bat winged woman.

Save the elf, Son of Durion.

Amerix shook his head and started toward Apollisian. "Bah. The woman is up an' fighting. I need to fight with the champion. Plus, his foe is larger and suits me better."

NO! Songsinger shouted in the old dwarf's mind, *You MUST save the elf, or all is lost!*

Amerix drew his twin axes, forged from the hammer of Durion, and charged the arch-devil. His boots crunched in the thick alley snow as he laid a deep slice down the back of Donathuku's leg. The devil arched his back in pain. He turned and slammed his heavy armored claw hand down. Amerix lunged out of the way as the claw struck the snowy alley floor, sending up a shower of rocks and ice into the air.

The old dwarf recovered quickly and slashed with a back-hand. His enchanted axe struck the arch-demon's left claw and neatly cut the top of it off. Amerix paused briefly and examined his enchanted blade. "Wow. Ye axes are better than any axe I ever had."

Donathuku angrily lunged in with his other claw. The thick chitin claw hit Amerix under his right shoulder and above his left. The force of the blow took him from his feet as Donathuku slammed his body into the side of the ally building. Amerix let out a moan as his air was forced from his body and bricks rained down on his helm from the damaged wall. The force of the blow knocked one of Amerix's axes from his hand. The shining brilliant blade fell into the deep snow.

"That was me good axe!" Amerix yelled as the arch-devil's claw struggled to crush the dwarf, but the general's enchanted armor seemed impenetrable.

"Eid uoy won!" The devil growled.

Amerix raised his other axe and squinted is eyes as he aimed. "Suck on me arse!" the old general growled as he hurled his other axe. The shinning brass colored blade hurled end over end through the cold snowy alley air, striking the arch-devil in the forehead.

Donathuku dropped the dwarf and staggered backwards into the west wall of the alley. His broad shoulders raked bricks loose as his large awkward claw fumbled at his face, trying to remove the axe. Amerix hit the alley floor hard. Bits of snow sprayed up around him. He struggled to get to his feet and began to look for his other axe in the snow. He knew he had just seconds before the arch-devil recovered. Amerix noticed the blade just a few feet from the pinned human champion. Amerix started toward him when the man screamed and pointed behind them.

Amyrillion cracked her whip, ripping open Alexis's left

arm. The elf weakly lunged in with her sword. She could hardly move because of the damage to her leg.

Amyrillion giggled in delight and pinched her breasts with her free hand. "I am going to enjoy killing you in front of your friend."

Alexis glanced over at Apollisian. Her gaze met his. Even from across the alley, his blue azure orbs were able to lock onto hers. She could see that the only thing left in his world was her. Alexis suddenly felt guilty that she might die. She couldn't die... she had to live for him!

Amyrillion cracked her whip around Alexis's neck. The much larger devil jerked forward and Alexis tumbled from her feet. Alexis narrowed her eyes and lunged in with her sword. She had to end this now.

Amyrillion sidestepped the feeble lunge and plunged her dagger into Alexis's back. Alexis shrieked in pain as the Abyssal cold dagger burned her insides.

"Noooooo! Apollisian screamed from across the alley.

Amyrillion cocked her head sideways. The pinned man and this woman were lovers. *How perfect,* she thought to herself. The arch-devil roughly grabbed Alexis by her hair and jerked her up.

Alexis fought for consciousness. That red bladed dagger the arch-devil used had some magical property to it. It felt like her insides were dripping from her body. Like, her soul was slowly leaking from her like the sands of an hour glass. Alexis looked down in the blood soaked snow and spied her sword. She was helpless to retrieve it. She started to try to wrench herself free when the cold burning sting of the dagger plunged into her back a second time. She felt her body go limp, as if paralyzed. She felt a deep sense of failure. She would die before the eyes of her lover. The sense of guilt and helplessness overcame her as her limp body was thrown to the alley floor. She struggled to breathe as warm hot blood drained from her mouth and began to pool in the cold snow under her head.

Amerix turned to see the elf woman as she was stabbed a second time and thrown to the snowy floor.

Damn you, Son of Durion! Your arrogance has doomed all of you, Songsinger groaned.

Amerix snarled and drew the chrome enchanted blade. "You can stick yer belly aching up yer scabbard, sword. I am tired of yer shit."

Donathuku was prone and managed to hook the tip of his claw under Amerix's enchanted axe. He delicately pulled the weapon free just as Amerix was swinging Songsinger down. The arch-devil lurched backwards but the celestial blade laid a deep gash across the arch-devil's muscled chest. The deep gash exposed odd red colored bones and bright bits of molten rock dripped to the snowy floor.

Amerix leaped to the top of the devil's gashed chest as the molten rock dripped down towards the monster's head.

Donathuku weakly glanced at the mountainous dwarf that stood perched atop of him. "Frawd, kcab eb ll'I.!"

Amerix narrowed his hawk-like eyes and slowly raised Songsinger above his head. The brilliant weapon gleamed in the pale alley light as snow fell around them.

Donathuku frowned as a honeyed voice echoed in his head, *There is no return for you, Athodrin. In the name of the Crowns of the Breedikai, I pronounce you judged.*

Amerix brought the celestial blade down and split the arch-devil's head in two. The thin blade cut through the devil's skull as easily as it would pass through water. The startled dwarf paused for a moment before hopping down from the beast's chest. As he made his way to the human champion, the arch-devil's body trembled and quivered as it crumpled into a pile of black soot and ash.

Amyrillion paused as she was about to plunge her dagger into Alexis a third time. "Why didn't he fade back to the hells!? How did you slay him here!?" Amyrillion screamed.

Amerix hurried to the pinned champion. His head was down and his long blonde hair hung over his face.

Amyrillion started toward the dwarf when the honey voice of Songsinger echoed in her head. "Go back to your master, Athodrin. Tell him Donathuku has been judged by

Panoleen. Do it now, lest I judge you next."

Amyrillion shook her head in disbelief, but quickly wove a bright orange portal and stepped through it. She did not know who this Panoleen was, but Azcarnicus must hear of this!

"Choices. Life is a myriad of choices with an even greater myriad of possibilities. Too many times people get caught up with the what ifs, or the maybe if I…

These are all falsehoods that mean nothing. As long as you have a good foundation and knowledge of oneself, there are no poor choices. You could no sooner make a bad choice than you could make a good one.

Now, I am not saying that one could not run into the dragon's lair and be eaten, or one could keep going. This is an obvious example of a good versus bad choice. But my point is this; if you are at one with yourself, you would consider running into the cave as a non-choice. It is not an option that you would consider, so there is no choice to make.

Apollisian was placed in a situation that he had two choices. He could let Alexis bleed to death and be with her as she passed. Or he could try to run and find me to heal her, thus risking the chance that she would die cold and alone in the snowy alley.

If he found me, the reward is an obvious one. If he stayed with her, the reward is a little unseen. The question is simple. Is the Champion of Justice in tune with himself enough that he can make the choice that is best for the both of them?"

-Lancalion Levendis Lampara-

16

Blood Oaths

Amerix reached down and grabbed the crumbled stone wall that was covering Apollisian. With a groan, his powerful legs flexed and the dwarf lifted the bricks. Apollisian turned to his belly and struggled to his feet. Amerix hoisted him up. "Tend yer woman. I'm going to find that wench and cut her from quim to skull."

Apollisian didn't reply as Amerix hurried off into the alleys. His heart felt like it would explode as he limped as fast as he could to Alexis. He plopped down in the snow and took her head in his arms. The light heat of her breath showed in the cooling air. He quickly shook his gauntlet from his hand and gently wiped the blood that ran from her mouth.

"I'm here."

Alexis opened her weak eyes and smiled through the pain. She delicately lifted her hand and placed it on his cheek. "I'm sorry. I fought her… the best I could."

Apollisian shook his head as tears began to well up in his eyes. "No, you did great. We ran her off."

Alexis smiled and let her arm fall to the snow. "I love you."

Apollisian felt the upheaval from his belly. Tears streamed down his face. "I love you. Just sit tight. I am going to find Lance."

Her smiled faded as she held his arm as firm as she could. "Please. Please stay with me to the end."

Apollisian felt a despair from his soul. His voice cracked. "No, I can't let you die. I can find him. I must find him."

A single tear streaked down from Alexis's smooth cheek. "And if you don't?"

Apollisian shook his head. "Please, my love. Please, don't make me watch you pass."

Alexis coughed and her face crinkled in pain. "Take a look in my eyes. See my love."

"You must let me find Lance, he can save you."

"Please. I am scared. Stay with me," Alexis begged through labored breaths.

"I must save you! I cannot live my life without trying."

Alexis pulled Apollisian close. Tears streamed down her blood soaked face. "You have saved me, Apollisian. Saved me from a life of suffering your death."

Apollisian buried his face in her neck and wept. "I cannot bear to lose you. I cannot bear to live a single moment without you."

"It'll be okay."

Apollisian pulled away as he held her bloodied and battered body in his arms. He stared longingly into her eyes as he sobbed.

"I love you, Apollisian. I always have," she said pausing to grimace in pain, "I loved you from the first time our eyes met in the market and I will love you until fate brings us together again."

Apollisian kissed her lips softly.

"I love you," Alexis strained to say with her dying breath.

Apollisian wailed as he held her body. He rocked back and forth in the snow like a mother would rock their child. The warrior of justice cried from his heart and from his soul as his empty tears fell into the lonely snow covered alley.

Petrovisk slowly rose to his tired feet. His hands and fur reeked of rotted filth from the fetid bodies of the walking dead. The mighty greyshalk glanced around the streets below him. The newly slain bodies were gone. Bodrell was not among them. Petrovisk shook his furred head sadly. Those that have fallen had risen up to join the ranks of their enemies.

The old warrior climbed down the waterspout and kept his keen ears to the streets. His tired feet were soothed by the cold snow that blanketed the streets. He made his way to the east, where his mate had decided to meet later. The tired old warrior wondered who from his family would be left to great him.

"Petrovisk."

The old warrior turned to see the dark elf, Artez. The light eyed dark elf had his kerstap tied to his back. The huge weapon looked awkward on the back of the small elf. The tired old greyshalk widened his stance and readied himself for battle. He had fought Artez in the orc wars.

"We've no time for old quarrels now, my friend," Artez countered, "The lines are broken. The Beyklans are trying to regroup in the coliseum."

Petrovisk nodded and thumbed the amulet around his neck. "I must find my family first."

Artez nodded, "They are to the north east, past the market. Come with me."

Petrovisk nodded and started to follow. Artez slung down the kerstap. The oversized weapon was as tall as the dark elf was.

 "Here, I found this in an alley. Thought you might want it."

Petrovisk smiled a wide grin as he picked up his old weapon. Perhaps the day was not going so bad after all.

Katrinal thumbed her light donjurik as she sat on the stone roof in Central City. Her father had arrived with the most peculiar looking elf she had ever seen. As she sat on the roof, the waning sun brought new sounds and terror for the night to come. The young greyshalk turned the blade over in her hand. It looked different now. It was no longer a tool her father used to scold her. Now, it had a purpose that was laid out clearly in front of her.

"Katrinal."

The young greyshalk turned to see her mother. The matre had climbed on the roof without her knowing. Moving silently and quickly has always been a talent of the ferocious Angelique.

"Yes, Mother?"

"Grogan is downstairs pestering your father and the elf. What are the dead doing?"

Katrinal glanced to the west, into the twilight. "They seem to be holding their lines. The Beyklans have regrouped and are trying to make walls in the city alleys."

Angelique nodded distantly. "Your father says those that have fallen have risen up and now march for the undead lord."

Katrinal scrunched her nose in disgust. "How does he do that?"

Angelique shrugged her furred shoulders. "I suppose that the body houses the magic needed to animate them. If the body is damaged, the magic slips out. That's why he can't reanimate corpses already destroyed."

"So is he picking them? It would take him forever to raise up everyone, we should strike now."

Angelique smiled at the wisdom her youngest was showing. "I think they just do it on their own."

"That makes sense. I have seen deer and other animals as well. He doesn't control it, it just simply works."

Angelique nodded distantly as she gazed toward the west. The sun flashed its twilight and disappeared behind the western horizon. "If any of us ever rise up, know that it is only our bodies. We will be dead."

Katrinal nodded, "Yes, Matre. But, surely there is a limit to how many he can control? Why not kill all those birds overhead? When his dark magic goes to make something rise up, it would be likely to pick a bird. They can't be near as dangerous."

Angelique glanced up to the hundreds of thousands of

birds that dived and rolled in the perpetual flock that hovered over the city. "My dear daughter, you are onto something."

Amerix wiped the sweat from his brow. That she-devil was nowhere to be found.

"Brohe-tah!"

Amerix turned to see the smiling face of Vlargcar running towards him. The massive orc scooped him up in his mighty arms and hugged him. Amerix's stubby legs kicked in protest.

"Put me down, ye ogre in orc's clothing!"

Vlargcar put Amerix down, but he beamed with a huge smile. "I knew you would come for me, Brohe-tah."

Amerix readjusted his armor. "I didn't come fer ye, ye blasted orc. I came to give this sword back. How come it took ye so long to escape?"

Vlargcar's smile faded. "It was hard. They didn't give you much chance."

"Bah! All that matters is that yer back."

Vlargcar's smile crept back on his face. "I did it, Brohe-tah. I learned to fight with two swords. I'm pretty good, too."

"That's good, Vlargcar. I have to give this sword back, then we can go to the under mountain."

Vlargcar's eyes lit up. "Under the mountain!?"

Songsinger's voice echoed in Amerix's ear. "Don't be a fool. You have already sealed the fate of the world, Son of Durion."

"Shut it, ye blasted sword. The world makes its own fate."

"No, sometimes it's determined by a foolish few."

Amerix ignored Songsinger as he and Vlargcar made their way back into the alley. His heart sank when he saw Apollisian cradling the elf's body. He felt a sting in his own eyes as he remembered what it was like to lose a wife.

The old general crunched through the snow and stood before the sobbing champion.

"Coming for revenge? Kill me, scum. For I have nothing

to live for."

The words echoed in Amerix's old ears. Songsinger must be allowing them to speak. "It's hard to lose a woman."

Apollisian did not look up. Tears dripped from his chin and fell into the cold snow. "How about a squire? Or the hundreds of other innocents you murdered?"

Amerix looked over to Vlargcar that was glancing to the west. Nightfall would be on them soon and the undead would surely use that to their advantage. The old general signed. "Aye. I have slain many. But now is the not the time for dying. It's the time for living." Amerix drew Songsinger and held the sword aloft in the pale evening light. The chrome blade glimmered in the dim alley.

Kill him, Son of Durion. Give him mercy.

Amerix turned the blade over in his hand and rammed it into the snow. The enchanted sword easily pierced the cobblestone street and lodged itself deep into the hard stone. "I carried this damned sword as a trophy to remind me of the champion that should have bested me."

Apollisian wiped snot from his nose.

"Take the blasted thing. Use it to inflict the pain on yer enemies that ye now feel. Use it to fuel yer need for justice."

No! Songsinger screamed in Amerix's ear, *This is not the way! You don't know what you are doing!*

Amerix turned to Vlargcar as he stepped away from Apollisian. "Come on, boy. I know some sewers near here that will take us into the undermountain."

Apollisian glanced up at Songsinger. The enchanted sword was stuck into the ground at Alexis's head. Like a symbolic tombstone.

Amerix walked past Vlargcar and into a side alley. "Come on, boy."

What about your path to your god, Son of Durion? You are turning your back on your creator!

Amerix gave a glance to Songsinger a final time. "Bah! He turned his back on me first!"

Vlargcar bounded after the old general as they made their way deeper into the alleys. "Where we go, Brohe-tah?"

"We have to get to the sewers. There's an old passage we

collapsed years back. It will take us to the undermountain."

Vlargcat scratched the small tuft of hair growing from his chin. "Why we go there? I want to go, but why now?"

Amerix glanced up at his hulking friend. "Well, 'cause I got some unfinished business with some dark dwarves."

Apollisian wrenched Songsinger free from the street and sheathed her in his empty scabbard. The cool west wind blew his blonde hair about his face. Small strands stuck to his wet cheeks as he stared at Alexis. She was gone. He gently scooped her up in his arms. He had carried like this before. Her head would nestle into his shoulder. But now, it hung backwards in death. He cried as he walked slowly through the snow filled alley. His boots crunched as he plodded to the north. He ignored screams that began to echo in the rapidly approaching nightfall.

I seldom spoke to you before, Songsinger said in his mind.

"Why start now, there is nothing to say."

There are those that still need you. Can't you hear their screams?

Apollisian narrowed his eyes. "What about what I need?"

Songsinger was silent as Apollisian stopped at the northern edge of the city. A wall of undead stood before him. The animated corpse of a woman in tattered yellow robes seemed to be leading them.

"Out of my way or I will destroy you," Apollisian warned.

Marzahna smiled. "Who are you? Has grief stricken you so, you dare come to our lines? You should be cowering like a hen while the foxes play."

"I am only going to tell you once, bitch."

Marzahna chuckled and waved her wrist. Dozens of necromantic weaves rocketed forward and surged into Alexis.

Apollisian gently laid his wife on the snowy earth. He wrapped her cloak under her head. He grabbed the necromantic threads with his hand and wrapped them around his fist.

Apollisian, how can you see those weaves?

"Because I want to."

There are too many. You don't have a link to Stephanis to call from. They are going to animate her. Take her head before they do. Do not allow her to be disgraced like this.

Apollisian narrowed his eyes and flexed his arm. To Marzahna's surprise, he ripped the tendrils from Alexis's body. The champion drew Songsinger and held her aloft in the snow.

No! Songsinger echoed as she began her shrill hum warning Apollisian of evil, *You cannot pull from him! You are not meant to follow him!*

Apollisian ignored her words. With a groan, he jerked on Marzahna's tendrils. The undead witch rocketed through the air. In one swift motion, Apollisian twisted back and cut the old witch in half. Her rotted body tumbled in two parts behind him sending up a small cloud of white snow.

There is no going back from this, Apollisian. This is a narrow ledge. If you fall…

The undead leapt into motion. Growling and gurgling, they charged through the snow.

Apollisian turned Songsinger over and held her, blade first, over the earth. "In the name of justice, I rebuke thee!" he screamed as he stabbed Songsinger into the frozen ground. A wave erupted in all directions. The earth cracked and rolled like an ocean wave. Snow was ripped up and hurled into the air. The undead were shattered like a melon under a sledge. Buildings toppled behind him and the air stood still.

Apollisian slowly wiped a golden strand of hair from his face as he surveyed his work. Thousands of undead lay around him, ripped apart. Several blocks of buildings were reduced to rubble behind him. The champion sheathed Songsinger once more and scooped Alexis up in his arms.

You cannot follow him, Songsinger pleaded, *You are sacrificing too much.*

Apollisian paused at the tree line outside of Central City. He waved his hand and the earth obeyed him. Dirt and stone tumbled away to form a grave.

See, Paladin. What god allows this? What god gives you pow-

er over earth and stone?

Apollisian kissed Alexis on her cold blue lips. A single tear drifted down his face as he laid her in her final resting place.

"The kind to give me justice."

No! Songsinger countered, *Not even Resh would approve this. If his power is so great then resurrect her.*

Apollisian waved his hand and turned back to the west. His cold blue eyes seemed distant. The frozen earth started to move once again and quickly covered Alexis. "He doesn't work like that."

And since when do you?

Apollisian lowered his head and marched to the west. "Since the death of my wife."

Songsinger's voice slowly drifted, *This is not justice, Apollisian.*

The paladin smiled out of the corner of his mouth. "It is for me."

Ehleeshuh trotted through the snow. Her once ivory hide was nearly black. She swished her equine tail in frustration. She didn't understand why her fur was changing color. It had to be a taint from the demon she was hunting.

Her blue eyes beamed ahead as she exited the forest. The unicorn paused at the spectacle. The sun was nearly set. A cloud of birds so thick that it nearly blocked out the sun hovered over Central City. The human settlement was blanketed by snow and an army was besieging it. The numbers of the attackers were so vast, they moved across the western plain like an army of ants. She had to hurry if she was going to navigate through the city streets to find the demon before it was too late.

"We must get with the others," Jude explained.

Kellacun distantly slid a lock of her sleek back hair behind her ear.

"Kellacun?"

She turned and nodded. "Yes.

Jude placed his large hand on her shoulder. He marveled at the texture of her armor. "It'll be ok."

Kellacun narrowed her eyes and knocked his hand from her shoulder. "I have seen worse than this, lummox."

Jude was taken aback. "You seemed upset, that's all."

Kellacun stormed off into the snow.

Jude glanced back to the west. The sun was almost set. He trotted after Kellacun. There was something about her that intrigued him. "Not because you were a woman that can't handle herself. But because of something else." Jude was no dunce when it came with women.

Kellacun didn't look at the large swordsman as they made their way from the collapsed inn. "Very perceptive. Yet, it is over and done. The task at hand is all we need to concern ourselves with."

Jude nodded. "So you seem to know this city fairly well."

Kellacun paused and turned to face the large man. "Do you not remember me? Surely you cannot be that stupid?"

Jude stepped back. "My lady, had I met someone with your deadly skills and ravenous beauty, I would have remembered."

Kellacun narrowed her eyes. "I am not some gutter strumpet that can be swooned with such pathetic compliments." *Joshua complimented her like that,* she thought.

"I am sorry. Maybe you have me confused with someone else," Jude said, "But we have to get moving. Dark will be on us and I am sure the undead will strike soon."

Kellacun narrowed her eyes and started walking east again. She would have to keep an eye on this fool. If he didn't remember her trying to kill the wizard he was running with a few years ago, he might lead her back to him. That boy was the only mark she ever missed.

"The simpler the mind, the less love it needs. A child requires the least amount of love compared to that of an adult, yet adults love each other least of all.

Some would disagree with me, but allow me to explain it like this: Let's take a war dog, or a domesticated wolf. One of the simplest minds we can use. The animal requires three things. Discipline, sustenance, and love. This is the proper order in which it needs them.

Discipline is the most important building block of affection. You must set boundaries and limitation to establish a foundation for love. I explained that there is no such thing as unconditional love. ALL love has conditions. Everything from devotion to fidelity. Culling activities that are not desired is discipline.

If you provide an animal or small child with things that it wants, or things that it needs to survive, it will feel loved. Just as you might surprise a romantic interest with flowers or an expensive dinner. This is the skeleton of creating love. If you did not give and only took, how far do you believe the relationship would go?

And finally, you must love to be loved. The funny thing is that even knowing this formula, understanding how love is little more than a trick that another can consciously place on your mind, most will still allow themselves to be lost in this farce of an emotion. The true trick of creating love is to simultaneously trick the other into the same thing they are trying to trick you into.

Perhaps true love then comes from willfully allowing yourself to be victimized like this with the faith that they have no ill intentions. A duality that is reciprocated by the other partner.

Love... will the gods even ever understand it?"

-Lancalion Levendis Lampara-

⌒❦17❦⌒
Enemies of Enemies

Katrinal sniffed the air.

"What is it?" Artez asked as he glanced to the dark alleys below.

"I smell the undead."

Artez moved to the edge of the roof. "Katrinal smells undead."

Petrovisk's smile faded as he enjoyed the company of his family. He snatched up his kerstap and moved to the edge of the old building. He raised his chin and sniffed the air. "It's not fresh. Could be a soldier."

Artez ducked low and moved to the edge of the roof. His yellow eyes scanned the darkening alleys. He relaxed and moved back to the edge of the crumbling roof. "It is two. A man and a woman. A big man."

Petrovisk stepped out into the snow covered alley. He thumbed the medallion around his neck. "Who approaches?"

"Jude and Kellacun," the voice replied, "The undead are preparing a second wave."

Petrovisk lowered his kerstap and glance back down at the medallion given to him by Bodrell. With this little trinket he could speak to tongue of the Beyklans. He wondered how many wars could have been avoided had they made this sooner.

Jude paused briefly when he saw the group. There was

a small dark elf and a family of greyshalks holed up in this crumbling building. He glanced down at Kellacun and recalled her transformation into the rat beast. Was he the only normal warrior fighting for Central City? Hell, it wasn't even his home and this was the second time he was caught in a war about it.

"No need to feel uneasy, Mister Jude," Artez offered, "Though we are unlikely comrades, we are still standing together."

Petrovisk waved his hand. "Bah. The elf is making pretty what is ugly. The undead have most of the Beyklans cut down. What are their numbers?"

Kellacun stepped forward before Jude could respond. "It seems as if it takes some time for the Abyss Walker to create new undead. The longer we sit here and do not form a counterstrike, the more forces he will gather up. Those that have died will have died for nothing."

Artez shifted uneasily when Kellacun said Abyss Walker.

Angelique thumbed her dirk. "What do you know of this Abyss Walker?"

Kellacun watched the greyshalk matre move. She was deceptively deadly. "I have heard whispers of him. My employer often mentions his role in a world event. I can only guess he was talking about this."

Angelique sniffed lightly. Kellacun had an odd smell about her. A coppery smell, like blood. Fresh blood. "Are you injured, Kellacun?"

Kellacun shook her head. "No, just eager to get back into the fray."

Grogan trotted from a southern alley. "Petrovisk, the Beyklans have regrouped near the collapsed bridge. They are several thousand strong and led by a wizard."

Jude thumbed his necklace as Kellacun looked confused. "We must go to them and convince them to lead a counter assault before the undead raise more to their ranks."

Petrovisk nodded as the others quickly gathered up their gear.

Kellacun glanced up to Jude. "How do you understand them?"

He thumbed the enchanted necklace. "Bodrell gave us these. They allow you to understand any language."

Kellacun smiled devilishly. She would have to get her hands on one of those before this battle was over.

Apollisian called forth the power that lingered around him. Somehow, he had become linked with a divine power that was close. Too close. A soft light encircled his hand as he called forth the power of this new god. He laid his hand on his chest and felt the warm tendrils of the divine weaves cover him. They healed his wounds, they gave him vigor, they gave him… power.

Apollisian marched down the cold snow covered street. The light wind blew his thick purple cloak behind him. The cape was tattered and torn and stained with his own blood. His armor was dirty and dented, but he stepped forward with a vengeful purpose.

This can be undone, Apollisian.

"I'm not interested, Songsinger."

She is gone, nothing is going to change that. You made the right decision to stay with her. She would have perished alone.

Apollisian ignored the biting wind as he marched into the abandoned streets of Central City. "I will have justice, Songsinger."

No, you will have vengeance. It will guide your decisions and cloud your wisdom.

Apollisian narrowed his eyes. "It will give me strength to defeat this monster. Alexis will not have died in vain."

It may give you power to defeat your foe, but at what cost?

Apollisian smiled wickedly. "I have already paid all that I have."

Petrovisk and Artez stalked through the snow covered

alleys. He often glanced back to make sure his family was safe. It was odd fighting alongside of them. While they gave him strength and warmth, they were also a distraction. He was not sure which one outweighed the other.

"We should be coming up on the Beyklans soon, Petrovisk."

The old greyshalk glanced down at the much smaller elf. It often amazed him how something so small could be so deadly. This one in particular. Elves just seemed so weak.

They group rounded the corner and met two Beyklan guards. They were adorned in their red and brass colored armor. Their helms were dirty and covered in ichor, but their capes seemed to be relatively clean.

"We are looking for the wizard and the Beyklans!" Petrovisk called out.

The guards seemed distant and uninterested at the spectacle standing before him. "Just keep going south. They are on the next block."

Artez smiled and thanked the guards as Petrovisk and the others pushed by.

The grouped rounded the corner of the next block and came into the Beyklan camp. They had set up defense fortifications. Hot oil cauldrons on roofs, as well as make-shift walls and spikes.

Jude placed his hand on Petrovisk's shoulder. "While you are handling the wizard, I will be examining our defenses. It seems they will be hard pressed to attack, now that they are sunk in."

Petrovisk shook his head. "They must attack if they want to live."

Jude nodded. He wasn't interested in being close to any wizard, except Lance. He had to search the ranks and find him.

"I'll go with, Jude," Kellacun offered.

Jude smiled. "That's fine. I could use a skilled sword."

Kellacun felt something warm inside of her. She had not been complimented in years. Maybe longer. What was his game?

Petrovisk clasped Jude by the shoulder. He could feel the feral power in the large Beyklan. "Try to convince any leaders that we must attack."

Jude nodded. "I will do my best."

Petrovisk nodded and motioned for his family to follow him. He liked being next to Jude. He was much like himself, but a bit younger. Full of honor and strength. Petrovisk glanced over to Grogan and bit his lip. Maybe Grogan wasn't as fine a kip as he thought. Odd how a human made the young greyshalk look weak and contemptible.

Jude rubbed his bare arms in the chilling air as he hurried through the western ranks. Kellacun kept pace with the large swordsman.

"Looking for your friend?"

Jude nodded. "Yes, Lance is his name. He is a good friend of mine."

Kellacun smiled. "The boy you ran with? The one with the black hair and the funny cloak?"

Jude paused. "Yes, do you know him?"

Kellacun smiled. "Yes, you two saved me from the dwarven attack. He is a handsome boy."

"Yes, he is a good friend. He was taken against his will. We both were."

Kellacun scanned the crowd. The soft tone in the big man made her feel warm inside. Maybe she wouldn't kill his friend. "Who took you? Slavers?"

"No, the elves of the Minok Vale."

"Why would they do that?"

Jude shrugged. "They believed he was the Abyss Walker, a fabled monster that was supposed to destroy them."

"Why would they think that?" Kellacun asked. Hector feared the Abyss Walker as well.

"He paid a rogue some money to steal these parchments that he thought would explain why his parents were murdered. Turns out they were some elven prophecy naming him the Abyss Walker."

Kellacun nearly choked. The boy she almost killed was

the Abyss Walker? The fabled monster that is supposed to destroy Hector?

"So is he the Abyss Walker? I mean, should we save someone who is supposed to destroy most of the known world?"

Jude shook his head. "No, he isn't the Abyss Walker. It's that damnable undead lord that we are fighting now."

Kellacun didn't say anything. There was no way Trinidy was the Abyss Walker. She heard Hector and Kalen talking about it. The Abyss Walker was a live man, not something that some dark priests created. "So why didn't the elves kill him?"

Jude shrugged. "How could they? He had not committed any crimes. I have recently learned that he was banished to Aten. The elves figured the she bitches would do their dirty work."

Kellacun nearly chocked again! That had to be the boy that the blue mother and Ramasiel fought over. Lance had to be the Abyss Walker? There was no other way to explain his survival despite so many treacherous odds.

"Your friend must be blessed as much as cursed to survive such difficult odds."

Jude paused and looked down into Kellacun's eyes. She had the prettiest eyes of any girl he had ever seen. "I guess you could look it at like that. I just want to find him again."

Kellacun poked Jude in the shoulder. "Well, I think your search is over. Is that him standing next to the tall dark haired woman?"

Jude felt his heart leap from his chest. "Yep!"

Petrovisk limped through the snow with the others behind him. The cold air was causing his old bones to ache. Artez hurried to match the greyshalk's long strides.

"General Bodrell?" Petrovisk called out.

A small thin man stepped forward. He had short brown hair that was graying. His hair line had receded with age, but his eyes still shined brilliantly behind his small round spectacles. "I am afraid the general has not arrived. I am in command."

Petrovisk looked the frail man up and down. The situation was worse than he expected. "I need to speak with whoever is in charge. Waiting for the monsters to attack is a folly."

"I am Arch-Mage Jonathon Klement. And unfortunately, I have become the reluctant leader of what is left of our forces."

Petrovisk scanned the street. There were maybe two thousand soldiers left. A few dozen elves and he didn't see any other greyshalks.

Artez pushed forward from behind the hulking Petrovisk. "We have deduced that the undead lord is using this time to raise our dead to join his ranks. Every second we wait, we make him stronger."

Jonathon shook his hands nervously and glanced off to the south for a moment before looking back. "Very well, we must begin our plan of escape."

"Escape?" Petrovisk snarled. "General, we must strike!"

Jonathon frowned. "I am no general."

"You are now!" Artez quipped, "You need to lead these men to victory, not run away. If we strike now, the undead lord will not expect it. We can catch him as he tries to raise more soldiers."

Jonathon but his lip and shook his hands again. "That explains the strong divine weaves that Lance said he saw to the west. I don't know how the boy can see divine weaves, but the others seemed to agree he could. I have never heard of a..."

"Stay on task, Genera!" Petrovisk snapped, "We need to hit him hard and fast. Like the Battle of Grimolakin Hill."

"We detected a large pool of necromancy coming from the coliseum. And that is where Lance said he saw the powerful divine weaves. If we were to strike there, that's most likely where the undead lord is."

Artez smiled. "Great! I will go rouse my brother elves. On your signal, we will strike!"

Petrovisk nodded slowly as the wizard hurried off. Finally, he was going to take the battle to the monsters.

"Jude?" Lance said as he turned towards the familiar voice. "Jude, it is you!"

Jude rushed forward and crushed Lance in his powerful arms. "I am so glad to finally find you again, my friend!"

Lance struggled to free himself. "Stop crushing me, oaf!"

"Sorry."

Lance straightened his sable black cloak. "How did you get here? I had heard you were a slave in the arena."

Jude nodded. "I was, but right before the undead attacked, they let us all free."

Lance smiled. "Good. It is good to see you. With all the magic radiating from the coliseum, I was worried my fath, uh, *Trinidy* had you."

Jude frowned. "Huh? Who?"

"Trinidy. The undead lord's name is Trinidy."

Kellacun nodded. "Yea about that, we have to hit him now. He is gathering his magic to raise all the recently slain soldiers to his ranks."

Jude nodded. "She's right. Oh, and yea, this is Kellacun."

Kellacun coked her head to the side and half curtsied. The silly etiquette almost made her giggle.

"Nice to meet you, this is my wife, Delania. We have little time to exchange pleasantries. We must let the arch-mage know what Trinidy is doing."

"Petrovisk went to do that. We will head out soon," Kellacun said.

Delania nodded. "Kellacun, you look familiar to me for some reason. Have we met?"

Kellacun knew that someone would recognize her. The assassin calmly smiled. "I don't think so, Madam."

Delania shrugged her shoulders. The woman was lying. She was sure Kellacun was the woman from Aten. The one that owned that gray elf. "My mistake."

"But, Sir. How will we guard the vault if we attack?" the soldier countered, "You know that's what the monster is after."

Jonathon nodded. "But, how can we not? If what they say is true, we have but a short hour before the undead lord completely restores his army… if not double it!"

The soldier stared at the snow covered ground for a second. "At the Battle of Stoneheart Hall, King Theobold sent his entire army into the Mist Valley. Half of it was decimated by the white dragon. While the fighting was going on, several scouts reported seeing the dwarves fleeing up the valley to their fortress. When we arrived, the doors were secured and we lost half our numbers again trying to break them down."

"And that means what? I am a wizard, son. Not a military man."

"If he had sent an excursion force, around the valley. He could have seen the dragon, and quite possibly, prevented the doors from being secured. You remember the Battle of the Torrent Manor?"

Jonathon nodded. "I do. Amerix sent his forces to attack the portcullis first. That move alone secured his victory with only a fraction of his army out from the tunnels."

"Exactly! Send a force of your best soldiers into the coliseum. They might draw the notice of the undead lord's main forces and they might be able to interrupt or stop his incantations."

Jonathon nodded. He knew full well that if a spell was disrupted, it would be nearly impossible to complete. "You are a great soldier. What's your name?"

"Sargoth, sir."

"I will ask the greyshalk to remain behind with us. I need you to go to the elves and ask them the same. We will need their talents to protect the vault."

"See the apex of the weave?" Lance pointed to the west. "Just above the coliseum."

Delania narrowed her eyes. There were so many weaves exploding from the coliseum she had a hard time discerning one school from another. "I see a lot of abjuration, Lance."

He nodded. "Yes, and the necromancy is woven into the abjuration. Whoever is casting it is making a portal."

"A portal?" Delania asked worriedly.

Lance shook his head. "Yea, and a big one, based off of the number of threads I see."

"Lance, if he is creating a portal that size, he is opening one to the Abyss!"

Lance frowned. "That's not possible. How could anyone do that?"

Delania tugged him by his cloak. "We have to get there and stop him!"

Lance motioned for Jude to follow him. "How is that possible, Delania? The Abyss is other worldly. Only windows can be opened. No doors."

Delania gave Lance a worried look. "There is much you have yet to learn, my love. Such a spell takes a lot of time to cast, but we must hurry. If we wait much longer, we may not be able to disrupt him in time."

Kellacun glanced back at the soldiers and then at Jude as he trotted off behind Lance and the sorceress. She felt a sadness to be leaving company with the large swordsman. Kellacun glanced back at the soldiers a final time before jogging after the trio. "Wait up."

"We all go through transformations in our life. Often, we don't even understand the emotion that sends us down the paths to these changes. For all the skill, ferocity, and resilience that Kellacun possesses, she is a great example of this truth.

Her father was slain, her mother raped and murdered by the duke's men and she became an agent against him. Pavicious catered to this and she became an assassin for him. The King of Nalir recognized her hatred for the duke and used it to help weaken the defenses of Central City when Trinidy attacked.

Despite all her power, Kellacun is as easily manipulated as small child. This is how politicians manipulate the masses to gain power. People cry about freedoms and tyranny so they can avoid the most important freedom of all, freedom of thought.

Kellacun began to enjoy the company of Jude, despite her original intentions of using him. She chose to indulge this idea. While she did this unconsciously, it was her first action she freely chose over someone else's manipulation.

Though, I cannot judge her. For even Lancalion Levendis Lampara himself was once led tight on the leash of manipulation. Unfortunately, my severing of that leash led to the most horrible conscious thought I would ever have to make. My love or my world."

-Lancalion Levendis Lampara-

Blood for Blood

Apollisian scanned the horizon. Bits of orange threads wrapped in black wispy ones danced and twisted over the buildings to the west. A soft glow that seemed to brighten with each passing second danced on the snowy central city surfaces.

"I can feel him. He is a god," Apollisian called out.

You can see the weaves, can you not?

"Yes, they are magnificent and ominous."

Songsinger sighed in his mind, *You are not supposed to be able to see them. He doesn't know how to distribute his power. You pull from it as a deer drinks from a stream.*

Apollisian tightened his grip on the sword as he stalked through the narrow alleys. "So what am I seeing?"

The bright orange glow is that of abjuration. A powerful school of magic used for altering reality. It is most often used to create portals, or to see into the future.

"So this undead lord is creating a portal? To where?"

The black tendrils that encircle the abjuration threads are that of necromancy. He is calling on an inherent evil.

"Then I will use my light to evaporate him. I will summon the righteous power of the boy and lay waste to this wickedness. I will do it for the people of Beykla, for Alexis… for me."

Songsinger hummed, *There is no righteousness to pull from. The power you pull from is from that of hurt and scorn. It is as dark as that in which you seek to destroy. You will not be able to stop Trinidy. You will fail.*

Apollisian chuckled. "Oh? And did I fail with the lich. Did I fail against those undead? They were shattered before me. Just as this 'Trinidy' will shatter before me."

No, Apollisian. You are not the one to do this. You will become lost. Amerix failed to see what he has done and you are playing into the hands of Bykalicus.

Apollisian narrowed his eyes as he marched. "I know not this Bykalicus. But he should be careful who he places in his hand. I am a scorpion ready to sting. I am a bee resting on his thumb, I am a viper poised to strike."

The champion of justice paused a block from the coliseum. He could see the bright orange tendrils whipping out from the inside like a giant coil of snakes. The undead in the distance turned to face him. They outstretched their arms and hissed menacingly.

Songsinger sighed heavily, *My boy, you may be all of these things. And your sting will be felt. But what happens to all of these things after they strike? They are crushed under a fist, or heel. This will happen to you as well.*

Apollisian set his feet wide and stretched Songsinger out before him as the undead savages rushed forward. "Let them try," he growled, "Let them try."

Trinidy sat on a stone throne looking out over the coliseum. His liches from the Lostom tower were encircled creating the largest portal he had ever seen. He was missing Marzahna, but he could no longer feel her. She must have been destroyed.

The death knight looked to his left at Nefertora. Her six arms were bound to her sides with his evocation. "I am going to deliver you to your master, bitch. You have failed."

The demon general's snake tail twitched in anger and

frustration. "Every second you tarry with me, you lose the opportunity to add to your ranks. We want the same thing. We want the Abyss Walker destroyed."

Trinidy removed his helm. His thin stringy black hair blew about his rotted face. He reached up and plucked a scorpion from his nose and hung it out in front of him. "No, I want you destroyed for what you have done to me!" he screamed, "Look at what I have become!"

Nefertora hissed in anger. She spit at him. Her acidic bile burned and sizzled on his face and armor. "My master created you. He will destroy you! He will rip your soul from that weak, rotting body, and he will punish you for an eternity!"

Trinidy's rotted face twisted in anger. He drew his blade and rammed it into the stone floor. The polished marble cracked and flaked under the power of the wicked blade. "You know nothing of torture, you worm!"

Nefertora laughed. Her long snake like torso coiled around her. "What will you do to me? This body is nothing. It is a manifestation on this realm. Go ahead and open a portal. The pull to kill the boy will keep you from entering. If you try, you will be destroyed and your soul will return to the Abyss. It will return to Bykalicus."

The liches stopped chanting. The bright orange weaves formed a complete circle. It was as wide as the coliseum floor and as high as the tallest seat. Bight tendrils snaked and erupted from the circle as black necromantic wisps danced around it. The entire coliseum took on an eerie orange glow.

"It is done, My Lord. All you must do is step to the edge and walk through."

Trinidy smiled. "I will kill your unsuspecting master. My liches have hidden this magic here. Bykalicus will not know I am coming until I am through."

Nefertora let out a sinister laugh. "You cannot get through fool, your job is not done."

Trinidy smiled. "I will right that which is wrong. The boy will come to me. I can feel him nearing."

"Oh, and what will you do, stab him? His power is more than you can imagine. You're a fool that will soon be crushed. You have not the power to destroy him,"

Trinidy laughed. "Destroy him? You stupid bitch. I'm going to bind him. Bind him into an eternity caught between the two worlds. He will roam the ethereal plane like a nomad amidst an infinite forever. And once I do, you will follow. He will have nothing but you to appease his desires and whims. I suspect you will not enjoy being the object of his attention."

Nefertora felt her body flush. Bykalicus would surely torture her for her failure. She needed to warn her master. "Yes, kill the boy. Do as you were created to do. Do as Bykalicus wants you to. You will obey, dog!"

Trinidy smiled revealing his rotted twisted teeth. "You wish to anger me now. Your words of carelessness are now focused. Why is that, she-demon? Why have your words changed?"

Nefertora hissed and spit. She struggled in her magical bonds, but she could not free herself. "You are a coward. Strike me down! You lack the strength. You are the lowest gweit that nibbles the shit from a spawn's ass!"

Trinidy chuckled. "And destroying you here would send you right back to the Abyss. So you can warn your master. You so much as gloated the fact earlier. Tell me, Nefertora. Are all the demons as stupid as you are? If so, I will easily conquer the Abyss in Bykalicus's absence."

Nefertora franticly scanned the weaves, she could break them if she had time.

"My Lord, the Beyklans have regrouped and now defend the vault of the city," one of the liches called out.

Trinidy narrowed his eyes before turning away from the demonic general. "What is significant about this vault?"

"We are not sure, but the Mark of Panoleen is on the door."

Trinidy felt his inner soul leap with emotion. The insects that scattered from his nose to his mouth fell from his face and writhed on the floor as their black shells turned white. His armor brightened and the wicked glow in his eyes dimmed. "NEVER say that name in my presence!"

The lich lowered her rotted head. "Yes, My Lord. But, what shall we do with it?"

Trinidy rubbed his chin as the light faded from him and the insects on his face blackened and resumed their skittering ways. "Take the ghouls, take everything, and capture this vault. The boy must be guarding it for a reason. It was not a coincidence that he returned here. Crush them all, and report back what is in the vault."

The lich nodded. "Yes, My Master. But, who will defend the portal?"

Trinidy chuckled as he ripped his blade from the stone floor. "I have poured a little of myself into this blade. I call it Renis-gnos. I learned the trick from my wife. The blade will serve me well."

The lich bowed deeply. "Yes, My Master. Are you sure this is wise? To guard the portal with just you and Renis-gnos? And what of the ghouls? We could use more in our ranks. Our numbers are but a third of what they were."

Trinidy's eyes began to glow brighter. "Why are you still here?"

The lich did not reply. She hurried from the coliseum loft and down the stairs to the ghouls.

Petrovisk sat in the snow and sharpened his great kerstap. He ran the whetstone down its edge slowly and meticulously, before deftly reversing his flow and running it back up the other side. Katrinal and the others sat beside him, doing the same.

"What are we guarding, Father?" Katrinal asked. "Why are we not with the Beyklan wizard and his woman?"

Petrovisk did not glance up from his weapon. "Because our duty is here. The Beyklans have something the Abyss Walker wants within their vault. We must stay here and buy our comrades some time."

Angelique roughed the fur on Katrinal's head with her claws. "Our little lover of colors has decided she wants to know of tactics and warfare."

The other girls chimed in with a guttural laugh.

"We should leave!" the legionnaires shouted. "There is nothing to be gained here."

Artez motioned for them to quiet. "The Abyss Walker wants what is in the Beyklan's vault. It has an ancient symbol on the door. That of the fallen goddess."

The others mumbled amongst themselves. "What of the other captains? What of Kendalerairy or Tylergaiden? Our captains are lost or slain. What duty do we have to remain?"

Artez hung his head low. "You have no duty but that which dwells in your hearts. If you do not sense it, then leave. I do not want to fight against my brethren that are already defeated."

"How can we leave? The undead surround us."

Artez pointed to the north. "There are none to the north. Several thousand have been decimated. Beyklan civilians have been funneling out to the north for several hours now. If you hurry, you can probably make it."

Artez watched sadly as his brethren started to get up and march north. A few went at first. Several turned into dozens and dozens turned into scores. The Abyss Walker need not fight for the treasures in the vault. His people might as well hand deliver it to him.

Apollisian marched forward through the alleys. The cold west wind blew his violet cape behind him as he walked. The streets were surprisingly bare of undead. Had the monster fled? Had the Beyklans been able to actually defeat him?

Apollisian rounded the corner of an old stone building and set his eyes on the coliseum. It was as great as the first time he saw it. The warrior of justice marveled at how something so beautiful could represent an instrument of vile wickedness. It was fitting that the undead monster hid within its walls.

"Turn back, Apollisian."

Apollisian chuckled. "My destiny awaits me within those stone walls. I have lost everything out here. In there I can reclaim some justice."

Vengeance, Songsinger countered.

"You may call a sword any name you wish, but it will remain what it is."

The only thing that awaits you in there is damnation.

Apollisian started up the snowy stairs of the coliseum. The great brown stones of the archway loomed over him as the great tabards of Beykla's royalty hung down. The silent banners slowly fluttered in the cold wind.

"Living without Alexis is my damnation, sword."

Apollisian, you have no idea what damnation is.

Apollisian started up the stairs. "Really? My father abandoned me and my mother when I was six. I nearly watched my mother raped on streets of Central City, forcing me to kill a man before I reached age eleven. I grew up in the academy with no family and the only person that I loved as an equal was murdered by a succubus."

That was not a succubus, Apollisian. That was something else.

"It doesn't matter. It could have been a tavern wench. Alexis is dead."

And you will be too if you walk through those doors.

Apollisian looked up to see several small stone archways. There were booths on each side, probably for ticket takers when the arena had matches. There was a deep orange and violet glow coming from inside. "See those, Songsinger? Those are the colors of Stephanis."

You no longer follow Stephanis. You have abandoned him for a god that doesn't even understand himself. He doesn't even know that you draw from his power.

Apollisian walked through the archway and gazed into the arena. His blue eyes feasted on a terrible and amazing sight. A bright orange portal that was several dozen feet high rested just above the arena floor. Great bolts of fiery arcs erupted from the edges of the portal as thin wispy black tendrils wrapped around them. The portal illuminated the entire coliseum with an eerie orange glow.

There is no turning back, Apollisian.

"Why would I want to?"

Because Trinidy has spotted you.

Apollisian turned to his left. He could see the monstrosity moving toward him. He wore a suit of thick plate armor that was littered with runes and skulls. His dark black cape was torn and fluttered in the light wind. He carried an odd sword that was much like Songsinger, except the blade was blood red. His shield was thick and looked too heavy to be wielded effectively. It bore a large bleached white demonic skull that had bright glowing blue eyes.

"Are you the monster that brought this undead to my country's door?!" Apollisian screamed.

Trinidy stalked forward. "I am the hero that is going to rid the world of evil."

Apollisian unstrapped his helm from his belt and placed it on his head. "Your devil's killed my wife. I am going to kill you."

Trinidy narrowed his rotted glowing blue eyes and brought his sword down. "I am already dead!"

Apollisian brought up his shield and deflected the blow. The strength behind the strike was unearthly. He staggered back as the death knight continued forward.

"You are a fool to come against me. You should have followed your wicked countrymen and ran like cowards."

"I will not rest until you are destroyed. You created me, monster. Now you must reap what you sow." Apollisian growled and slammed his shield out and then stabbed low with Songsinger. Trinidy parried the strike with Regnisgnos. The shrill ring of the two swords striking one another echoed throughout the coliseum.

Trinidy sliced his shield in high at Apollisian. The blow caught the paladin off guard. Apollisian staggered back and parried a thrust from the undead lord. The enchanted blade sliced a thin groove in his chest armor. Apollisian was forced down the stairs towards the center of the coliseum. He started to feel weak and tired. His armor was beginning to feel heavy.

Songsinger quipped in, *You are dying, Apollisian. The evil from this monster is aging you. I can shield you from his aura, but I am not sure how long I can prevent it.*

"What do you mean we stay here?"

Stieny munched on a small dried apple and relaxed on the top of an ale barrel. "Just what I said."

Fehzban brushed dust from his sleeves. "The entire inn has collapsed on top of us. We're stuck in this damned cellar."

"So?"

"So?!" Fehzban shook his head. "So our friends are out there fighting the undead. Where we should be!"

Stieny stuffed the last bit of dried fruit into his mouth and popped the cork on a small wine bottle. "And do what? The monsters have surely broken the lines. Our friends aren't stupid. They'll flee."

"And what if they can't?" Fehzban countered. "What if they are stuck up there and need our help?"

Stieny took a long swig from the bottle. "What will we do? You don't seem to be a warrior. You said yourself you can't wield Leska's power and I am clearly not suited for warfare."

Fezbhan grunted as he pulled a piece of broken timber from the stairs. "We do what we can. Anything we can."

Stieny rolled his eyes. "Fine. You're gonna get us killed you know."

"Just shut up and help me move these rocks."

"Steel yourselves!" Petrovisk growled. His yellow eyes took in the horrid site of the undead as they pierced the edge of the alleys and began to bore down on the remaining Beyklan forces.

"Just like old times?"

Petrovisk glanced to his right and gave a broken fanged toothed smile. "King Minostak. You've survived thus far."

"I couldn't let you have all the fun."

Petrovisk nodded and turned back to the advancing

wave. "Steady, girls. Don't break rank yet. Let them come to us then funnel them down this street to the Beyklans and the wizard. Give them a clear line for his wizard fire."

"My enemy's enemy is my friend? How often I have heard this mentioned. But what happens when my enemy's enemy is also my enemy?

No, those that wish to have a victory must learn to align themselves with those they must. But, all the while understanding that just because an enemy is not attacking you does not mean he is your friend. I find those that live the longest are those that grasp this truth. Well, at least before their enemies do."

-Lancalion Levendis Lampara-

19
Tooth and Nail

Petrovisk brought his kerstap down in a wide slice. The heavy weapon took two undead down at a time with each stroke. King Minostak ducked and sliced with his morning star and shield. It was good to be fighting next to his mate and his king.

"Why do they have to be filled with such rotten ichor?" Angelique growled.

Katrinal chuckled as her slender donjurik made thin slices that felled her foes without spilling much of their fetid black blood. "I'm not having much difficulty, Matre."

Anglique snarled. "You're using that skinning blade. I am using a real warrior's weapon."

Katrinal smiled curtly. Her mother wielded heavy blades that affixed to her wrists. Katrinal couldn't remember what they were called. But, clearly her donjurik was much better for cleanliness.

"Don't sass your matre, Katrinal!" King Minostak warned as his heavy morningstar crushed one of his foes. "Her weapons are perfect for fighting normal enemies. Normally, the sheen of her enemy's blood covers her fur."

"Gross." Katrinal stabbed an undead under his chin.

Petrovisk smiled. "It inspires fear in her enemies and the coppery smell of their blood fills her nose with fury."

Cathena flinched as a large flash of light followed by

a boom ripped a dozen undead into several pieces. Their writhing mangled bodies continued to twitch as the hole in the ranks were soon replaced. "What the hell was that?"

Cheural chuckled as she skewered another undead with her spear. "I call them poppers."

"Is it magic?" Katrinal asked.

Angelique quipped in. "You know Cheural is a gadgeteer, Katrinal. Just another one of her gadgets."

Petrovisk crashed his fist into an undead's face. The rotted skull exploded into a shower of ichor and fetid brain matter. "That's a popper."

They all had a hearty laugh.

My God, Jon thought to himself. The wave of undead seemed to pour out from every city orifice. If he and his defenders had destroyed any of them, the numbers were lost in the sea of undeath.

Jon glanced all around. His lines were broken, his soldiers were swept under like a castle of sand before the rising tide. The tired middle aged wizard wiped sweat from his brow. He steadied himself atop the small stone platform under the statue of the late King Thoebold. The screams of dying men and the dull sound of their undead attackers filled his ears. Yet, the wizard summoned. He pulled in hundreds of abjuration weaves.

"My Lord, what are you casting?" a young wizard asked.

Jon twisted and turned his body as he gathered up weave after weave like a sailor gathering up a mooring line. "I am going to take us and the vault from here."

"But where will we go? How will we get back?"

Jon did not answer. He began to cast the weaves out around them. The bright orange threads anchored themselves in a circle around the defenders.

The young wizard blasted out weaves of blue evocation, shattering the rotted bodies of several undead.

Jon set the weaves. The thick orange bars slammed into

the cobblestone street sending up bits of rock and debris. "Anywhere is better than here. The fight is lost, we must stop the Abyss Walker from reaching this vault."

The earth around Petrovisk exploded like thousands of great spikes were rammed into the cobblestone street around him. The mighty greyshalk sliced down and cleaved an undead from skull to groin. The two halves twitched and writhed before him. "Careful with your tricks, Cheural."

"Not my tricks, Father."

Katrinal frowned. "Father, I can see them. A strange orange light, but like a rod. There are thousands of them."

Angelique slashed down and twisted her weight to bring her other blade across, severing the head of her attacker. Black ichor oozed out and covered the street." I don't see anything.

"Nor I," Petrovisk growled.

Katrinal slashed in with her donjurik. "That doesn't change the fact they are there. And they are growing. It is forming some sort of net."

"I don't like this," King Minostak growled, "Get out of here. Take your family to the south. I will meet you there soon. This is likely foul dark magic of the Abyss Walker."

Petrovisk nodded. His weary old bones were glad to be moving. He earned no satisfaction in defeating these foes. "Come on."

Angelique motioned for the girls to follow. They ducked out of the skirmish and went south. Several undead turned to see them leave, but they were not followed.

Petrovisk glanced back to see King Minostak, and the front lines, falling back deep into the growing orange dome. Every second a score of Beyklans fell. The old greyshalk couldn't see any of the Darayal Legion among their ranks. "We have lost."

"What's wrong, Brohe-tah?"

Amerix sat in the dark underground cavern. His bare feet dangled in the pool as small beovi nibbled his toes. "Just thinkin' bout that Beyklan champion."

Vlargcar dangled his monstrous green feet in the pool as well. "We should go help him. You are good at all things. Even better at feet fishing."

Amerix glanced over to see that Vlargcar was moving his feet too much for the beovi to even want to come close. "I think I should go back. Ye should stay here, Vlargcar."

The giant orc shook his head. "No, Brohe-tah. What if something bad happens?"

Amerix smiled and patted the orc on the shoulder. It seemed as he had been carved and not born. "Nothin' to worry about, boy. This is more a personal errand. I'll be back for certain. Ye stay here and work on feet fishin'. Some roasted beovi would really hit the spot."

Vlargcar nodded. "Okay, Broh-tah. You hurry back. I'll catch a lot of fish for us."

Amerix smiled and sighed. He never would have thought he would come to love an orc as his own child. The grizzled old general reached over and snatched up his stockings. He slid his damp feet in and began to place on his boots. How many more times would he do that before he died? It began to dawn on the old dwarf that he had missed many of the finer things in life. When he returned, he would enjoy them with his only friend.

"This is eerie, Lance," Delania offered as she thumbed her necklace. It seemed to be getting warm.

Jude trotted forward. He moved his muscular arm in front of Delania, Lance, and Kellacun. "Stay behind me as we move in. I'll meet the first wave."

Kellacun frowned. *Was he serious? What kind of fool believed he was more equipped with a sword than two skilled magic users?*

"It's okay, Jude. I've progressed much since we last met. Plus, Delania is more powerful than I am. There's no need for you to risk yourself."

Delania nodded and thumbed her necklace. It was defiantly growing warmer. "While your intentions are appreciated, warrior, let me and Lance handle this. Save your sword for a more worthy foe."

A more worthy foe? Jude thought to himself.

Kellacun could see the pained expression on the large man's face. She placed her gloved hand on Jude's shoulder. He felt thick and powerful-like a good horse. "No worries, you can keep me safe."

Jude offered her a half-hearted smile. "Never fear, Kellacun. I'm no dunce. Once upon a time, he would have died without me."

Kellacun smiled. "I'm sure of it. But now, let's allow them to deal with this undead lord."

Jude nodded and followed Lance and Delania up the snow covered coliseum stairs. The bright orange and violet wisps of light seemed to flicker and dance, lighting up the sky above them.

Delania pulled her cloak tight around her. The colored clouds reminded her of the Abyss. They tumbled and danced within themselves like muddy billows in a murky stream.

"Be careful." Lance started up the stairs. "I hear sword fighting."

Petrovisk limped around the corner of a building. His old leg was beginning to slow him down. Angelique tried her best to help him move as the girls covered their retreat.

"They're not following us," Katrinal offered in surprise, "The undead are all fixated on that vault."

Cheural pointed to the growing bright orange dome. The brilliant threads of magical energy had woven a near perfect transparent dome that covered several city blocks. The soldiers had fallen back well within its borders and the thousands of undead were driving towards the vault. Several of Trinidy's liches were summoning deep necromancies. The wispy threads encircled the rotting sorceresses as they channeled them.

Cathena cocked her head to the side. Her pointed ears twisted forward. "What are they doing?"

Petrovisk placed his head on the cold brick wall. It felt good on his weary head. He lowered his kerstap and leaned on it like a cane. The round pommel fit his hand perfectly. He was too tired to look. "Just tell me when the undead are coming."

A low hum began and the ground began to tremble. The snow that covered the streets began to sift within itself and covered the greyshalk's tracks. The orange dome began to grow brighter.

"We need to get farther away," Petrovisk growled. He forced himself from the stone wall. He continued to use his giant sword as a cane as he limped south away from the dome.

"Come on girls," Angelique said.

Katrinal backed off, but kept her eyes fixated on the brilliant colors. The swirling dome was so beautiful.

Angelique grabbed Katrinal by the arm. "We need to…"

The dome erupted in a white hot flash. A circular wave blasted out from the dome incinerating all of the undead around it. Their torn fetid bodies were reduced to a thick black vapor that was quickly mixed with the brick and stone debris of the surrounding buildings. The force of the blast leveled several circular blocks and sent rocks, dirt, and stone raining down around them. The building next to them shook, and the snow was blown clear.

Petrovisk kicked in a side door. "Get inside."

Angelique hurried the girls in behind their father. His kerstap was at ready in case any undead were hiding inside.

Rocks began to rain down. Some were the size of small boulders. They crashed down through the roof of the small building sending up a cloud of dust and debris.

The greyshalks huddled together. Petrovisk covered them. He was afraid. Never in all of his days had he seen such power, or felt the earth tremble. Several minutes passed. The dust settled and rain of debris had ended.

Katrinal poked her head outside of the door. "In Larunthus's name..."

Petrovisk and the others moved to the door. To their surprise, the dome was gone. All that was left was a several hundred foot deep hole in the earth. It looked as if someone had taken a giant spoon and neatly gouged out a hole in the city. Sewer passages were exposed and leaked water into the crater. Around the crated every building had been annihilated. They had been reduced to small lines or rock outlining their foundations. The city's civic building stood like a rebellious beacon at the edge of the blast radius. But to the greyshalk exhilaration, it seemed as if all the undead had been destroyed.

"What happened?" Cheural asked.

Petrovisk let out a long sigh. "The wizard either destroyed himself and the vault they were protecting, or the undead witches did. Either way, they all are gone."

"But, had we not moved..." Katrinal said as her eyes welled up with tears.

Angelique placed her furry arm around Katrinal's shoulder. "Then we would be dead too."

Cathena stared on quietly. Her yellow eyes took in the destruction in quiet contemplation.

Cheural turned to Petrovisk. "Now what, Father?"

Petrovisk reluctantly took his eyes from the devastating scene. "We came to help the Beyklans protect the vault and defeat their enemies. It seems neither exists any longer. We'll return home. I think it may be time for me to retire."

Angelique smiled absently. "I've been telling you that for years."

"Some say you know when it is time to hang up your sword. Your muscles get old, your reflexes slow, but are they?

How could someone see what they once were without coping with what they are now? A master swordsman learns to cope with his body's aging. His fighting style changes, but as long as his mind is sharp, he can cope. But even then, there will come a day that he recognizes he must stand behind the protection of others until death claims him.

A wizard has no such sensibilities. His body is not needed to wield his power. No, there is no great balance. There is only his mind. There is no grace a wielder in the arcane arts can have when it is time to slink back into the soft chairs of retirement. No, the curse and blessing of being powerful while your body wanes is like that of a bursting waterskin. You don't know your time is coming until it's too late. I often wonder what a wizards last thought is? I guess time will tell."

-Lancalion Levendis Lampara-

~20~
Father and Sons

Apollisian's head rocked back from the blow of Trinidy's shield. He stumbled down the stairs. His metal armor grated against the stone railing of the coliseum. Blood dripped from the gash in his face like a drizzling faucet.

"I'm going to kill you." Trinidy stepped down the stairs slowly. His rotted face shined orange in the glow of the large portal.

Apollisian weakly leaned on Songsinger as he forced himself to his feet.

"You're resilient, boy." Trinidy mocked.

Apollisian, you must get away. Regain your strength, Songsinger warned.

Apollisian lay on the stone rail and gently tried to lower himself to the center of the arena. His weak body failed and he fell. His armor made a dull clang on the arena's dirt floor.

Apollisian could feel his strength returning.

Songsinger pleaded with him, *Apollisian, you must flee. This foe is beyond you.*

Apollisian stood defiantly and backed to the center of the arena floor. The massive orange portal hummed and chimed behind him as its flickering power lit up the cloud covered night sky. His tattered and torn blood-soaked cape fluttered in the wind. The warrior of Stephanis pointed Songsinger at the undead knight. "Come to me, monster. Come to me so that I may slay you!"

Trinidy's rotten face cracked a twisted smile. The stones from the coliseum twisted and shook. They formed a small staircase in front of the death knight and he casual walked to the arena floor.

Apollisian could feel his strength beginning to wane… and then he felt it again. That power he pulled on when he buried Alexis. It was near. Apollisian pulled from it. He could feel it coursing through him.

Trinidy stepped to the coliseum floor.

He is not your foe, a strange feminine voice echoed in Trinidy's ear. It was a dark powerful voice.

"He stands in the way of my destruction of evil. Those that defend evil are evil." Trinidy answered.

Ignore her, Apollisian, Songsinger countered, *She has been forged from pain and misery.*

Apollisian rushed forward. He pulled the power he felt inside and channeled it into Songsinger. He placed both hands on the ancient blade and brought it down. Trinidy moved Rengis-Gnos and deflected the strike. There was a tremendous flash as both weapons collided with one another. The death knight side stepped the blow and struck Apollisian in the back. The holy warrior fell forward. He landed awkwardly and rolled to his back. Trinidy continued to spin and brought his wicked crimson Abyssal blade streaking down towards the helpless paladin.

"There!" Lance pointed. They could see Apollisian standing in front of a massive portal to the Abyss. Great winged demons danced and darted in a black and yellow sulfurous sky on the other side.

Delania quickly surveyed the scene as Kellacun and Jude rushed down to help the paladin. Her blue eyes fell onto Nefertora, one of Bykalicus's demonic generals. "Be careful, Lance. You deal with the undead. The real monster is here."

Lance stopped on the stairs. "It's not my father? I mean,

Havrion. It's not Havrion?"

Delania pointed to the glowing green bars that held a shadow figure in place. "Not likely."

Lance glanced down as Kellacun and Jude leapt over the edge of the balcony. "She looks trapped. Maybe we should help them instead?"

Delania smiled. "We need to send her back to the Abyss first. Shouldn't take too long.

Lance nodded and reluctantly followed.

"Nefertora, you fucking snake. Why are you here?"

Lance frowned. "You know it?"

The demonic general writhed in her magical bonds. Her long serpentine tail swished angrily. Her six arms struggled against the thousands of tiny green rings, but she could not move. "How do you know my name, wench?" The arch-demon answered in her demonic tongue.

Delania smiled and began harnessing her own orange weaves. The strands of abjuration whipped around her. "Not all of us are bound to this realm by deceit and magical anchors."

Lance glanced back at the battle. "Hurry, Delania. They may need our help."

Delania ignored the taunts and threats from Nefertora. She quickly encircled the trapped demon and with a quick tug and collapsed the orange globe on top of her. With a small flash, she was gone.

"What'd ya do?"

Delania hooked Lance's arm and started toward the others. "Demons can't exist on this realm without an anchor. Like any ship in a harbor, if you pull up their anchor they'll float out to sea."

Lance nodded and narrowed his eyes. "Okay, let's finish this. I'm tired of running."

Kellacun rushed down the stairs as she quickly transformed into her hybrid form. Her face elongated and her eyes darkened. The assassin's smooth pale skin was replaced by shimmering black fur. She drew her twin blades as her nimble feet landed on the stone coliseum rail and launched her high into the air. Her dull black eyes looked down on the undead lord as he approached Apollisian.

Jude watched in awe at how quickly Kellacun transformed from seemingly delicate woman to vicious monster. He found himself awe inspired at the feral ferocity that the woman possessed. The large man drew his great sword from his back and rushed down the stairs into the arena.

Kellacun turned her swords over in her hands as she plummeted towards the death knight. Her hybrid visage snarled and stabbed her blades deep into Trinidy's shoulders. She quickly withdrew the enchanted blades and tumbled to the ground next to Apollisian. Black ichor dripped from her keen swords.

Trinidy stabbed Regnis-Gnos into the arena floor and summoned a powerful glove of evocation before hurling it at Kellacun.

Apollisian extended his shield in front of Kellacun. The blast from the globe sent out a flash that lit the arena like a lightning bolt lights up the night sky and knocked them from their feet. Smoke and steam poured from the red hot shield. Apollisian struggled to remove it as the molten metal began to burn his arm.

Jude growled as he brought his blade down. The heavy weapon struck Trinidy's thick back plating and severed his long tattered cape in a jagged slash. The death knight whirled and struck Jude in the chest with his shield. The large man tumbled from his feet.

Delania channeled a globe of evocation and hurled it at Trinidy. The blast struck the undead general in the chest. He staggered backwards and clutched the red hot breastplate. The soft blue glow from his eyes intensified and the black insects skittered across his face excitedly. Long tendrils of necromancy erupted from his shield. They snaked outwards like a spider's legs and then shot into the hard arena dirt floor.

Apollisian shook his singed shield from his arm. "I don't

know what you are, rat. But this foe is beyond you."

Kellacun smiled wryly. Her black bulbous eyes gleamed under the orange hue of the dark portal. "Men and their egos," She said as she leapt at Trinidy.

"What's he casting, Lance?" Delania asked. "There are so many weaves. I never seen so many."

Lance strained his eyes. "It looks as if he is creating something. But, he isn't guiding them. It's coming from his shield."

Kellacun rushed forward with her swords extended behind her when the arena floor shook and trembled. The hard compacted dirt cracked and shifted.

Apollisian grabbed Songsinger and ran to Kellacun. "Get back!"

In moments a creature emerged from the depths of the coliseum floor. It was formed of hundreds of bones from various races and animals. The monstrosity stood nearly twelve foot tall. A soft blue glow, much like that of Trinidy, shone from inside the monster's body. It had seven heads that orbited a central ball of azure energy. The golem outstretched its arms as if to roar.

Lance ran to the arena rail. "Jude! You and Kellacun deal with that thing. We'll take Trinidy down!"

Jude charged the bone monstrosity. The apparition turned and hammered its fist into the arena floor. The crumbling dirt shot out in a cloud of debris and knocked Jude from his feet.

Kellacun leapt through the air. Her keen enchanted blades slashed deep groves in the fiend's thick bone legs. She ducked a swipe and tumbled away from Jude.

"Try to hold him!" Delania shouted as she hurled blot

after bolt of evocation.

Lance pulled from the weaves he had created in Aten to wrap the undead lord in a full bar hold spell. "I can't seem to get them to form around him. It's like they can't stick to him."

Delania continued to hurl bolt after bolt. Trinidy deflected each strike with his shield, but the force of the blasts were keeping him off balance.

Lance hopped from the ledge. He gathered a thin form of the energy from inside of himself. He created a knife of glowing transparent energy that wrapped around his hand. In a swift motion he brought the blade down and severed the thick black tendril hat connected himself and the death knight.

Trinidy howled in pain. His blue eyes lit with fury and his rotted face contorted in pain and anger, The death knight ducked low and hurled his shield. The circular shield whistled through the air and struck Delania in the chest. She let out a muffled cough and was hurled backwards into the stairs.

Apollisian rushed forward. He lashed in with Songsinger. The enchanted blade easily cut through the dead lord's armor and went deep into his shoulder. Pieces of metal and rotted flesh fell to the arena floor. Hundreds of black centipedes and scorpions drained out like a spray of animated blood.

Trinidy howled in pain. He stepped backwards and deflected another slice from the champion of justice and forced his blade to the side. He punched Apollisian in the side of his head. The stunned paladin lost his footing and went to his knee. Trinidy raised his empty hand and stabbed down with his elbow. The thick black spike from the death knight's armor pierced through Apollisian's plate. The champion of justice howled in pain. He weakly tried to reach the elbow spike.

Trinidy raised Regnis-Gnos for the killing blow. "You were a fool to stand against me."

Lance rushed forward. His spells seemed useless against the death knight, but he was not going to let Apollisian die.

He shouldered his body into the Trinidy. Apollisian rolled out from under the spike and struggled to his feet.

Delania lay on her back and stared up at the night sky. Her ears were ringing and her vision was blurry. She turned her head to look at Trinidy's shield. The hard skull covered metal disc had begun to melt. The edges of it were floating away in a soft blue magical glow that seemed to drift away into nothingness on the evening breeze. She tried to sit up, but her chest hurt too badly. She coughed up a warm sticky substance that drained from her mouth and pooled on the cold arena seats. *Blood?* She thought to herself, *How can I be bleeding?* Delania rolled to her belly. She could feel her ribs grating against one another. The pain made her swoon and took her breath. The thought of standing made her want to cry, but she couldn't leave Lance to fight that monster alone.

Kellacun leapt backwards through the air over a swipe from the awkward bone golem. Her nimble body landed on the arena stone rail. The beast smashed its powerful fist down a second time. Kellacun sliced out and severed the monsters wrist before tumbling into the stands. A shadow caught her eye. She turned to see a corpulent silhouette tossing a woman over his shoulder. She narrowed her eyes and stared in shock. "Pav-co?"

The fat guild leader tossed Delania's injured body over the back of a large black unicorn. The animal's unusual red eyes seemed to shine in the eerie night.

"That's right, wench. Seems Kalen suspected you'd fail him. Working with the boy instead of killing him? Pathetic. All you had to do was steal this necklace!" Pavicious ran his finger under Delania's pearl necklace. "Well, consider your contract voided. Tell the boy and your new hunky friend that if they want this bitch alive to come get her. Hector will be waiting."

Kellacun started toward them then glanced back at Jude. He had severed the leg of the golem, but it had his neck in the grip of its good hand. "You tell that scrawny chicken armed elf, we'll be done as soon as we finish with this toy of his." Before Kellacun could leap back into the fray, the unicorn disappeared in a flash of black smoky dust.

Trinidy slammed Regnis-gnos into the ground. Great chunks of rock and stone debris shot out around him. They swirled and spun like a circular globe. Thin bright weaves of evocation danced and flowed between the stones. A soft blue glow appeared on Trinidy's left arm as his shield began to reform. "You should have not stood against me, son. My anvil of righteousness will soon crush you and your wickedness."

Though I know you will not, this is your last chance to flee, Apollisian! Songsinger warned, *Destiny will deal you a fate that has no redemption.*

Trinidy used the energy from the globe and hurled the rocks outwards. One struck Lance in the head. He quickly fell unconscious on the hard arena floor.

Apollisian shielded his face with his arm. The heavy stone struck him in the chest. The wind was knocked from his body. He held Songsinger out in front of himself and rubbed the large dent in his chest plate. Another rock struck him in the leg and knocked him from his feet. He tried to sit upright when another struck him in the arm and sent Songsinger sliding across the dirt floor.

"It's a pity I couldn't have raised you, Apollisian. Lancalion was such a disappointment." Trinidy motioned to Lance's unconscious form. "Look at the pathetic wretch. Felled by a single stone."

Apollisian struggled to his feet. He couldn't put any weight on his leg and his arm hung limp. Bright blood drained down from his shoulder plate. His hair was dirty and matted with blood and sweat. His violet cloak of Stephanis was tattered and torn.

Trinidy grasped Apollisian by the shoulder and placed Regnis-Gnos at his abdomen. The cold crimson blade turned the air around the armor into ice. Bits of frozen air drifted down like a small snowstorm. Apollisian's armor cracked and aged before his eyes. His hair grayed and his skin wrinkled. "Aren't you going to beg for your life? Aren't you going to pray to Stephanis for justice?"

Apollisian stared into Trinidy's lifeless empty orbs. "There is no justice for me, monster. Do your worst, for I am already dead."

Trinidy heard footsteps behind him. He turned to see the arena sewer grate open. There was a large dwarf. He was wearing some sort of gold colored metal plate. He had an odd shaped helm with ram horns facing forward. The dwarf was surely the largest Trinidy had ever seen. He held Songsinger in his right hand and a small hand axe in his left. The dwarf's gray streaked braided beard fluttered in the evening wind. "I will be with you shortly, fool."

Amerix chuckled. "I wait fer no one. You'll be with me first!" The dwarf slashed in.

Trinidy parried the strike and smashed out with his shield. Amerix lifted his axe arm and left the plate strike him in the shoulder. He ducked low and spun with Songsinger. The large weapon moved slowly. Trinidy Parried with Rengis-Gnos. Just as Amerix had intended. He quickly rose and rocketed his axe in an uppercut. The enchanted blade easily slid between the death knight's defenses and laid a long gash up the monster's chest plate and into his face and helm.

"I thought you were this great foe? Yer a joke!" Amerix taunted, "That would have killed anyone else. Ye got lucky cause yer already dead."

Trinidy growled in anger. "I don't need to strike you down, mortal. Just from being near me your wickedness will drain from you and take your soul with it."

Amerix chuckled as he backed away and squared off. "Ye got to be the dumbest dead guy around. Aint no evil gonna drain from me. I ain't never been evil and ain't got none to drain."

Trinidy hurled his shield. Amerix barely had time to put his head down. The thick plate struck him in the helm. The blast knocked him from his feet. Amerix tumbled backwards and fell. He quickly rolled to his feet. He picked up his damaged helm. It had a long red hot dent in it and the horn was severed on the right side. "Ye done pissed me off now. It's one thing to whoop up on the boy and his stupid churchy friend. But I draw the line at messin' with me hat."

Trinidy rushed forward. Amerix met his strike with Songsinger and struck the undead lord in the thigh. Black ichor shot out all over the arena floor. Trinidy shot out his arm and grabbed Amerix by the throat. The death knight slid Regnis-Gnos down Songsinger's hilt and pressed the tip of his demonic blade into the soft underarm of the dwarf, pinning Songsinger harmlessly against his ribs. In a single motion he hoisted the renegade from his feet and slammed him back against the arena wall. "Now you die, Son of Durion."

Amerix felt the blade slide through his thin chain under armor and into his ribs. The Abyssal cold blade seemed to tear through his soul as much as his flesh. The pain caused him to drop his axe. He would have dropped Songsinger too had she not been pinned under the death knight's arm. Amerix tried to shift his weight, but his feet were not touching the ground. He tried to push off of the arena wall, but the demonic sword stabbed deeper into his side. He could feel the blade sliding past his ribs. He knew he would be dead soon. The renegade reflected over his life, his battles, his achievements. His own god had discounted him and called him a coward. Why not die here? Why not give in. Surely his muscle would fail and the death knight's blade would end his life. Amerix thought about all the foes that deserved the right to say they slew him, and this monster was not it.

Amerix gritted his teeth and struggled in vain to stop the Abyssal cold blade from killing him. He could feel his life slipping away and his muscles were weakening.

Give in, Son of Durion, Songsinger said soothingly, *There is no dishonor in this death.*

"Fuck you!" Amerix growled. He turned his body and let the weapon slide in. The old general knew that even though the wound would be fatal, he would have time for one last strike before he died. He would not make a mistake like he did with the dragons. He would fight to win.

Trinidy tumbled forward against the wall as the dwarf slid out from under him. Amerix grabbed Songsinger in his meaty hands and sliced down. He put every ounce of hatred and anger into the blow.

NOOOOOO! Songsinger screamed.

Trinidy tried to parry with Regnis-Gnos, but he was too late. Songsinger crashed down into the monster's exposed neck. The enchanted blade severed the undead knight's head and shattered. Amerix shielded his face from the explosion as bits of metal and magical energy flashed across the arena.

Kellacun started towards Jude when a flash of light across the arena lit up the night sky. The bright blue glow from the golem dissipated and it fell into a massive pile of yellowish bones. Jude collapsed and gasped for breath. Kellacun quickly changed form and rushed to his side.

"Are you okay?"

Jude smiled and glanced up. His deep brown eyes locking into hers. "I am now."

Kellacun felt her legs buckle and her heart swooned. Her face flushed and she felt embarrassed and angry at her body's reaction.

"Come on, get up before the others think you some sort of wimp."

Jude smiled as he stood. Her warm body next to his made his pulse quicken. He pretended to be a little weaker than he was so she would keep her arms wrapped around him. "I think it's over."

Apollisian weakly watched the great portal slowly unravel inside of itself and dissipate into nothingness. The hundreds of thousands of birds that swirled overhead quickly flew away as if they were never there. The storm clouds dissipated revealing a starry moonlit night. Almost instantly, the air began to warm to its normal spring warmth and the snow began to melt and drip from the rooftops.

Apollisian looked at Lance and then at Amerix. The old general leaned weakly against the wall. The tired paladin struggled to his feet and walked over to the giant dwarf. The two stood in silence as they stared at one another.

Amerix sighed and raised the broken shaft of Songsinger. "Sorry. I broke yer weapon."

Apollisian nodded. They shared a moment of understanding. "It was just a sword."

"I wish it had been you that killed me."

Apollisian glanced down at Amerix's side. He could see the vicious wound that Regnis-Gnos had left. "Yea, that doesn't look good."

"A fitting end for me, I guess."

Apollisian glanced back over at Lance. "Hold on."

Amerix chuckled then winced in pain. "What fer?"

Apollisian drew a dagger from his boot.

"A hollow victory, but ye deserve it."

"I'm not going to kill you, fool." Apollisian cut the side straps on Amerix's armor. "I'm going to heal you."

Amerix fell to his knees. The loss of blood and pain was too great for him. Apollisian took a deep breath and pulled on the inner power he felt before. It was not Stephanis, but it was strong. And close. He placed his hand on Amerix's wound.

"Why would Stephanis want to heal me?" Amerix asked through gritted teeth,.

Apollisian unfastened his cloak and let it fall behind him. He channeled his new god's power into the dying dwarf. He smiled as the wound closed. "He doesn't. But my new god does."

Amerix marveled as he felt his strength returning. "That's how you survived the fire."

Apollisian narrowed his tired eyes. The memories of all the deaths, all the lives shattered because of this dwarf that stood before him.

"Don't judge me from the eyes of me enemy," Amerix said, "Look at me through the eyes of a man wronged. Sometimes those that get in the way of yer justice are as guilty as those who committed it."

Apollisian turned his head and glanced up at the stars that shined down on the macabre scene in the coliseum. The soft spring breeze blew his dirty blonde hair about his face. "Yes. The soldiers of my enemy are my enemy as well."

Amerix sighed and placed his hand on Apollisian's battered shoulder plate. "It was a pleasure fighting alongside of you for once."

Apollisian nodded.

"I guess you can have this hilt. The magic in it still works for me to understand you."

"No. It's this necklace." Apollisian thumbed the charm Bodrell gave him. "The magic of Songsinger is lost."

Amerix nodded. "I've got to get back to me boy."

Apollisian gave the renegade a half-hearted smile and watched the old general climb back down the sewer grate. He felt his eyes burn and tears well up. The battered warrior picked up his tattered and dirty cape. He thumbed over the symbol of Stephanis. It was torn and ragged. He had nothing left. He lost his father at age six. He lost his mother while at the academy. Victor was lost, then Stephanis, and now his one true love. He had spent his entire life fighting for others. Maybe now it was time to fight for himself.

Apollisian tossed down his old cape and started towards Lance. The boy was being attended to by Jude and Kellacun.

Jude glanced up. "He's coming to."

Lance opened his weak eyes. "Apollisian?"

Apollisian loomed over. "I'm here, boy. Your father is dead. The Abyss Walker has been defeated."

Lance smiled weakly. "Where's Delania?"

"The world will rejoice and the heavens will reunite in the wake of a great victory. But the Abyss Walker lingers in the death of himself. His love will fuel his fury until the time comes for him to unleash his wickedness upon the world. Woe to those who have understanding, for even Arketeuthus does not know the Abyss Walker's time is nigh and that his impiety revels under our sun."

-Found scrawled on dried sharkskin
in the islands of Aboe-
(Author is believed to be a shark god cult member.)

Epilogue

The eastern sky was beginning to brighten. The morning glow would soon wash away the stars of a long night. Apollisian stared down on Alexis's grave. He could hear the cheers and cries of elation from the surviving townsfolk of Central City. But, there was no victory for him.

"Goodbye, my love. I shall be with you soon enough."

Apollisian placed the splintered remnants of Songsinger in the ornate box. He stared at the shattered hilt one last time.

Let her go. She had her own agenda. She didn't care for you like I do. Besides, there is much to be done, the feminine voice echoed in his mind.

Apollisian closed the box and placed it in the small hole he had dug near Alexis's grave. He drew his sword and stared at it as the sun crest over the eastern sky. He turned the blade in his hand and marveled at the cool red Abyssal steel. "We defeated the Abyss Walker. What is left for us?"

Regnis-Gnos gleamed in the morning light and whispered in his mind, *There's much for us to do, Apollisian.*

Apollisian sheathed the wicked blade and started his trek to the west. "Don't call me Apollisian. I was named after my father. You can call me... Havrion."

Glossary

Aboe- (a-bow) Kingdom on the southern-most peninsula of Terrigan. The kingdom has little or no army, but does not fear being conquered due to the great mountain reaches that surround i's borders. Kingdom is wealthy and home of merchants and pirate alike. Of all the kingdoms in Terrigan, it is the most racial diverse with humans, dwarves, and elves, holding political offices.

Aclia - (uh-clee-uh) Black skinned dark angel. She is the most warrior like.

Adoria- (a-door-ee-ah) Kingdom just west of Beykla. It waged a bloody civil war against its western half, Andoria.

Alexis Alexandria Overmoon- (a-lex-us / al-ecks-zan-dree-uh / Over-moon) Daughter heir of King Christopher Calamon Overmoon. High Lord of the Minok Vale. She travels with Apollisian Bargoe, the paladin of Justice, trying to learn the ways of justice to aid her when she becomes queen.

Amerix Alistair Stormhammer- (am-er-icks / ali-stair / storm ham-er) Dwarven general of Clan Stoneheart, formerly of Clan Stormhammer. His clan was wiped out before him, when he was a young man, by dark dwarves and a white dragon. He fled with a few survivors and was welcomed into clan Stoneheart where he excelled in the art of war.

Amyrillion- (amur-ill-yun) Arch-devil of pain.

Androdius- (an-drode-ee-us) Evil black dragon of immense power that lives in the swamp west of Aquabar.

Angelique- (anj-ul-eek) Grayshalk wife of Petrovisk

Apollisian Bargoe- (a-paul-issi-in / bar-go) Paladin of justice that was sent from his order in Westvon keep to oversee the negotiations between the humans and the dwarves from Clan Stoneheart, in attempt to derail a conflict, when he was caught in the middle of the war.

Andoria- (an-door-ee-ah) Formally western Adoria, this kingdom's brief history came when it declared its independence from Adoria. It waged an eight month long war with Adoria, but was eventually re-conquered.

Androdius- (an-droe-dee-us) The great black dragon imprisoned in the swamp west of Aquabar.

Aquabar- (awk-wuh-bar) Capitol of Aten. Lies near the great swamp and the Mountains of Meara.

Arluda- (are-loo-duh) Blue Mistress and friend of Delania.

Artamanake- (art-man-uh-key) Dark dwarven general.

Aten- (a-ten) Queendom to the far west that is ran solely by women. Males of any race are considered inferior and are immediately made into slaves, or killed at birth. Only a choice few males are kept alive for reproduction purposes only. The women of Aten are adept sorceress and keep a rigid society of back stabbing and political maneuvering.

Artez Undermoon- (are-tez) Captain of the Undermoon Darayal Legion

Athodrin- (uh-thod-drin) Souless beings that are created by gods. Demons and angels are some of these.

Ayden- (a-den) Powerful salomen that used Therrig to

gain control of a large clan of dark dwarves.

Barbetin- (bar-bet-in) Also known as the Lake of the Damned. It is the lake in the Abyss where damned souls are thrown into the be tortured for eternity by the demons that swim among it.

Beovi- (bee-o-vi) Subterranean fish that live in the deepest freshwater caverns of the underworld. They are a delicacy to dwarves, dark dwarves, dark elves and other subterranean races. These fish can grow to unlimited size, depending on the lake or river in which they live.

Berylys-Quieness- (berry-liss / kwee-uh-ness) Great White dragon. She disappeared and is rumored to be dead.

Beykla- (bay-kla) Human kingdom on the northeastern corner of Terrigan. The kingdom is well to do, militantly powerful, and well patrolled. It has never, in its long history, been conquered.

Blue Dragon Inn- Inn in Central City that is closets to the Dawson river and the Dawson river bridge, where Lance, Kaisha, Ryshander, and Apollisian battled the dwarven horde, until the king arrived with re-enforcements.

Borkin- (bore-kin) Small wooden device that is inserted into the mouth that keeps the wearer from closing their jaws.

Bureland- (bur-land) small hamlet, in the southern part of Beykla, where Lance spent most of his childhood and early adult life with his adoptive father, Davohn.

Breedikai- (bree-da-kii) Original gods, or gods that were created. They have no soul and most dwell in Merioulus.

Broyed- (broid) Male incubus dark angel.

Bykalicus- (Bye-kal-eh-kus) Powerful arch-demon that controls much of the Abyss.

Cadacka- (ka-doc-uh) Black ceremonial robe worn by elves when they have lost a love one and are mourning. Most elves never remove the cloak once it is donned.

Calours- (ka-loo-ers) Non-sedimentary rocks found in the underworld. Subterranean races, mostly species of dwarves, use them to heat to cook meat on.

Calito, battle of- (kuh-lee-toe) Battle that took place in Adoria near the town of Dolzan. Adorian knights fought against an evil necromancer named Randolph Forelinger who commanded over a thousand undead soldiers.

Carcarass- (kar-kar-us) Training school that raises and trains Aten born pureblood males to be slaves as they age.

Casen- (kay-sin) Name applied to animals that grow to giant size. Named after the halfling wizard Nermal Casen that accidentally created them.

Cathena- (Ka-theen-uh) Falconeer, daughter of Petrovisk.

Central City- City just south of the Dawson Stronghold that is in the center of the Beyklan nation.

Cheural- (Share-uhl) Gadgeteer, daughter of Petrovisk.

Christopher Calamon Overmoon- (Kris-toe-fur / Kal-a-mon / O-ver-moon) High king of the Minok Vale.

Clan Cutstone- Clan that makes its home under the Lalin Plateau in Southern Beykla.

Colonel Mortan Ganover- First lieutenant of Duke Dolin Blackhawk, and acting mayor when the Duke is gone. Is considered responsible for the slaughter at central City by the dwarves due to his inability to act on the paladin Apollisian's recommendations.

Commander Fehzban Algor Stoneheart- (fez-ben / algore) Commander and loyal follower of General Amerix Stormhammer. Was tried and convicted of treason after the Torrent manor and the Central City campaigns.

Copel Nin- (cope-ul) Fat keeper of the gladiator slaves in the arena in Central City. Copel was once a gladiator champion but in the fight he earned his freedom he was severely injured, ending his career as a fighter. He was hired by the duke to be the keeper of the slaves. Copel always worked hard at the job but as he aged, his injury and time took its toll on him preventing his ability to stay in shape. He soon became fat, but he enjoyed his job at the arena as he longed for the days to hear the roar of the crowd once more.

Council of Wise- Consists of ten elders that sit on the governing seat at Monk Vale, though not all ten are usually present at meeting, There has to be at least six to hold a vote.

Cranetium- (krane-tee-um) Official title given to an elven high mage. The title means little to other elves, save for the wizards and sorcerers of their Vales.

Crowalta- (Crow-all-tah) Mother of the Black Sept in control of the Gearian.

Dadramedion- (day-drom-uh-dee-in) Powerful arch demon and enemy to Bykalicus.

Dargruden- (Dar-grew-din) Male leader of the Gearian.

Dall-kal-Mour- (doll-kal-moo-ur) Title given to blood born men from Aten. They are the only males that are allowed to reproduce. They are expensive slaves and only the highest ranking, or wealthy own them. It is a status symbol for Mother's, or heads of septs, to own more than one, since they will never give birth.

Dolzan- (dol-zahn) Small city in the north western side of Adoria.

Darayal Legion- (dar-ray-all) One hundred of the finest elite elven rangers that patrol the Minok Vale in pairs. They are skilled swordsman that wield a weapon in each hand during battle. They are as feared as they are awed.

Darious Theobold- (dare-ee-us / They-bold) Eleven year old son of king Theobold.

Dark Dwarves- Dwarves that live solely in the underworld. They have pupil-less eyes that have adapted over time to see in the dark by detecting heat patterns. They hate bright light as it is painful for them, and have turned to wicked and evil ways as a society.

Dargruden- (dar-grude-in) Dal-kal-mour that runs the Gearian.

Darren Brightson, Duke- (Dare-in / bright-sun) Duke of the Adorian lands just to the east of the northeastern border of Aten. Governs over the small hamlet of Lostom.

Darrion-Quieness- (dare-ee-on / kwee-eh-ness) Great wyrm white dragon. Oldest of all white dragons and most powerful. His lair is in the mountains of Nalir, but he roams all over the realms. He often leads lesser races against their enemies, and takes the majority of the treasure after the victory. His last major campaign was in aide of the dark dwarves against the dwarven Clan Stormhammer.

Davohn Ecnal- (da-von) Adoptive father of Lance. He is a woodcutter that made his home in Bureland and found Lance when Lance was only six years old. He raised him as his son until Lance left when he was seventeen.

Dawson River- Largest river that runs in Terrigan. It stretches from the Sea of Balfour, north of Beykla, all the way through the southern kingdom of Aboe.

Delania- (duh-lane-ee-uh) Beautiful succubus that dwells in the Abyss.

Delker- (Dell-kur) Wizard bent on creating an alliance between powerful allies across terrigan that are interested in defeating established kingdoms.

Demphinshile- (Dim-fin-shy-ul) Dark elf city deep in the under mountain.

Dicermadon- (die-sir-ma-don) God of gods, Dicermadon plots with demons to kill the son of a goddess, drawing the wrath of the gods that he governs.

Diltz Quest- (Dilts) Ceremony in which Dal-kal-mours, Aten full blooded males, compete in a gladiator style competition to be selected as a mate for the queen.

Dolgo seeds- (dole-go) A tasty mountain nut found on the steepest slopes of the highest mountain. Considered a delicacy by all dwarves and mountain people.

Dome of the Rock- Ancient dwarven temple that was supposedly built by Durion himself. The dwarven Mountain God. The temple is rumored to be atop the Lalin Plateau.

Donathuku- (Don-uh-thue-koo) Arch-devil of terror.

Donjurik- (Don-szhur-ick) Small thin greyshalk sword. Rarely used in combat. Primarily ceremonial.

Donk- Aten word for the penis. It is an insulting word in their culture and is associated with weakness and stupidity.

Doogan Raymer- (doo-gun / ray-muhr) Northern noble from Dawson. Doogan is a conniving tactician who has made his estates through double dealing and backstabbing. He shows his family tree as being distantly related to the king, and hopes to one day return his house the throne.

Dorcastig- (door-cast-ig) Tall muscled priest of Rha-Cordan. Follows under Resin Darkhand. One of the priests that participated in the DeNaucght.

Durion- (doog-a thee-in) Dwarven Mountain God.

Dregan City- (dree-gan) Home of the Clan Stormhammer before it was wiped out by the dark dwarves and a white dragon.

Drunda- (drun-duh) The god the orcs follow. It is not known if he actually exists, or even if he is male.

Earth Oath- Oath an elf makes that they will give their lives trying to up hold.

Ecnal- (eck-null) surname given to all orphans of Beykla before they were all killed by unknown assassins.

Eckwon- (Eck-qwon) Trinidy's warhorse when he was alive.

Edsil Strongbow- (Ed-zuhl) Darayal captain of the Strongbow Vale.

Ehleeshuh- (Uh-leash-uh) White unicorn.

Elder Bartoke- (bar-toke) Elder of the Minok Vale, member of the Council of the Wise, and Keeper of the Sealed Passing.

Elder Darmond- (dar-mond) Elder of the Minok Vale, member of the Council of the Wise, and Keeper of the Passing.

Elder Humas- (hue-mass) Elder of the Minok Vale, member of the Council of the Wise, and Keeper of the Passing.

Elder Varmintan- (var-mint-ton) Elder of the Minok Vale, member of the Council of Wise, and Keeper of the Passing.

Elecksixs- (uh-lecks-ick) Succubus leader of the dark angels.

City of Eldred- (ale-dread) Small town that brews their own specific ale that is not revered by most other Beyklan towns.

Erik Stromson- (stahm-son) General of the Beyklan Western army and hero of the orc wars.

Eucladower Strongbow- Oldest Elder of the Minok Council of Wise and Keeper of the Passings.

Famen's Tree- (fay-mens) Large tree three miles east of the Dawson River Bridge. The tree was named after Jeddis Famen, a Central City militia leader that held off an orc attack. After the battle he led a group militiamen after the fleeing orcs, and managed to slay one of the orc leaders as they fled. He nailed the orc's head on a spike to the tree as a message to any other orcs. That was the last orc battle against Central City during the orc wars. The people believed the orcs were afraid of him, but in truth they were massing to finish the elves at the Minok Vale.

Fezbhan Algor Stoneheart- (Fez-ban) Commander of the Stoneheart Clan and cleric of Leska.

Fig root- Strongbow root that is dried and soaked in spirits

Flunt- God of Fire, and one of the four elemental gods.

Funis- (Fu-niss) Strong straight line of waxed bowstring that was at the draw of all the Proudarrow Bows from the Darayal Legion. This device allowed them to shoot several arrows at once with deadly precession.

Freedom Festival- Holiday celebrated in Beykla to commemorate the end of the twenty year-long orc wars.

Galla noodles- (ga-la) Thin noodles often prepared with butter.

Garlibane- (gar-lee-bane) High mage and Elder of the Council of Wise in Minok Vale.

Gearian- (Gear-ee-in) Collection of incorrigible sudas that exist for the sole purpose of raping and killing women in Aten who have been convicted of the most serious crimes. The women are stripped of their power and thrown into the pit for spectators to watch as they are raped repeatedly over many days until they are killed or die.

General Laricin West- (lair-iss-in) Late general for the northern Beyklan Army that was responsible for scattering the orc horde, in the battle that was later referred to as; The Quigen. General Laricin and his men fought to the last man, keeping the orc horde from wiping out what was left of the elven resistance.

General Thatcher- (Thach-er) Southern general of the Beyklan Army that embraced the southern Beyklan nobles when they announced their independence.

Gorsan- (gore-sahn) Dwarven brew master who is a distant relative to Fehzban. Gorsan lives in Dolzan and sells dwarven ales to the locals.

Greyshalk- Tall furry humanoids that have strong beliefs in family, tribe, and warfare.

Gregory Herwain- (her-wane) Southern noble that is chairmen of affairs in southern Beykla. He is leader of House Herwain that is well known for saying much and doing little. He hosts the monthly meetings of the southern nobles in the city of Motivas at the House of Affairs.

Grimolikin Hill, battle of- (Grim-mole-uh-kin) Battle where greyshalks were forced from their land by the Beyklans during the orc wars. The Beyklans were actually trying to route several tribes of kriel that were helping the orcs.

Gweits- (ga-weets) Tiny insect like demons that dwell on the rocky floor of the Abyss. They feed on flesh, and burrow under skin with their horrific claws and hooks.

Harbor Mountain- Large city state on the Dalgun island

of Aboe.

Heart of the rock- A gemstone mounted on a gold ring that is aid to have magical properties that can prevent the wearer from being harmed by dragon's breath.

Hector De Scoran- (heck-tor / day-skore-an) Evil warrior wizard that is the King of Nalir. Believes that Lance was prophesized to destroy his kingdom, and will stop at nothing until the boy is dead.

Henrious- (hen-ree-us) Ex-Diltz quest gladiator and Dalkal-mour that helps Tonya of the White and the Freedom Movement.

Hiramem- (her-uh-mem) Old female sorceress that lives in Aten. She often works for Ramasiel in the red tower and has a limited ability at foretelling. She often uses old chicken bones, stones and other small objects that she tosses about on a board with elven skin stretched over it. She is from Beykla originally. She grew up in Sineuvia.

Hourid Thigguard- (hor-id / thig-guard) Master of Arms and father of Mylaneia.

Ian Silverman- (E-uhn) Human knight under Duke Darren Brightstar. Fought in the Battle of Calito. Has two sons, Ian Silverman the Second and Myer Silverman. Both are adventures and Ian does not agree with their lifestyle.

Ickten Norris- (ick-ton) Ranger that works for the Hentridge Farm south of Central City. He is an expert tracker and skilled swordsman. His favored enemies are orcs.

Illilander tree- (ill-lee-land-er) Largest trees in the realms. Over five hundred feet tall.

Iratus- (eye-rat-us) A rare form of a personality that has the ability to gain great strength from anger.

Jon Klement- Arch-mage of Central Beyklan Army.

Jordan Gersian- (jor-dun / ger-see-in) Southern Nobleman that is leading the plot to pull southern Beykla away from the north.

Jude- (Jewd) Mercenary swordsman from Bureland. He

sold his sword to fight brigands, polecats and other minor enemies of Bureland. He is also Lance's best friend.

Jurnda Undermoon- (jern-duh) Dark elf legionnaire that fights with two axes. Big brother to Artez.

Kai-Harkia- (kay-hark-ee-uh) Mountain kingdom northwest from Beykla. Its people are dark skinned, dark haired, heavy chested, nomad swordsmen. They seldom form static villages, though some do exist.

Kalen Al-Kalidius- (kay-lin / al-kal-id-ee-us) Grey elf ex-stepson of King Overmoon of the Minok Vale. Kalen has turned to the shadow and hungers for power, hoping to take over the throne of Nalir when Hector dies.

Kalistirsts- (kal-eh-stirsts) Underground mole people with no eyes that live in the underworld.

Kalliman Theobold- (kall-eh-man) King of Beykla.

Kalliman Castle- (kall-eh-man) Castle and home of King Kalliman Theobold.

Kareeg Hut- (kuh-reeg) Nobleman that owned more land than any other noble in all of Beykla. His lands where in the north that extended from just south of the Torrent Manor all that way west to the border of Beykla and all the way east to the Dawson River right up Dawson itself. His brother was a Captain that was stationed at the Torrent manor when it fell and he hates the dwarves more than any other Beyklan.

Katrinal- (Ka-trine-uhl) Greyshalk daughter of Petrovisk.

Katykop- (Kate-ee-cop) Abyssal for mischievous/feline.

Kellacun- (kell-eh-kun) Wererat assassin that worked for the guild in central city before it was destroyed. Now she works for Kalen in attempt to kill Lance.

Kendalerairy Overmoon- (ken-doll-ler-air-ee) Captain of the Overmoon Darayal Legion.

Kerstap- (kur-stap) Mighty curved two handed greyshalk sword.

King Minostak- (min-oh-stack) Greyshalk king.

Kings, Game of- Game similar to Chess.

Kingsford City- Largest city in Terrigan. Capitol of Ladathon.

Kornicus- (corn-uh-cus) Demon imp and servant of Delania.

Kuma- (koo-muh) Blade attached to the end of the Strongbow's bows for melee fighting.

Kriel- (kree-uhl) Smaller thinner greyshalks with darker fur with spots. Hyena like.

Ladathon- (lad-uh-thon) Southern country, south of Tyrine, where mysterious animals live in thick jungle. Kingsford City, the largest city in the world, is its capitol.

Ladathonian Warhorse- (lad-uh-thone-ee-un) A breed of war horse from Ladathon that stands nearly eighteen hands high and weighs nearly three thousand pounds.

Lalin Plateau- (lay-lin) large plateau that is the middle of southern Beykla. It is covered by thick lush forest and is nearly impossible to scale it's thousand foot high sheer rock walls. Stories tell of ancient ruins at the top, but few have climbed to its summit to validate the claims. What makes the plateau so unique is that the Dawson river runs through the inside of it in a great river cave.

Lance Ecnal- Adopted son of Davohn Ecnal. Lance's birth name is Lancalion Levendis Lampara. His natural mother was Panoleen, the goddess of mercy. Lance is prophesized to bring plague and death on the world, though he sees himself as nothing more than an orphan trying to discover his past.

Lancalion Levendis Lampara- (lance-uh-lion / lev-un-dis / lamb-par-uh) Birth name given to Lance Ecnal.

Larunthus- (lar-unth-this) God of the Hunt.

Leska- (les-kuh) The Earth Mother Goddess. She reins over all living things while they are alive, including plants and animals. She is one of the four elemental gods.

Lirlithe- (lear-lith) Short haired mischievous dark angel with curved horns.

Lostom- (lose-tom) Small Hamlet on the border of Aten and Adoria

Lostos- (low-stoes) Name for the underground complex of the Severed Heart Guild of wererats in Central City.

Lukerey- (lou-kear-ee) God of Luck and Mischief.

Lunarian- (lou-nar-ee-in) Enchanted wells that priestly elves, or other good forest creatures, bless by the powers of Leska to rejuvenate and to heal one another.

Lyndall- (lin-doll) Gladiator champion in Central City. A skilled swordsman that had fought over two hundred forty fights.

Markus- (mark-us) Suda in Ramasiel's tower that is secret lover with Reena

Marlana- (mar-lane-uh) Backstabbing Mistress of the Blue Sept that conspired with Ramasiel to overthrow the Mother of the Blue Sept in order for her to control a second vote in the senate.

Marzahna- (marr-zohn-uh) Mother of the Yellow Sept that was banished for wanting to marry. She built a smaller tower on the border of Aten in the hamlet of Lostom.

Mary of the Yellow Robe- Mistress of the banished yellow mother, Marzahna.

Master David Hentridge- (hint-ridge) Leader of small mercenary guild that is disguised as a farm, just south of Central City. King Theobold uses them to hunt and kill orc's that he does not want the public to know exists, keeping their awareness of the actually amount of the green skinned beasts that still live in his kingdom.

Merioulus- (mare-ee-oh-you-lus) City of the Gods. Set on a form of the astral plane.

Mersaat- (mare-sat) Great Blue Dragon that lives in the Desert of Tyrine. A scroll was stolen from his lair by a hapless thief. The scroll was sold several times until it ended up at the great library in Kingsford City where Ladathon scholars identified the text as draconian. What made the scroll unique was that it was written in humanoid size. Few humans know draconic. It gave credibility that there is a secret sept of priests that worship the great serpents, but it led others to believe that the once the beasts fully mature, they gain the ability to transform into a man-like creature. All of these theories are yet to be proven.

Mershaulk- (mur-shalk) God of Serpents. Some believe the god does not exist and is only worshipped by a cult following known as the Sept of Serpents. Mershaulk is also the term referred to for men who go into berserker rage in in battle. The rage is so intense the men do not feel pain, can continue to battle long after their body has died, and have a hard time differing friend from foe on the battle field. Mershaulks are as feared as they are respected as warriors, though they never fight with comrades as a Mershaulk often claims the lives of those around him in his rage.

Midagord Milence Stormhammer-Amerix Stormhammer's deceased father.

Minok Vale- (my-nock) Name of the elven sovereignty that is set in Beykla.

Mordrik- (more-drick) Dark Elf mercenary that resided in the under mountain. Amerix Stormhammer hunted him and killed his band one by one for killing a Kalistirst friend of his.

Mortigalus- (mor-tuh-gal-us) Arch-Devil of Gluttony and Torture.

Motivas- (moe-ta-vis) Southernmost city in Beykla. City is built on a large brick foundation that is rumored to be ruins of an ancient civilization.

Mountain Heart- Home city of Clan Stoneheart, located in the Pyberian Mountains.

Mount Steeple- The largest mountain on Terrigan. The mountain is rumored to hold the road way to Merioulus as its peak cannot be seen as it ascends into a permanent veil of clouds.

Mowaka- (moe-walk-uh) camouflage cloak like blanket that elven archers, and sometimes rangers, use to spy on their enemies.

Myer Silverman- (my-er) Son of Ian Silverman of Lostom.

Mylaneia Thigguard- (my-lane-ya / thig-guard) Young daughter of Hourid Thigguard, and courtier of Tharxton Stoneheart.

Nalir- (nall-er) Evil southern empire that is made up primarily of swamps and quagmires. A militantly powerful nation that worships most of the evil gods.

Necromidus- (neck-rom-eh-dus) A collection of the first four tiers of necromancy spells.

Osimar- (Ossy-mar) City on Dalgun Island that makes the best wine in all of the realms. Most expensive.

Oswald Thorrin- (oz-wald / thor-in) Captain of the Royal Beyklan Guard and bounty hunter, though he only collects on lawful bounties set by the magistrates.

Panoleen- (pan-oh-leen) Goddess of Mercy that was banished from the heavens.

Pav-co- (pahv-coe) Fat wererat guild leader in Central City.

Petrovisk- (pet-roe-visk) Old greyshalk champion from the orc wars.

Plaatu- (pla-two) Kalistirsts friend of Amerix that was killed by one of Mordrik's dark dwarves.

Pyberian Mountains- (pie-beer-ee-an) Mountain range in the northwest corner of Beykla, near Adoria.

Quadry Proudarrow- (quad-ree) Darayal Legionnaire of the Minok Vale.

Quigen- (kwi-jin) Elven word for sacrifice. Most widely known as the name of the great battlefield where General Laricin West scattered the orcish horde by fighting until every man in his army fell in the Serrin Plains.

Ramasiel- (ram-uh-zeal) One of the three mothers of the

red order in Aten. She is a powerful sorceress and a political power in Aquabar.

Randolph Forlinger- (ran-doff / four-ling-er) Powerful necromancer that was defeated and slain at the Battle of Calito.

Reagle, The- A fancy clothing store in Aquabar that makes dresses and other articles of women's clothing. It does not make any article of clothing that could be used in an intimate way to make the women more attractive. Atenians believe that men have no right to be attracted to women, that the act should be gratifying to the woman only.

Reena- (ree-nuh) Third sorceress, also called third sister, of the red sept in Aten. Second only to Ramasiel herself.

Rha-Cordan- (rah-kor-don) God of Death and Dying. Not inherently evil, he reigns over the placement of souls when they enter the afterlife, though he has been known to be incredibly vengeful to those who prolong their lives through magical means.

Salomen- (sall-oh-men) Subterranean humanoid species with powerful mind controlling abilities.

Samarkel- (suh-mark-uhl) Large frog-like demon from the Abyss.

Serrin Plains- (sare-in) Dangerous expansive grassland just south of Minok Vale where most of the evil races that live in Beykla dwell.

Sha-Shor'Nai- (sha-shore-nigh) God of the Sun and Light.

Shanorian- (sha-nore-ee-uhn) General of devils.

Sierra Blackhawk- Duke Dolin Blackhawk's granddaughter.

Silas Proudarrow- (sigh-less) Darayal Legionnaire of the Minok Vale.

Stephanis- (stuh-fawn-is) God of Justice.

Stieny Gittledorph- (stie-knee / get-tull-dorf) Halfling thief who became mixed up with the dragon Darrion-Quieness.

Stormghast- The great stone doors that seals Mountain Heart from the dark uncharted reaches of the undermountian.

Suda- (sue-duh) Title given to all non-eunuch slaves in Aten. A suda is looked as a lower form of a man by the Tuda, or eunuch.

Surelda Al-Kalidius- (sir-el-da / al-kuh-lid-ee-us) Ex-wife of King Overmoon and mother of Kalen Al-Kalidius.

Surshy- (sir-she) Goddess of Water. One of the four elemental gods.

Tallnok- (tal-knock) Young wizard that works for the Hentridge Farm south of Central City. Occasionally hires himself out for specific jobs.

Talwin- (tall-win) Young apprentice war wizard that joined the Western Beyklan Army instead of staying with the mage guild in Dawson..

Targavian Hollen Stoneheart- (tar-gave-ee-in / hall-in) New general promoted by Tharxton after the betrayal of Amerix and his officers.

Terrigan- (ter-eh-gun) Name of the continent that all known civilizations exists.

Tharxton Stoneheart- (tharx-ton) Young king of Clan Stoneheart and political rival with Amerix Alistair Stormhammer.

Therrig Alistair Delastan- (ther-ig / al-eh-stair / del-eh-stan) illegitimate son of Amerix Alistair Stormhammer. Therrig is living proof of Amerix's and Therrig's mother's infidelity.

Thomas Smith (Arwar)- (are-wahr) Blacksmith that was worked at the Torrent Manor before Amerix attacked. He was head of the liaison between the two peoples and He learned dwarven from his many dwarven friends at Mountain Heart before he retired and moved back to Poria.

Tonya- Former mother of the white tower, who staged her death so that she could anonymously lead the Freedom Movement of Aten.

Torrent Manor- small keep northwest of Central City that was built specifically for enforcing the trade embargo on the dwarves that dwelled in the Pyberian Mountains, and the Adorians in the civil war.

Tracy Ross- Young girl that lives with her family at the Junction outside of the Torrent Manor.

Trinidy- (trin-eh-dee) Dead paladin of Dicermadon, that was raised from the dead by evil priests of Rha-Cordan creating the first death knight.

Trishal- (trish-uhl) Multi-armed female demon with human torso and snake body.

Tuda- (too-duh) Title given to all eunuch slaves in Aten.

Tylergaiden Proudarrow- (tyler-gai-den) Darayal captain of the Proudarrow Vale

Tyrine- (tie-reen) Kingdom south west of Beykla..

Valley of Mist- Lush green valley that is just below the entrance to Mountain Heart in the Pyberian Mountains.

Vendaigehn- (vin-day-gun) Type of horse from the Plains of Vendaiga. The steeds are marked with white spots n their flanks, and are taller than most horses with longer, thinner legs. Legend says that Vendaigehn steeds are the off spring of a pegasus and a unicorn, though hat has never been proven.

Victor DeVulge- (day-vul-juh) Slain squire of Apollisian Bargoe.

Vinr- (Vin-er) Greyshalk word for friend.

Vlargcar- (va-larg-car) Orc whelp saved by Amerix when he and his mother was ordered killed by their tribe.

Vrescan Alistair Delastan- Therrig's father that was killed fighting side by side with Midagord Stormhammer in defense of Dregan City.

Walter Thigpen- Middle aged royal guard crossbowman and longtime friend of Captain Oswald Thorrin.

Westvon Keep- (west-van) large keep and hamlet to the

far east in Beykla on the banks of the Dawson River.

Whisten- (wiss-ton) God of Air, and one of the four elemental gods.

Yahna- (ya-nuh) City in the heavens where mortal souls, blessed by their gods, dwell.

Yohr-Acht- (your-awk-tuh) Great green dragon that makes his lair atop the Lalin Plateau.

About the Author

Shane Moore grew up on a farm in rural Illinois. An only child that was six miles from his nearest peer, Shane often created wild tales of heroes and villains during his many trips into the deep woods that surrounded his rural home.

Shane was accelerated in his class and started his senior year of high school at age sixteen. After graduating and getting a waiver for his age, Shane joined the United States Navy to pay for college. He participated in campaigns; "Provide Hope" and "Secure Democracy" during the Yugoslavian civil war. Shane received several naval awards and citations and was one of the highest trained members of his ship.

After getting out of the service, Shane began college. He was soon hired by the Carlinville Police Department, beginning his multiple venue police career. Shane retired as a detective for the Gillespie Police Department after serving twelve years. His police career was quite notable with awards for bravery and with one life saving medal. He was named Officer of the Year in 2005.

A lesser known truth about Shane is that he played eight years of semi pro football with the Central Illinois Cougars. Shane is the team's all-time tackle leader and holds the record for most special teams tackles in a season and the most tackles in a game. Shane received many awards including Defensive Player of the Year in 2005.

January 14th, 2008. Shane retires from his police career to be a professional novelist.

Mr. Moore resides in Central Illinois with his son, Dakota.

www.ingramcontent.com/pod-product-compliance
Lightning Source LLC
Chambersburg PA
CBHW060306260626
47160CB00007B/2518